Prittik's Will

David Lewis Paget

Barr Books

To my old mate
Mark Hamilton

ISBN 978-0-9596876-6-8

Chapter One

Alex Prittik staggered in through the front door looking grey and old. He was only forty-three, but the casual observer at that moment might have taken him to be anywhere between sixty and seventy. He stood for a moment in the hallway, caught a sight of himself in the mirror, and groaned.

'Not now, for Chrisesake! Can't you see I've had a shock?' He was halfway into the lounge room before he realized that the stranger in the hallway had been his own reflection, and that between ten o'clock and ten thirty that morning he had managed to age thirty years.

'Brandy,' he gasped at his wife, as he staggered through the doorway and flopped down into an easy chair. 'Brandy, for God's sake!'

Jocelyn Prittik looked up from her crossword and momentarily ceased to buff her nails.

'Oh dear! Is that his master's voice? Back from the doctor's already,' she remarked, disinterestedly. 'And did you find out the cause of your tummy ache, oh lord and master?'

'Don't give me a hard time, Joss. I've just had a terrible shock,' said Alex, staring up at the ceiling.

'I thought you said it was only a routine visit? What's the naughty doctor said to upset my Alex,' she pouted.

She looked down at the generous breasts struggling to come to terms with their imprisonment in her bikini top, and ran her hands over them in satisfaction.

'I suppose it's all that sex, Alex! You've been overdoing it! I told you that it wasn't good for you, but what would I know? I'm only the little woman after all. I'm just here to sate your carnal desires – that's what the vicar said, anyway! That's what he said about you... a carnal man, Mrs. Prittik, that's what your husband is!'

'Oh, fuck the vicar, Joss! Just get me a brandy will you?'

Jocelyn got slowly to her feet a look of disapproval on her face. She was ten years younger than her husband, and would have been attractive except for the rather vacant expression she had cultivated in the mistaken impression that it was irresistible to men other than her husband.

She had been a bottle blonde since the age of twenty-two, and had an intellect to match. She thought that the word Bimbo equated with a cuddly Disney character, and would preen whenever she overheard the term used in reference to herself.

'The master has spoken,' she said, sarcastically, as she made her way over to the large and well-stocked bar on the other side of the room. She took a brandy balloon from the shelf and poured a generous allowance of St. Agnes into the glass. Then she took it over and handed it to her husband, making an effort meanwhile to look concerned.

'Thank God for brandy,' he said, as he downed three quarters of the glass in one hit. He experienced an immediate twinge of pain, and doubled over in his seat.

'Well aren't you going to tell me what's the matter?' said his wife, after waiting patiently for the ten seconds she felt she had to spare on him.

'You're not going to like it,' Alex said, as he grimaced with the pain. 'You're not going to like it at all!'

Jocelyn sighed deeply and perched on the arm of his chair. She looked down at the top of his head, began to twiddle a finger through his dark, wavy hair, then thought better of it and went back to buffing her nails.

'What won't I like, Alex? You're always saying I won't like something, and then nine times out of ten I don't mind at all.'

'You won't like it this time, Joss. It's for keeps this time!'

'Well, you tell me what it is, and then I'll tell you whether I like it or don't like it. That's the easiest,' she said, suppressing a yawn.

'Well, you know those tests I had done... two weeks ago? They weren't sure at first, but now they say there's nothing for it but to tell me straight out. They said I'd just have to take it like a man!'

Jocelyn looked confused.

'But of course you'd have to take it like a man, Alex! How else did they think you were going to take it?'

Alex stopped for a moment, then looked up at his wife, incredulously. He was never quite sure if Jocelyn was really as stupid as she made out, or whether she was taking a rise out of him.

'It's all down to the big 'C', Joss...'

Jocelyn stood up suddenly and went back to the table, annoyed.

'I wish you wouldn't talk in riddles, Alex. What's a big 'C?'

5

'Oh for Chrisesake woman! Where have you been all your life? I'm talking about cancer… that's right, bloody cancer, Joss!'

Jocelyn paused, looked back at her husband and furrowed her brow.

'But you're a Scorpio, Alex! You've always been a Scorpio. I know because I've always been a Pisces. I read your stars every week.'

Alex spluttered over his brandy.

'Not that sort of cancer, woman! The real thing!'

'What? Real cancer! Like the cancer that kills people?'

'Yes, the cancer that kills people, Joss! That's what I said! I've got cancer!'

There was silence for a full minute. Jocelyn went to speak, then thought better of it, and began buffing her nails again.

'Do you mean you've got cancer,' she said finally, leaving her nails for the moment, and staring at him with an ever-increasing frown. 'Does that mean you're going to leave me?'

'Well, I haven't really got much choice, have I,' said Alex, exasperated. He looked over at his wife, who went back to buffing her nails. Suddenly he snapped.

'I do think that you could at least show some interest in the imminent demise of your husband, Joss! Once I've gone, you can do what you bloody like, but in the meantime could we at least have some semblance of grief… Just a couple of little tears, maybe, or an expression of condolence, like, 'Oh God, I don't know what I'm going to do without you, dear!''

Jocelyn came back and sat on the arm of his chair, and stared at him from behind her false eyelashes.

'Well I was going to say that, Alex, but you didn't give me a chance. You know I'm not very good at thinking these things up.'

Alex stood up, and looked at her balefully.

'What's so hard in saying I'm sorry, for God's sake? What's so bloody difficult in that?'

Jocelyn flounced around to the other side of the table, as if putting a bit of distance between him and her. She pouted.

'Now that's not fair, Alex, and you shouldn't say things like that. I didn't give you the stupid cancer! Why should I say sorry?'

'Oh, for heaven's sake,' said Alex, and kicked the door open, out to the patio. He stormed through it, and slammed it, hard, behind him.

II

The patio of 'Dolphin's Retreat' looked out over the blue waters of Break-Mast Bay, named after some old British Clipper that had languished out there with a broken mast in the 1840's. It was on South Australia's west coast at Meddleton, a hundred kilometers or so from Port Lincoln. The house was actually situated on a small tidal promontory called Crab Island, three hundred yards off the coast, with a narrow causeway giving access from the mainland at the low water mark. Prittik had engaged contractors to dump thousands of tons of filling between the island and the shore to try and raise the level of the causeway, and the sea had just as determinedly washed it away again. This meant that visitors could only access the island for a few hours, twice a day, unless they wanted to get very wet.

They could swim, of course, the downside of that being the rather large number of hungry white pointer sharks that persistently circled the island, just waiting for the inhabitants to put a foot in the water. The only other access was by boat, but Alex had sworn off boats after a huge wave arriving from points south had dumped him and his party into the briny, dashed them against the rocks and swept two businessmen, a debutante and his bank manager three kilometers out to sea on the rip. It was only thanks to a lone fisherman that the accident hadn't proved to be fatal.

Once the boat had gone, the only emergency craft remaining was a blow-up rubber dinghy with outboard, but few were game to use it.

The house had been built on the seaward side of the island, and looked out towards the cold waters of the Antarctic. It wasn't the sort of place you would want to spend a winter, and in fact the Prittiks' didn't. In addition to 'Dolphin's Retreat', valued conservatively at seven million dollars - including the island of course - they also had a large mansion in Adelaide, a comfortable town house in Melbourne, and a matchbox sized flat facing the beach at Bondi, in Sydney. You could say that the Prittiks' had done all right for themselves!

You would be quite wrong, of course! Alex Prittik had done all right for themselves, while Jocelyn Prittik had gone along for the ride. He was an ingenious man who had a knack for inventing items that no one had previously thought of. His earlier inventions had not paid huge dividends, but five years before he had come up with a whopper of an idea that had made him an instant multimillionaire, and which had endeared him to the yuppie brigade.

The invention was a solar powered wristwatch that could communicate with a man's home, raise the garage doors, switch on the air-conditioning, heat the swimming pool, turn on the roast, adjust the blinds, and a hundred other little jobs all on the way home from work. As long as a system was installed and configured so that it could operate remotely, the *'Prittique'* could do it. It was a boon to a workaholic bachelor, a toy for the burnt-out businessman, a must-have for a female executive and a trophy for the ambitious middle manager. The idea had caught on so fast amongst the upwardly mobile brigade that the first question asked about an applicant to an upper management or administrative position became… 'Yes; but does he have a *Prittique*?' The answer to that question often sealed the fate of a promising new talent.

The watch didn't come cheap. As Alex always said, 'we all have to pay for life's little luxuries,' so at $15,000, people paid! Approximately $6,249 of each sale ended up in Alex's personal account, and once his idea had caught on in Japan, there was no stopping him. The money had poured in like an avalanche, and for the first time Alex had been forced to employ an accountant to deal with the nuts and bolts of his empire, to shuffle his money and investments backwards and forwards through various tax evasion schemes, buy and sell shares, deal with his foreign currency account and keep his rather vacant wife out of his hair.

Lindsay McCrae was the accountant in question, a thirty six year old bachelor who for the past eighteen months had been fully employed under the auspices of Gunther, Hamilton, Weatherall and Trebilcock, Chartered Accountants, who attempted to control the money machine that was *Unique Prittique Ltd.* Always with an eye to the main chance, McRae had recently left his former employment, set up on his own as a Financial Adviser, and had taken the *Prittique* account with him. Now that he could operate unobserved, so to speak, it was remarkable how much of his only client's money seemed to end up in McRae's personal account. Indeed, McRae was on his way to becoming a millionaire in his own right.

Alex was worldly enough to realize that in this age of greed, it didn't really matter which accountant he used, there would no doubt always be a steady leakage of funds into the pockets of the leeches he was forced to employ, and in that knowledge he had already forgiven McRae his personal peccadillo's. It is questionable whether he would have been so forgiving had he been aware that McRae was also porking his wife.

As Alex disappeared onto the patio to ponder his fate Jocelyn, meanwhile, had repaired to the bedroom where she was already on the phone to McRae, informing him of this new development.

'Oh Snookums, is that you,' she said, knowing perfectly well that it was. 'No, I know Winsey-Pinsey, I know that I'm not supposed to phone you at the office... Yes, I know your secretary has got big ears, lovey-dovums! But I just had to phone my Snookums to tell you something... something important!'

'Well can you just tell me without all the ooky-wooky bits, Joss. I'm snowed under here!'

McRae sounded irritable.

'It's just that Alex has got cancer, Duckums. Yes, real cancer! He says he's going to leave me.'

There was a short exchange.

'No, leave me for good... die! Yes, that's what he meant. No, I don't know where the cancer is, should I? I never thought to ask!'

At his office, Lindsay was straining forward across his desk, a fine sweat breaking out across his forehead. His complexion had gone a ghastly white, the colour of uncooked pasta. Death would mean probate, a will, lawyers, other accountants, an audit... then possibly jail and a stripping of his assets. McRae had good reason to turn white.

'For Chrisesake, Joss, just for once can you be more explicit? How long's he got?'

'Like I said, I never thought to ask him. Does it matter?'

At the other end of the line, McRae gave a reasonable impression of someone having an apoplectic fit.

'Of course it bloody matters, woman! Unless you want to see your inheritance disappear into the pockets of fifteen lawyers, you'd better start taking an interest in your husband's affairs while he's still alive. Has he made a will, for instance?'

The urgency in Snookem's voice finally communicated with the atavistic self-preservation principle lodged somewhere in Jocelyn's sinuous spine, and she felt the hairs begin to rise on the back of her neck.

'Now you're beginning to frighten me,' she wailed, a little too loud for a private, secret conversation being held in a bedroom, only yards from the subject of that conversation.

Out on the patio Alex pricked up his ears and walked along to the bedroom window, curious as to the subject of this sudden phone call. From there, he could hear his wife's side of the conversation clearly.

'Well, you're going to have to tell me what to do, Winsey-Pinsey. You know I'm no good at *real* things. I only know how to *spend* money, not how to get it... Alex has always done that! Can't you sort it out with him? You *are* his accountant, after all! He'll listen to you.'

The response at the other end was almost palpable. Jocelyn shrank back against the wall, and clutched herself tightly at the throat. If it had been possible for her skin to go any paler than it already was, she would have been an albino.

'Yes... all right, all right Snookums! Yes, I understand! Do you think I should write it all down so I don't forget any of it?'

There was a roll of thunder down the line as McRae choked on his asparagus and champignons sandwich, provided for him thoughtfully by his secretary, Janelle. This was just one of her extra-curricular duties, one of the few that she could accomplish with her underwear in place.

'All right - Will? How long? Where's the cancer?' Jocelyn paraphrased, ticking the items off on a neatly manicured finger. 'I'll get onto it straight away, Winsey!

Anyway, while we're on the phone, when are you coming up?'

'It'll have to be soon, especially now,' McRae grunted, as Janelle massaged the back of his neck. 'Tell Alex I need to get some signatures, and I'll bring the papers with me on Friday. Then I'll stay for the weekend.'

'I think he's going away on Sunday,' said Jocelyn, conspiratorially. 'Maybe you should bring your little camera, Snookums, and I'll get my broomstick out. You *do* remember my broomstick, Winsey?'

Jocelyn had once, during her misspent youth, been a model for a pornographic photographer.

McRae felt a cold sweat break out on the back of his neck at the vision of Jocelyn, naked from the waist down, astride an old-fashioned swish broom.

'Th.that would be nice, Joss,' he spluttered. 'But we have to be careful, especially now! With so little time left it would be a pity to spoil it by getting caught.'

'Oh, we won't get caught, Snookums…' she began to say, but Alex on the patio had heard enough. Reaching for his *Prittique* he pressed the appropriate button, brought up a three-digit number on a tiny liquid screen, and a message from his phone message service interrupted their call.

'Hi! You have reached the phone of Alex Prittik! I can't be with you just now, so I have recorded your call. Once I have played it back I shall call you… so don't forget to leave your number now!' The message ended with Alex's version of a diabolical laugh.

Jocelyn collapsed onto the bed, staring in horror at the phone on her lap. McRae rolled his eyes up into his head, and dropped the handset back into the cradle. How many times had he told Joss not to phone him? He put his head down and beat on the desk with both fists.

Out on the patio, Alex paced his short frame energetically backwards and forwards along the side of the swimming pool. So that was their game! How come he hadn't seen it coming? His wife, and his accountant... how cozy!

Alex had never given his wife credit for having much in the way of brains. He had married her for the sex, and appreciated her for her decorative qualities. As long as she didn't actually have to *do* anything, she was a positive asset at social events, and he was the envy of many of his business associates who reflected on their own dull, practical wives, and felt cheated somehow. Here was this Johnny-come-lately to the world of entrepreneurial wealth, who had a wife that reeked of sex and sensual pleasure while their own little women prided themselves on their potato-bakes. It just wasn't fair!

Jocelyn in her turn knew what was expected of her at these soiree's, and kept her end up admirably. She flirted and teased Alex's male guests unmercifully, until the indignant wives seized their husbands by elbows, ears or other appendages and dragged them off home to repent. Alex had gained intense amusement from these antics, as long as he thought his wife was being totally faithful to him. But the for the past eighteen months the rot had set in. Jocelyn had become withdrawn and sullen at times, and he had dealt with her peremptorily, like a misbehaving pet. This had just made her worse, and she now affected a disinterest in him and his affairs that he had misread as temperament. He now knew it was more than that!

So McRae, the dirty dog, had been dabbling in more than his accounts. Alex began to think back, to the many times that he had been called away on business, leaving McRae and his ever-beloved together in the house. God, he was a fool! He should have known that something like this would happen. When the cat's away the mice will play! And where Jocelyn was concerned, he should have realized that someone who believes that her prime purpose in life is to lie on her back and make loud, reassuring noises to the fellow on top, isn't going to change her spots because he's not around!

Alex wondered how many others had probed his wife's defenses over the years. Today it was his accountant. Yesterday it could just as well have been the Vicar! She spent enough time over there, listening to the man's asinine pronouncements about the morality, or otherwise, of her husband's lifestyle. It was a short step from there to a full-blooded repentance, doggie-fashion, behind the altar. If Alex knew anything, he knew human nature, and he didn't absolve the religious from occasional lapses into the pit of lust. But what to do about it, that was the question!

His initial gut response was to sack McRae and throw him to the wolves. He had no doubt that there would be ample evidence for fraudulent conversion once the auditors went over the books, and a spell in jail might be revenge enough. But that would make him into a martyr, and Alex knew how attractive martyrs were to dim-witted, gullible women. No, he wouldn't make McRae into a martyr. His revenge on them both would have to be more subtle than that, because – hey! He was going to die!

Alex came to a standstill beside the pool, rigid with shock. It hit him as if for the first time! He, Alex Prittik was going to die, and those two were going to be left behind with his money and his estate. Suddenly his knees went weak at the thought, and he staggered over to a bench and sat down. Looking down, he saw that his hands were shaking.

Chapter Two

Alex had visited Doctor Proust earlier that morning, in response to a summons from the doctor's secretary.

'Doctor Proust asked me to call you, Mister Prittik, to arrange an appointment with a view to discussing the results of your recent tests.'

'Oh, yes... those!'

'Doctor Proust informs me that it would be in your own best interests to attend.'

'Oh yeah... found something, have they?'

'I'm not at liberty to discuss the matter over the phone, Mister Prittik, but the doctor has put aside a time for you... 10 o'clock. Would that be convenient?'

'What... 10 o'clock... *today?*'

'Yes! Would that be convenient? It's the only time available, I'm afraid. The doctor is very busy at the moment.'

Alex looked blearily at the copy of the tides table that he kept on the set of drawers, near the bed. The tide was out at ten.

'Oh, I suppose... if I must, I must!' Alex was far from gracious at that time of the morning.

'We'll expect to see you at 10 o'clock then.'

Alex had crawled out of bed – it was 8.30am – and staggered out to the shower. These bloody doctors... thought they could summon you at will, like some foreign potentate!

In the shower he got gel in his eyes, and cursed roundly. When he had recovered his sight, he stepped out and stood before the mirror. He needed a shave! There was three days of growth on his chin, and that always made him look a bit like a wild man.

In actual fact, he was on holiday... or considered himself to be, and he always made a point of never shaving on holiday! It was bad enough having to do it every other day of the year, when he was in the city. But Crab Island was his retreat from all that, and although he was often called away in the middle of a long siesta, he still tried to maintain that holiday spirit as long as he was there.

Alex stared at his reflection in the mirror. No doubt about it, he was starting to pass over that imperceptible hill called middle age. His hair was still intact, though rather less bountiful than ten years ago. His Zapata moustache was as luxuriant as ever. It made him look like an older, more weathered version of Ché Guevara. He liked that, even though it never occurred to him that he was a considerably shorter version. Alex was only five foot eight, but in his Cuban heeled boots he always imagined himself as being taller than the next man.

It was his skin that worried him. That youthful bloom had long gone from his cheeks, and the imprint of stress had worn its way onto his features. What the hell, it gave him character, he told himself, and smiled, showing a perfect set of teeth.

Over all, he wasn't a bad looking fellow was his ultimate conclusion, though that didn't explain what was going on in his interior, as the twinges of pain that had begun to make themselves felt three months ago were now full-blooded, agonizing spasms that bent him over double in their extremity. Usually after meals, always after booze, he had found it necessary to curtail his annual intake of brandy and bourbon, and reduce them to a trickle. For a party animal like Alex Prittik, this was not good!

If there was one thing that Alex enjoyed, it was throwing a lavish party. He had a lot of friends in the city, and a lot of business acquaintances, and it did his ego good to be at the centre of a group of hard drinking executives. It wasn't the same when you had to stand there, sipping lolly water!

But that was city life! Crab Island was Alex's retreat from the world, the place where his other self, the hermitic version, could enjoy the simplicity of fishing alone, evening strolls, and the peace and quiet that you could never get in the city. Three months of that, and he had usually recharged his batteries, ready to return to the fray.

At the doctor's surgery, he was waved to a seat and asked to wait. The doctor was with another patient. Alex looked at his own personal *Prittique*. It was 10.05am, and he sat there for another twenty minutes while the doctor's door remained firmly closed.

'Bloody amazing,' he thought. These damned doctors made appointments for a set time, dragged you halfway across the city – when you were in the city, which of course he wasn't – and then proceeded to keep you waiting well beyond the time of your appointment! Nothing made Alex madder than being made to wait!

He began to drum his fingers on the small table next to him, and the receptionist took due note. She leaned over and smiled sweetly.

'Doctor Proust won't be too much longer, Mister Prittik. Sometimes things take a little longer than you'd expect.'

Five minutes later the door opened, and a portly Bishop dressed in his full robes issued forth into the reception area, and went over to sign the Medicare form. Alex heard his name called, and he got up to enter Proust's inner sanctum.

'Just been getting your daily dose of salvation, doctor?' he said flippantly, nodding his head over his shoulder. 'What's up with him... got a full dose of gripe water by the look of him!'

Proust looked up from his desk, over the top of his glasses, and cast a disinterested eye over Alex's figure.

'Please sit down, Mister Prittik! Bishop Bagwort is a very old friend of mine. We grew up together. He went into the ministry, and I took the other direction, that of ministering to the body. Between us, you might say, we keep body and soul together!'

Alex looked at Proust suspiciously. He suspected that he had just been firmly put in his place.

'My speciality, as I'm sure you're aware, are the inner organs. In your case, we're talking about the pancreas!'

'Oh... yes...' said Alex, looking humbly repentant, and hiding his smile behind his hand.

'Now I have the results of your tests back, and I'm sorry to say that the prognosis is not good, not good at all. I think you'd better take a deep breath, Prittik!'

Alex looked at the doctor with an amused boredom. He still hadn't grasped the seriousness of his situation.

'What exactly do you mean by not good? Do you mean *not-good-but-not-all-bad*, or do you mean *bad-bad*? When my accountant says not good, it usually means I've lost a hundred thousand dollars on the stock market!'

'I'm afraid you're going to have to brace yourself, Prittik,' said Proust, now acting more like a headmaster, with a cane hidden up his sleeve. 'The results of your tests were positive.'

'But that's good, isn't it? Positive's good!'

Proust gently shook his head.

'In the world of medical science, Prittik, positive quite often means bad whereas negative means good. In your case the result for you is positively negative, where both positive and negative are bad! You have in invasive cancer of the pancreas. I suspected as much when I first saw you. In addition to this, you also smoke, Prittik… far too much to be of assistance to you in this case!'

Alex went slightly pale, flexed his shoulders and cleared his throat.

'Aaarrrrum! So, cancer! Of the pancreas!'

Proust nodded.

'So what can you do? Can you take it out? An operation, is that it?'

Proust shook his head.

'Unfortunately, it's gone too far for that! If we catch it in the early stages, then that is certainly an option. But once it breaks out and begins to attack nearby organs, gets into the lymph glands and sends out secondaries, then the only thing we can advise is palliative care, which may include chemotherapy and radiation treatment.'

Proust went on to describe how the inevitable might be delayed for some time by various methods of treatment, but in the end result, the finale to it all was the finale to life itself!

Alex was barely listening at this stage. He had fixed his gaze over the doctor's shoulder, and was watching two children playing in the gardens outside the clinic. They were ducking in and out of the rose bushes, laughing and carefree at the beginnings of their lives, while the end of his was being detailed to him in, what was now a grim, grey office.

'So there's no hope at all, doctor,' Alex said, thoughtfully.

'Oh, I wouldn't look at it like that, Prittik! It's no good being negative about things. We should rise to the challenge and give it our very best shot.'

'I'm sure you should,' said Prittik. 'It's not your pancreas!'

Proust was silent for a while.

'We can pretty well deal with the pain these days. At least, you won't have to put up with that. We can make you comfortable, and... who knows, you might just prove me wrong and live for six months longer than I'd give you at this particular moment.'

'And how long would that be, Doc? How much would you give me... not counting the six months, of course.'

'About eight weeks... could be as much as twelve, but plenty of time to put your affairs in order, anyway. I'd certainly be making immediate arrangements to draw up your will… if you haven't already done so, of course! Sorry I can't be more positive.'

'I think you've been positively negative enough – in terms of medical science, anyway,' said Alex, bitterly. 'If I undergo these treatments… this palliative care; what are the side effects likely to be?'

Proust explained about the anaemia, the vomiting and diarrhoea, the hair loss, mouth sores and general weakness. He spoke at length about the nausea, the jaundice, the narrowing of the bile duct and the weight loss. He waxed lyrical about the breathlessness and poor resistance to infection, the fevers and headaches and poor appetite, and was rhapsodical about the reddening and burning of the skin due to radiation treatment. Finally he described in detail the lessening of the sex drive, and the difficulty Alex might find in engaging in intercourse at all, due to lower back and abdominal pain.

'In short, Prittik, a rather unfortunate end to life!'

Alex looked at him, angrily.

'Well, aren't you a barrel of laughs! Do you get a kick out of this, doctor? What *are* you… a death junkie?'

'Now, now! It's usual to feel threatened at these times, Prittik!'

'Threatened? Too bloody right I feel threatened! You've just told me I'm going to be dead in eight weeks!'

Nevertheless, you must rise above it… try to enjoy what you have left… Live as if you had another fifty years ahead of you!'

Alex declined his invitation to make appointments for palliative care, seized his scripts for painkillers, and stormed out of the surgery looking murderous. He jumped into his classic, rebuilt, E-type Jaguar, and drove through the township of Meddleton, and down to Meddleton Beach.

From there he could see his island, sitting out in the bay like a jewel in the sun. He got out and walked along the line of the tide at low water mark, the water occasionally sweeping in and covering his shoes. He was oblivious to it! He walked with his head down, thinking furiously about the immediate future, and more, about the way his life had suddenly turned. Eight weeks!

Forty three years, and unlikely to make forty four! His whole life spun in front of his eyes, the years of failure, the years of challenge, and the final success. But he wasn't going to be allowed to enjoy the fruits of his labour. It was all going to be snatched away from him in an orgy of vomit and diarrhoea. It was all so hard to believe because, standing there, he felt as fit as he'd ever done. There was just the odd twinge of pain in the abdominal region, and the occasional feeling of nausea. But he knew now that the symptoms would magnify day by day, and within a matter of weeks he would be confined to a wheelchair, or his bed, looking drunkenly out at the world through a miasma of morphine and painkillers.

Well, it wasn't going to happen to him… not like that! Alex's sense of justice recoiled at the idea of allowing some influence outside his own reason to decide when and where he would part company with his body.

No! He would go when he was ready. He would plan his own demise! But it would have to be soon, or the decision would be snatched from his grasp.

Looking up, he saw that he had wandered over a mile from the car, so he sat at the verge and dialled up the Jag on his *Prittique*. The car roared into life, startling two young lads who were peering through its windows at that moment, and causing them to scatter when it put itself into gear and reversed out from the curb. Using its own satellite tracking system, and beaming out its radar in an arc of ninety degrees to cover the road ahead, it threw itself into first, took off with a squeal of tyres and executed a deft manoeuvre around a woman with a pram before eventually pulling up alongside Alex, and allowing him to climb aboard.

On the way home he called his solicitor in Adelaide and told him that he wanted him to call in to see him, just over three weeks from today. If he wanted special transport from the city, Prittik would lay on a helicopter. But he must not forget to bring a new will form, as that would be the prime purpose for his visit.

II

Prittik's sister Hilda was down at the local supermarket, struggling under the weight of five shopping bags while her daughter, Darlene, wandered unencumbered behind her. Every now and then Darlene would wander off to the cheap clothing racks and riffle through the halter-tops, causing her mother to stop and wait for her to catch up.

'I wish you wouldn't get sidetracked, dear. We've only got so much time to get this done, then I have to get home and make your father's tea.'

Darlene threw a top bad-temperedly onto the floor.

'Oh, for god's sake, Hilda, don't be in such a hurry. He can wait!'

Hilda thought about the idea of Greg waiting for anything, and shivered. She knew him better than anyone, and rather feared his haughty, overbearing manner.

'Now don't be unfair, dear, you know how irritable he gets when he doesn't get his meals on time.'

Hilda and her husband, Greg Tressor, lived in the rear section of the house on Crab Island, not by choice but by necessity. Their two teenage children lived with them. They had once owned their own home in Adelaide, where Greg had worked as an insurance salesman. He was ginger haired, tubby, and jolly when he had to be, which meant when he was with potential customers. At home he was taciturn and withdrawn most of the time.

Bringing up two children on commission hadn't been easy, but Greg was the sort of fellow that liked people to think he was a Mandrake where it came to financial wizardry. After years of belittling Hilda's brother's inventions, and lording it over his brother-in-law, it galled him considerably when the *Prittique* took off and made Alex an instant millionaire. Stung into action, he re-mortgaged the family home, and went all out to prove that his theories of incredible wealth were attainable through judicious paper shuffling on the stock exchange.

He almost did it, too! Getting onto the dot.com boom early, he was at one point worth almost three million dollars, and he would visit Alex and swagger about in front of him, offering to share his savvy with the amateur.

'I don't know, Greg,' said Alex, shaking his head. 'These dot.coms... they look a bit dicey to me!'

Greg found difficulty in not curling his lip in contempt. Alex was slim, tanned and fit looking, something Greg would never be. That, in itself, was a source of resentment. He even resented Alex his Zapata moustache, which he saw as an affectation. The fact that he couldn't grow one himself had nothing to do with it.

'Nonsense old fellow! Wave of the future! You mark my words, one of these days ninety percent of all business will be done over the Internet. But you need to get on the bandwagon early, old chap, or you're going to miss out.'

'Correct me if I'm wrong,' said Alex, 'but from my understanding, not one of these dot.coms has so far made a profit. They're just spending the investors money!'

'Merely a hiccup, old chap. Bound to be a few teething problems. New technology, you know! But everyone who's anyone has made a bomb so far. If I cashed in today, I'd be worth... well, I won't tell you what I'd be worth because you'd be green with envy, old chap. Wouldn't do it to you! Have to maintain a certain modesty you know!'

'Well, I'm glad you're doing well,' said Alex. 'It's nice to know that Hilda is being looked after.'

'I could sort something out for you, too, Alex. Get you a good bundle of shares for, what... two mill? You'd have a couple of mill spare, wouldn't you, Alex,' Greg said, goadingly.

'I might have had, Greg, but I put it all into futures. Not doing too bad either!'

Greg looked at him as if he was mad.

'Futures! Hah! You'll come a cropper there, my lad. God! What futures?'

'Lentils,' said Alex, noting the other's amusement.

Shortly after the dot.coms collapsed, and Greg and Hilda were turfed out onto the street, Lentils went from $300 to $650 per tonne. It was Hilda that went to Alex, cap in hand, asking him for help.

'Poor Greg's not very well, Alex. This whole business has hit him very hard. We've only managed to rent ourselves a little flat in Enfield, but there's only two bedrooms and the children are squabbling like cat and dog. I'm afraid he might do something desperate, Alex… He might kill himself!'

Alex looked at his sister with sympathy. He noted the worried, hunted look of her, the disappointment that seemed a permanent feature of her eyes, the disillusioned downturn at the corners of her mouth. Hilda had been a good-looking woman when she'd met Greg. Now she was haggard and middle-aged before her time.

'Now don't you worry about that, Hilda. I can't spare the room in Adelaide, but the place on Crab Island is pretty big. We only go over there for the summer months, so you could stay there until he gets back on his feet. It's like two houses really, because there's a large area set up at the rear for guests. It has its own kitchen and there are en suites to the bedrooms. Just do me a favour. Keep the youngsters out of the front of the house, I wouldn't want anything damaged or disturbed.'

Hilda had relayed the good news to Greg where he lay on his sickbed.

'Couldn't you have got the house in Adelaide, Hilda? What good is it to me over at Crab Island? It's hundreds of miles away. I do think your brother could have put himself out a bit. I mean, we are family, after all!'

'But he needs the Adelaide house for himself, Greg. That's where he does most of his business!'

Greg raised himself up on one elbow and looked splenetic.

'Business! Hah! The fellow's just been lucky, that's all. He wouldn't know business if it jumped up and bit him, Hilda.'

Hilda bridled at this.

'Well at least he's still got *his* money, Gregory, *and* his houses. I think the proof of the pudding is in the eating!'

'So! Taking his side, is it? If I remember rightly, I was the one that suggested the *Prittique* to him in the first place!'

'No you didn't,' Hilda said, firmly. 'You were just bragging about your new remote garage doors, and they've been out forever.'

'Well anyway,' said Greg, suitably rebuffed, 'did you get any money? We need money to live on, Hilda.'

Hilda looked shocked.

'I most certainly did not, Gregory. I wouldn't demean myself! I think Alex is being very generous as it is, without us expecting him to keep us. You'll just have to get a job.'

'How the hell am I supposed to get a job at Break-Mast Bay, Hilda? I'm an insurance salesman!'

'Well, you'll have to go on the dole then! We have to eat, and the children need money for clothes and things.'

'The dole!' Greg groaned, and fell back on the bed. His humiliation was complete!

Later, at 'Dolphin's Retreat', Greg sidled up to Alex and tried to pry a lump sum out of him.

'Sorry about the inconvenience, old chap. Just a temporary snarl. Those dot.coms, caught me with my pants down a bit. Of course, nobody could have foreseen it! Just the vagaries of the American economy, really! I feel sorry for Hilda, though, having to go without. She shouldn't have to rough it like this!'

Alex raised one eyebrow.

'Oh, I wouldn't call living rent free in a seven million dollar mansion, on its own private island, 'roughing it!''

Greg managed a sickly smile.

'No, no, I didn't mean it like that. But you know what she's like, Alex. She likes her little luxuries. And she feels badly about not being able to supply Darlene and Jason with the things that kids today take for granted, you know, computers, Play Stations, Nike shoes.'

'Probably the best thing that's ever happened to them,' said Alex. 'I always said you spoiled those two, Greg. A bit of deprivation might drag them into the real world.'

Greg took a step backwards, and swallowed hard..

'You can't mean that, Alex. You're their uncle, after all! We've always tried to do our best for the kids.'

'Meaning that you bought them everything they ever asked for, spoiled them rotten. What about the discipline, Greg? What about *spare the rod and spoil the child*?'

'That might be your philosophy, but it's not ours, Alex! If you'd ever had kids of your own…'

'I wouldn't let them go around destroying other people's property, Greg, like they do around here. I wouldn't allow them to talk to me, or their mother, as if you had just come in on someone's shoe. I'd demand a bit of respect! I wouldn't have them calling me by my first name.'

Greg shuffled from side to side, and looked embarrassed. This was not going as planned.

'Well, kids today… it's not as easy as you think, old chap!'

'It is for me! I'd kick their little fat arses for them, and lock them in their rooms. They wouldn't treat *me* like shit, Greg! Which reminds me. As you don't seem able to control their rampages through my home, I would remind you that although I have consented for you and Hilda to live here rent free, your two teenage monsters are here under sufferance. The rent's free, but the breakages will be charged for. If that's the only way that I can get you to accept responsibility for their appalling behaviour, then that's the way it will have to be. I've made up a list of items that they have so far destroyed or damaged beyond repair, and I have to inform you that the total stands so far at $2344.50. You can pay it off at $50 a week.'

Greg's jaw dropped, and he seemed, again, lost for words. Alex waved one hand, signalling dismissal. Then he turned again.

'Oh, and by the way… if the total creeps over $5,000, I will be turfing them out on their ears. You can stay, but they won't!'

Greg relayed the message to Hilda in high dudgeon.

'That's it, Hilda! We leave this place today! I will not be spoken to like that by your brother, or by anyone else if it comes to that. The hide of him!'

'And where exactly do you think we're going to go,' said Hilda, wiping an angry tear from her eye. 'Are you going to pitch a tent, or rent a caravan? You're just going to have to learn to put up with it, Greg, until things turn for the better. You should never have gone to him in the first place.'

'I was only doing it for you, Hilda. But perhaps you're right. *You* should ask him! You are his sister, after all. He'd obviously like to get rid of us all!'

'And how much should I ask for,' she said, sarcastically, 'a hundred thousand dollars? Two hundred thousand! How about the amount you lost on your stupid investments, Greg... two hundred and forty five thousand dollars!'

Greg stood with his back to her, leaning against the mantelpiece. Suddenly he straightened up and turned to face her, a hopeful look on his face.

'Could you? Yes, well why not! Ask him for four hundred thousand... just a gnat bite to him. Make it four hundred and fifty thousand. Sounds better than half a mill. With that sort of capital I could recoup it all with a few smart investments. Only take six months and we could be swimming in it.'

'Oh Greg,' said Hilda, and burst into a flood of tears.

Chapter Three

Jason Tressor was only sixteen, but he already had the attributes of a hardened criminal. After a lax upbringing by a timid mother and a misguided new-wave father, he had learned that authority was there to flout, whether it came in the form of parents, school authorities, police or outraged citizens. Magistrates and social workers he had a special contempt for. They took one look at him in the dock, affecting his teary-eyed impression of the lost adolescent, and then indulged in a paroxysm of do-gooding, like the bleeding hearts and clucky matrons they were. His misdeeds would be put behind him from now on, they thought. They would expect him to succumb to their overtures for '*a fresh start for a pure heart*' routine, gratefully accept the money that the social workers would throw at him as an advance reward for behaving himself, and they would then put him back on the streets to wreak havoc. Jason would curl his lip as he dashed off to freedom, and think of them as pathetic, weak and ineffectual. Almost as weak and useless as his parents!

Jason wasn't big for his age, in fact he was rather stunted. He had untidy mousy hair, squinty little eyes and a way of looking slyly sideways to see if anyone was watching him. As a small child his mother had treated him like an undernourished runt, and he had repaid her by becoming more and more demanding as the years went on, throwing tantrums if he didn't get what he wanted. If it worked for his older sister, he figured it would work for him too. They were a good pair.

Greg Tressor and his wife Hilda were the sort of parents that Alex Prittik hated. Even though Hilda was his own sister, Alex favoured her with an amiable contempt once he discovered that she had surrendered to her husband's philosophy of plaintive reasoning with the children, and obsequious compliance with his every demand. What really galled Alex was their policy of abstaining from corporal punishment under any circumstance. To Alex, reasoning with children was like trying to reason with baboons. It made no odds that you were only trying to feed them. The first slip, and they would be at your throat!

In their turn, Greg and Hilda thought that Alex was not far short of a barbarian in his attitudes regarding the upbringing of children, though it was noticeable that when Darlene and Jason addressed him, they never resorted to their time honoured 'what do you want, bitch,' routine, which they used on their mother, or dared to call him 'the old bastard!' Alex got a sullen 'yessir', or 'yes uncle Alex!' This was especially pronounced now that they were living in his house, though they tried to make up for it by clandestinely destroying his possessions, one by one.

On one occasion when a police officer had called with regard to an escapade of Jason's, the parents being out, Alex had dragged Jason to the front door by his ear.

'I'm going to have to give you a warning this time, my lad,' said the constable, sticking strictly to his warm and fuzzy routine.

Alex got impatient.

'I'd rather you gave him a bloody good flogging,' he said, 'give him something to think about.'

'Err, that's not the way we do things nowadays, sir! And I must say that holding the lad like that, between finger and thumb, might just constitute assault!'

'You mean like knocking that woman over when he was riding his bike on the pavement? Wasn't that assault?'

'That was more of an accident, sir – an avoidable one, I'll give you that! But an accident just the same! If the woman hadn't been there…'

'Walking innocently along the footpath, which is what it's provided for,' added Alex…

'Well, yes sir. What you say is true. However, for some years now insurance companies have maintained that there is no innocent party in an accident; there is always a percentage of blame ascribed to each party.'

'Bugger the insurance companies, what does the law say?'

'Well,' the policeman took off his hat and wiped his perspiring brow. 'To tell you the truth, the law seems to have followed the reasoning of the insurance companies.'

'Not to mention the United Nations Charters on the Rights of the Child, the rights of minorities, the rights of everyone except that of the victim, in fact,' said Alex, annoyed. It was a pet hobby-horse with him.

Meanwhile, Jason had bored of the conversation and squirmed away, running off to hide in his bedroom. The policeman, lost for a reason to be there, booked Alex for leaving the gate to his swimming pool open, thus endangering neighbourhood children who might wander in and drown.

'But this isn't a neighbourhood,' Alex protested. 'It's a private island... or didn't you notice the signs as you drove across the causeway?'

'No one is above the law, sir! You have children in your house here. They must be protected too.'

'They're sixteen and eighteen years old!' Alex said, frustrated. 'In fact, they're the ones who leave the bloody gate open all the time.'

The policeman shook his head, got into his car and drove off before he felt the need to write a ticket for Alex's dog, that was running unfettered along the island's private beach.

But on this day, Jason came sloping around the side of the house onto the patio, totally oblivious to the fact that Alex was sitting on a bench, close to the bedroom window, after listening to his wife's conversation. When he threw the bomb of red dye into the swimming pool, therefore, he was startled by the roar of anger from his father's host.

'Why, you little shit! What did you do that for?'

Jason panicked and tried to run, but Alex was fairly nimble for his age and grabbed him by the collar.

'No you don't you little bastard. Your father's going to deal with you, and if he doesn't birch you, I will!'

Jason struggled and wriggled to get free of his coat, so Alex grabbed him by the hair and hung on. The only way Jason was going to get away, was bald!

'You can't touch me! I'll have the law on yer. Lemme go you deadshit! Just 'cos you're rich, doesn't mean you can hit me! You'll go to jail!'

Alex looked down at the squirming figure of his nephew, and across at the rapidly spreading stain of red that was obscuring the bottom of his pool.

'You're a little ratbag, aren't you? Not enough discipline, that's your trouble you little jerk. Well this time you're going to pay!' With that he dragged young Jason over to the edge of the pool and threw him in.

Jason came up spluttering to the surface, his struggles spreading the dye in waves. Soon the entire pool was red, and it was impossible to see the bottom. He splashed his way over to the side and tried to hang on, screaming and swearing at the top of his voice. Alex was almost incoherent with anger. He grabbed the long bug net, turned it around and shoved the handle into the boy's chest.

'When I said you're going for a swim, I meant a good long one you little creep.' He pushed him off from the side, and Jason went under. By the time Darlene heard her brother's yells and came running around to find out what was going on, Jason had been ducked four times.

'What's going on – hey, you're going to drown him!' she yelled, running up to her uncle and trying to wrest the net handle away from him. Alex grabbed her by the hair and spun her around. She did a neat little pirouette in mid-air and headed into the pool herself.

'Don't you dare interfere,' Alex yelled as she surfaced, spluttering. 'A good bath will do the two of you good, maybe wash some of the shit out of your liver,' he shouted, beside himself with anger.

'I'll tell my father on you, I'll call the cops,' Darlene yelled, madly dog paddling in the centre where he couldn't reach her.

'Go ahead, tell your father… and I'll throw the lot of you out on your ears! You can go and live in a one-room dogbox – that's all you two are fit for anyway. You're a bloody disgrace to your parents!'

'My Dad'll kill you for this,' Jason spluttered. In response, Alex trod on his fingers as he tried to grasp the side, and he howled in pain, then pushed off into the middle and tried for the other side. Alex was there before him.

'He's going to drown us… he's going to drown us,' Darlene screamed hysterically. Joss came running out, along the patio, and stood there indecisively, trying not to get splashed.

'Oh dear, why's the water red?' she quavered.

'Because this little shit threw a dye bomb in it. I watched him do it! So I'm just making sure he gets the benefit of his own handiwork.'

By this time both Jason and Darlene were distinctly red in the face, and it wasn't from exertion. Their hair had gone the colour of a pillar-box.

Alex finally let them out after ten minutes, by which time all their clothes, their hair and skin were distinctly red. He made them shiver on the far side of the pool while Joss went off for towels and a change of clothes.

'You can't make us get changed here. We'll catch pneumonia,' Jason snivelled.

'I'm too old to get changed in the open. I'm not taking my clothes off in public,' Darlene whined.

'But not too old to take them off for any one of ten boys in the town, eh Darlene! Don't deny it! You're the town bike! Don't think I don't know about the abortion!'

Darlene went breathlessly quiet, shocked to the core. The abortion was a dead-set secret between her and her mother. Even her father didn't know.

'I don't know what you're talking about,' she bluffed.

'Oh, you know all right! Where do you think your mother got the money from – the lamington stall at the fete? Your mother doesn't have access to that sort of money, and neither does your father anymore. She came to me! And let me tell you something, that's the only chance you get. Come home pregnant again, and you'll be left carrying the baby. See how that screws up your life, you stupid little trollop!'

Darlene went silent, then collapsed onto the tiles and began to sob. At that moment Greg and Hilda arrived, and rather than explain, Alex just indicated the water in the pool.

'I suggest you get started right away, Greg. There's about a thousand dollars worth of water in that pool, and I want it cleaned out, replaced, and as good as new by tomorrow evening.'

A twinge of pain hit him in the abdomen, and he flinched. Then he recovered himself and stalked off into the house, taking Joss with him.

II

As Alex stormed off into the house, he realised that it wasn't that he disliked his sister's kids; he hated them! That Darlene was a slutty little beast, foul mouthed and

39

contemptuous of everyone. Why Hilda ever put up with her talking to her the way she did, he would never understand.

Their own father, Ulrich Prittik, had been a convinced disciplinarian, and neither he nor Hilda had been allowed the laxity that these two enjoyed. As children, if they did anything wrong, they were walloped, either by a ham-sized hand on the back of the legs, or later with a shoe, a wooden spoon, or any other implement that came to hand. And yet Alex didn't remember his father as an unkind man, quite the contrary. His father was a loving man, who showed his children a great deal of affection. He didn't shower them with gifts, and he didn't try to buy their affection in return; he didn't have to. Both Alex and Hilda loved their father, and accepted the justness of any punishment that was meted out. He was of the old school, and used to say as they got older: 'If you can't accept discipline from without, how can you build discipline within?' Alex had adopted the credo as his own. Hilda had given in to her husband, Greg, as she felt it was only right to do. Perhaps if she'd been a little more assertive, this state of affairs would never have come about.

As a result, Darlene had been a problem since the age of eleven. She'd got to the mouthy stage very early, and instead of a sharp slap to reinforce the boundaries of acceptable behaviour, Greg had sat down with her and wheedlingly tried to reason with his precocious daughter.

'Now why won't you be a good girl for Mummy, Darlene?'

'Cos I don't want to!'

'But you've always been a good girl before, Darlene. What's upset you to make you act like this now?'

'She makes me eat eggs, and I *hate* eggs. And she won't give me my chocolate!'

'But eggs are good for you, Darlene. Mummy's only trying to make you grow up big and strong.'

'I don't care, I don't *want* to grow up big and strong. I want my chocolate!'

Greg turned aside to Hilda with a weak smile.

'You see dear, I told you, there's always a reason. You just have to ask the child, and she'll tell you.'

'I know why she's playing up, Greg, I'm not stupid!'

'Well, why don't you give her the chocolate then, dear, and then she will probably eat her egg.'

'I won't, I won't,' said Darlene. 'I hate her, Daddy!' She had learned very young that an appeal to 'Daddy' was far more effective than an appeal to 'Greg', which was her usual form of address.

'Now, now, you don't mean that,' said Greg, revelling in his role as mediator. 'And you know you don't call someone 'her', do you? Who's 'her?''

'Hilda! I don't like Hilda. She's mean to me, all the time. When you're not here she hits me!'

'I hope that's not true, Hilda,' said Greg, menacingly towards his wife. 'We don't believe in hitting children, do we Hilda?'

'She's lying, Greg. Can't you see that she's lying?'

'Now, you shouldn't go saying things like that, Hilda. Children are sensitive. You'll *make* her hate you if you say things like that.'

'So you only want the truth from her, Greg, you're not interested in my truth!'

41

'You're the adult, Hilda. You're the grown-up! I should be able to rely on you to contain your feelings on these occasions, especially with a helpless little girl like this. Now come on you two, make up!'

Hilda often went off into her bedroom for a good cry after confrontations of this kind, but it didn't change anything. Greg went blindly along his chosen path, and as he was away most of the day, didn't get to hear the foul and insulting remarks that began to litter his children's speech. By the time he did, it was too late.

When she was fifteen, Darlene turned to her father with a look of contempt.

'I don't care what you say, *Greg!* I'm going to the disco, anyway!'

'I said you're not going,' said Greg from behind his paper.

'You're a real slime ball, do you know that, *Greg!*' said Darlene, as she stomped off to her room. Later she let herself out of the window, and went anyway.

Greg went to Hilda in the kitchen, his mouth open in shock.

'Did you just hear what she called me – *slime ball!* I can't believe it!'

'Doesn't surprise me,' said Hilda, looking at him scornfully. 'You're not here most of the time, so you never get to hear what they call me... or you, behind your back if it comes to that. You've brought it on yourself.'

'Now don't put this onto me,' said Greg, puffing himself up. 'After all, you're the one that's here with them all day. They're taking their cues from you, Hilda.'

'No, they're running out of control, Greg, I've been telling you for years. Well now you're going to reap the harvest... serves you right!'

'I've tried to bring those children up under the best model there is,' he huffed, 'as civilised, reasoning human beings.'

'No – as undisciplined little brats, Greg, that's what your 'model' has produced.'

'Well why didn't you take matters in hand, Hilda? You were the one on the spot. You're the mother figure!'

'Yes, with my hands tied behind my back. You said don't hit, so I didn't hit. They saw how easily they could manipulate you, and now they just hold you in contempt... me too, I might add.'

'Now I'm sure that's not right,' Greg said, shocked. 'Darlene's just having an off day. Maybe she's got, you know, woman's troubles. She is fifteen, after all!'

'Whatever you say, Greg,' Hilda sighed, and went back to the dishes.

Greg went along and tapped on Darlene's door.

'Who is it?' she yelled out.

'It's just me, honey bunch. I think we should have a talk.'

'Fuck off, Greg! You're an arsehole,' was the muffled reply.

Greg staggered back as if he'd been physically assaulted. The veins around his temple began to pulse, and his face turned the colour of ripe beetroot.

'What did you say... I said, what did you say, young lady,' he yelled. Then he pounded on the door.

43

'Open this door, Darlene. Open it this minute!'

There was no reply.

'I said open this damned door, or there'll be trouble!'

Still silence.

When Greg finally overcame his own rule of only entering the children's rooms on their invitation, and kicked Darlene's door in, the room was empty. The curtains blew ineffectually at the open window, and Darlene had disappeared into the night.

Chapter Four

The Reverend Elder Berry visited Jocelyn that afternoon. He was young for a vicar, only twenty-nine, and he took his duties seriously. Each Friday he set out from the vicarage and covered his parish on foot. A number of his parishioners needed that extra spur of a home visit to ensure their presence at the Sunday service, and Vicar Berry was proud of his attendance record. In times of religious drought, he still managed to boast an average attendance of between forty-five and sixty, rising to a hundred and fifty at weddings and on special occasions. Some of the less charitable might have said that his visits appeared to favour the rather better endowed of the opposite sex, but that would be unchristian. He occasionally visited men too, when they were dying, or when their tithes had fallen below a certain red line on a chart in the vestry.

Alex saw him coming, plodding along the causeway shortly after the tide had gone out.

'Good God! Word spreads fast around here,' he groaned, imagining that the visit was for him. The vicar had tried repeatedly to save Prittik's everlasting soul, via the solicitation of a massive donation to the local church, but Alex had refused to cooperate.

'God doesn't need my money,' Alex had said at the time, 'and if he does, then I'm sure he can get a loan off the Pope. He's got plenty!'

'But Alex, the Roman Church and the Anglican Church are two totally different entities, I'm sure you appreciate that.'

'Well, which one does your God go to? If he goes to theirs, why would I want to give money to yours?'

'He doesn't go to any particular church, Alex. *We* go to *ours!*'

'Then what would be the point, if he's not there?' said Alex, being deliberately obtuse. He loved to watch 'his Elderness' as he liked to call him, going red in the face and struggling for comprehension.

On this particular day he decided to make himself scarce.

'Jocelyn,' he yelled. 'You'd better put on a clean pair of knickers... the vicar's coming! I'm off for a walk.'

So saying, Alex fled the house and skirted around to the beach, walking swiftly towards the high point of the island on the western side. If he was careful he could hide out by the cliff, and not be seen from the house.

Jocelyn hurried to check herself out in the bedroom mirror before answering the door. She stripped off her cargo pants and donned a short, leather skirt, matching that with a bra-less, halter-top, that left little to the imagination. That was her little quirk. There was something kinky about turning a vicar on.

'Good afternoon Jocelyn,' the vicar smiled, puffing a little from the exertion of crossing the causeway. 'My word, you look a picture today, my dear.'

'Oh, thank you, your reverence,' she gushed, trying very hard to blush at the same time.

'Err, that's 'Reverend', Jocelyn. I'm not quite so high up on the ecumenical scale as that, though it would be nice.'

Jocelyn giggled nervously, and led him into the lounge. She always giggled when a comment surpassed her understanding. It covered up for a gaping chasm of ignorance.

'And is your good husband about the place?' the vicar enquired, stretching his neck in various directions. He was hoping the answer would be no!

'I think he just went for a walk, your worship. If he reappears I'll give him a call. I'd like you to talk to him at the moment, anyway. He's got me really worried.'

Berry affected a look of concern. He was very good at it... it was one of the crowning talents of his profession.

'I'm sorry to hear that, Joss. Perhaps if you come and sit near me you can tell me all about it.'

He was sitting on a two-seater divan, patting the seat beside him, and Jocelyn sucked playfully on one finger as she appeared to be making up her mind. The vicar stared at her legs, mesmerized, and Jocelyn, aware of this, turned one foot in and posed.

'Oh, very well then!'

She smiled coquettishly, and hurried over to sit beside him.

If he hadn't been a vicar, Joss would probably not have given him the time of day. He wasn't that good looking, though he *was* four years younger than her, and that was a plus. He was very tall and thin, with a hooked nose that dominated his face, and a prominent Adams Apple. His eyes, in contrast, were small and beady, and his mouth a thin, disapproving line. About the rest of him, the only things worthy of note were the long, tapering fingers on each hand, the backs of which were covered in fine dark hairs, making each one look a little like a spider. Joss looked down at them and shivered deliciously. She knew where at least one of those hands was going to end up!

'Now you tell me the problem, little girl,' he said, and patted her knee, reassuringly. Jocelyn leaned back and revealed a length of thigh, while crossing her arms and thrusting her breasts up and partly out of the halter-top.

'Well, it's like this. He's going to die on me, vicarage. He's got cancer and he's going to die!' She screwed up her eyes, and with intense effort managed to squeeze a couple of tears out at the corners. Then she began to sob.

Berry sat up straight in surprise. He hadn't expected this!

'Oh you poor, dear girl,' he said, and reached over to comfort her. He had long arms, and as he was encircling her his hand, by chance, wrapped itself firmly around her left breast. After a couple of comforting squeezes she disentangled herself and he had to content himself with stroking the inside of her thigh.

'I'm so sorry to hear it,' he continued. With an effort he then remembered his spiritual role, and added: 'of course, the lord must have other plans for him. Who is so wise that he can tell the ways of the lord?'

'That's all very well, Mister Vicar, but where does that leave me? He's going to go away, and I won't have anybody to look after me. He's always done all the money things. I wouldn't have a clue! I don't even know how much we've got in the bank.'

Berry sat and thought for a moment. Maybe this was his chance?

'Well, Jocelyn! Help is closer than you think. In fact, it's right at hand. You never need worry about anything with the right friends around you!'

'You really think so,' said Joss, sitting up and looking guilelessly into his eyes. 'I'm still a young woman, parson, with my whole life ahead of me. I don't feel like being a widow for forty years and having to wear all that black... yeccchhh!'

She shuddered. Joss's sensitivities were assaulted at the thought of wearing black. Berry patted her leg again, then stroked it suggestively.

'Aaaarrrrum. We're not bound, you know, in the cloth... you understand... err.. not like the Catholics. I mean, it is possible for a vicar to... err... marry you know!'

Joss sat bolt upright and stared into his face.

'Is that right? I'm so pleased for you, your eminence. When did they change that rule... just recently? Oh, goody! You'll be able to bring your wife over to meet me!'

The vicar looked nonplussed.

'I... err... don't have a wife, Joss. I was just saying that I... err... could have one if I wanted. Maybe in the future... the... err... *near* future.'

Jocelyn clamped both hands over his hand and, apparently unconsciously, slid it up to the top of her thigh, as if in congratulation. The black hairs on the back of his hand stood up and danced.

'Won't that be exciting for you! Promise to tell me when you've picked one out. I'll help you to decide whether or not she's suitable for our favourite holy man!'

Berry sat frozen in his seat. He could feel the edging on Jocelyn's knickers, rubbing against his little finger.

'Ahh… huh… what about you, Joss? You know, when the inevitable has happened and Alex has gone to meet that other fellow… Will you marry again?'

'Oh, dear me no,' said Joss, sliding his hand up and down her thigh in a fury. 'No, no, no! I'll have too much money for that! No, I'll just have a string of lovers, Vicar, like racehorses!'

'But I thought you said you were no good with money, Joss? That you needed help?'

Jocelyn sat and thought for a moment.

'Well, I've changed my mind. I suppose I can spend money pretty well as much as the next person, probably better! No, I think it's a mistake to let anyone too near the moneybox,' she whispered, conspiratorially. 'Don't you, Vicar?' She lifted his hand off her thigh, and pushed it aside.

Berry sat there bemused. The double entendre danced in his brain. There was no clear path to follow from that point.

'No, I suppose you're right. Still, you may change your mind once it happens. That idea of yours… racehorses, I think you said. Not a good idea, Joss. I don't think he'd like that very much!'

'I don't care much what he'd like,' she pouted. 'He'll be dead, won't he, so he won't have any say in it.'

'I didn't mean Alex,' Berry hastened to reply. 'I meant *him*, you know, up there.'

'Oh, you mean God? Well he shouldn't have made me so good in bed, should he? I mean, it's like the parable of the talents, isn't it. You have to use them, don't you, or he gets cross. Well, I intend to use mine from now on, and I've only got one talent that I know of.' She turned to the vicar, put her hands around his collar and pouted. 'Of course, I might have others, but I need someone to show me what they are, Father. Maybe I've got talents that I don't even know about.' She blew up her cheeks, and looked suggestively at his Elderness.

'I... err... wouldn't know about that.'

The vicar struggled to his feet, and looked around desperately for the door. It was so hot in there. He needed some fresh air, before he made a fool of himself and surrendered to some long suppressed litany of lust.

'I'll tell Alex that you called,' said Jocelyn to his retreating back, and smiled as he stumbled over the doormat.

'Aren't you sweet,' she said to his distant figure, as she watched him plod heavily back over the causeway, trying to work out what had gone wrong.

II

On the other side of the island, Prittik was sheltering under the cliff in Stingray Cove. It was a particularly beautiful spot, a natural swimming basin where the water was a light azure blue, clear through to a bottom that consisted of fine, white sand. At its deepest point it was sixteen feet deep, with a natural rock shelf around it, a foot under the surface, that made it appear like a swimming pool carved out by nature. The only drawback was that the stingrays liked it too, and often came to bury themselves in the sandy bottom. The first indication that they were there would be a flap of the great wings, which would send a plume of water six feet into the air. Then they would appear out of the sand and retreat at incredible speed, sliding across the rock shelf and heading out to sea. As long as you kept out of their way, they were harmless.

Alex sat back in the shade of the cliff, safely hidden from the house, and attended to his business on a cell phone. With such little time to spare he felt the urgency of the condemned man. His first call was to an old army buddy of his that he hadn't seen for years.

'Hi, Jack? Jack Delaney? So it is you, you old bastard! It's me, Alex Prittik. Don't say you don't remember me. That's right, 'C' Company, Engineers.'

'Well, where the hell have you sprung from,' said Jack, wiping the grease from his hands onto his overalls. He was a mechanic these days, and owned a little repair shop in Gawler.

'I know it's been a long time, Jack, but I've got a situation, and I need your help. Are you still *au fait* with pyrotechnics?'

Jack raised an eyebrow.

'Don't tell me you've joined the IRA, Alex. Or is it Al Quaeda?'

'No, nothing like that,' Alex laughed. 'No mate... I want to put on a firework display, like no firework display you've ever seen.'

'Well I can still handle that all right. I haven't done it for a while, mind you. It's hard to get the licences these days, and it's priced out of the pockets of most people.'

'Cost isn't a factor, Jack. In fact, what if I told you I've got half a million dollars to spend on it?' Alex could hear the sudden intake of breath on the other end.

'God almighty, Alex! Where are you going to hold this… on the Sydney Harbour Bridge?'

'No, in my own backyard! I've got a little island off the Eyre Peninsula, Crab Island. The fact is, Jack… that I'm dying! Cancer of the pancreas! The quacks have given me eight weeks, so I want this done in the next fortnight. Can you do it?'

Jack found a chair and sat down.

'Jeeze… not on my own, Alex! It would take a team of guys. There's a lot of planning goes into something like that, you know, timing each burst, what direction you're going to fire it off so one display doesn't interfere with another. It all has to be coordinated.'

'Well what about three weeks, and you can hire whoever you want?'

'What's in it for me, Alex? I've got a little business down here, just a one-man show. I'd have to close it for the duration, which means two to three weeks of lost work, plus no work to go back to if you know what I mean. It could take a month to recover.'

Alex leaned back against the cliff face, and stared out to sea.

'What do you make a year, Jack? Not turnover… net profit!'

'Oh, about forty five thousand, Alex, plus a few perks.'

'I'll give you sixty thousand dollars in cash, and ten thousand dollars a man. How does that sound? What's more, I'll pay you in cash. Where you hide it is up to you. Keep it out of the bank, and you won't pay any tax on it. Same with the others!'

At the other end, Jack began to chuckle.

'Are you fuckin' serious! You just got yourself a pyrotechnics expert. In fact, a fucking team of them.'

'Great! I'll make arrangements to have the necessary fireworks and powder flown in. We'll use a whole pile of traditional stuff, then I'll get you to make up some special skyrockets and starshells, and some huge bangers mate. If this doesn't scare the shit out of my guests, then I'm going to be disappointed.'

'If you want me to make up some specials, I'll have to give you a list of equipment I'll be needing. Have you got anywhere on the island, away from the house where we could work. It has to be dry and well ventilated.'

'There's a large boatshed about fifty metres from the house. We sank the boat, so it's empty at the moment. You can use that. As far as accommodation is concerned, let me know how many guys you're going to hire, and I'll provide caravans.'

'Four… no more than four of us! Any more would just get in the way.'

There was a sudden silence as the two men reflected on the situation. Jack spoke first.

'Look… this cancer thing, Alex! Jeeze, I'm really sorry to hear it. Three or four of the old crew are dead already –

remember Alan Golding? He's gone. Bowel cancer! And Ricky Marshall... another one! He found out he had Parkinson's, and topped himself. They found him hanging in his shed.'

'I'm sorry to hear that... I liked Ricky,' said Alex, sombrely.

'When did you find out?'

'Just yesterday morning, Jack I couldn't believe it. I'm only forty-three you know.'

'Yeah, it's a pisser, mate!'

'What really galls is the fact that I'd finally made it. You remember all my plans, back in the old days. When I came up with the *Prittique* it made me a multi-millionaire.'

There was a gasp on the other end of the phone.

'So that's yours! *Prittique*! Prittik! God, how stupid am I? I didn't even put two and two together.'

Alex smiled. It was a long time since the army days.

'Anyway, I'm not going to let nature or some pissy little cancer dictate when I get to leave this planet, Jack. This show will be my big farewell. I'm going to push off before the pain becomes too much to bear.'

'So that's what the fireworks display is for. You're going to do it that night!'

'That's right, mate! I reckon a couple of bottles of Jim Beam and a hundred aspirin will sort me out, quick smart. I don't want to wake up the next morning.'

'Well in that case, Alex, we'll make this a show fit to blast you into hell and back. They'll be talking about this for years.'

After he hung up Alex looked down into the blue waters and muttered, 'they will, mate. They certainly will! They're not going to forget Alex Prittik in a hurry.'

Alex peered over the top of the cliff to see if the coast was clear yet. He couldn't see any movement about the place, but from where he was he couldn't see the causeway, either. He decided that it would be imprudent to return just yet, and slid back down the cliff to a narrow rocky ledge. It was this that they usually dived from, into the crystal clear waters of the basin.

He carefully made his way along the ledge and around the corner, and presently stood in the entrance to the Grotto, a cave eaten out by the sea's constant worrying at the cliff face. The Grotto was merely an entrance to a long tunnel, usually filled with water, and lit by a couple of narrow overhead openings where the roof had caved in. It actually ran underground as far as the house. In fact, it was doubtful whether the original owners of the site had been aware of its extent when they built the house, as the western side of the building stood over what was a wide underground chasm. If they'd known, no doubt they would have built the house further back.

Alex wandered into the cave and made his way slowly along to the end, stepping carefully along ledges and through shallow water until he reached the part where it opened out into a circular cave. There were a few stalactites formed from the lime in the soil above, but no stalagmites, as the floor area was always deep in water. Alex looked up at the formations, strangely lit now by the afternoon sun, reflected from the surface of the water. It looked timeless to him… above and beyond time! Alex called it 'The Cathedral', because it gave him a feeling of reverence, almost holiness. It was probably the only thing in life that did. He had long ago resolved that if he was going to have to die, this was where he would like his body to lie, staring sightlessly up at those beautiful formations for eternity.

He sat down on a ledge at the side, leaned back and enjoyed the glint of the water's reflection off the ceiling. It was moving, constantly moving! It reminded him a little of looking into a kaleidoscope when he was a child.

There were worse things! The inside of a coffin lid, for instance. The sudden orange glare of gas jets, igniting in a crematorium oven! Oh yes, there were worse things than being sealed up in a Grotto, forever, and at one with the sea!

The wind picked up outside, and cautiously found the mouth of the cave. At first it whipped around at the entrance, searching for a clear way in. Then it began to flow through the tunnel in gusts, producing a high-pitched humming drone as it rounded the curve into the main chamber. All Alex could hear was the sound of the Valkyrie, calling his name.

Chapter Five

The following day, Hilda managed to waylay her brother as he was making his way down to the beach, in full retreat from Jocelyn's whining. She had launched a full scale assault on him after the vicar had left, and continued it whenever she saw him, determined to extract from him the three things that McRae had demanded over the phone. 'Will? How long? Where's the cancer?' Alex had steadfastly refused to divulge anything.

Jocelyn was now on the outer, though she didn't know it yet. She had jumped into bed with his accountant, and that constituted the end of his marriage as far as Alex was concerned. There wasn't time for a divorce, nature had seen to that. But there *was* time for revenge! Alex took note of the old saw that pointed out that *'revenge is a cup best supped cold!'* He had no intention of forewarning the adversary by throwing a tantrum, and letting himself down. No, he would wait, and plot, and plan their downfall, step by step!

'Alex, I need to talk to you,' Hilda called out, hurrying after him towards the beach. Alex shot an exasperated look behind him, and increased his pace. After the swimming pool incident, and the subsequent abuse from those brats of hers, Alex was not in the right frame of mind to shower Hilda with brotherly love.

'Alex! Don't be childish. I said I need to talk to you, and I won't stop following you until you do. This is only a very small island you know!'

Alex looked over towards the causeway and noted that it was still covered with at least three feet of water at this time of day. It would be another two or three hours before the tide went out far enough to allow access to the mainland. She was right. It was a very small island. Alex went and sat on the beach, allowing her to catch up and sit down beside him.

'What the blazes do you want, Hilda? I'm not in the mood for family chats.'

'Yes, and I know why! Why didn't you tell me, Alex? I thought we were closer than this. Joss has been running around with some story that you're about to expire on us!'

'Is that what she said, is it? Well, you know what Joss is like. If you told her you'd caught a cold, she'd tell you to let it go. She's very literal is our Joss.'

'Now don't give me that, Alex. I've known you a long time, forty-three years to be exact, and there's something up. I've been noticing it for days.'

Alex looked at her and smiled. Then he reached out and put his arm around her shoulder, and gave her a squeeze.

'Sorry, Sis! But you're in the enemy's camp these days. I can't be too careful you know.'

Hilda looked back at him and smiled, sardonically.

'If you want me to swear that not a word of what you're about to say will get back to Greg…'

'Should I even have to ask that,' said Alex, quizzically. 'Do we need words now, to communicate what we both understand?'

Hilda shrugged.

'No, I suppose not. I know you don't like Greg, never did! I was hoping that you two might be able to overcome your differences in time and hit it off. But I can see now that it's not to be.'

They were silent for a moment. Alex pulled a face in answer to her reproving stare.

'Well, it's no good looking at me like that, Hilda. I'm well aware of what *you* think of *Joss*! *You're* not exactly bosom buddies, are you?'

'Well, she's such a... a floozy, Alex! There, it's out! I never could see what you saw in her. I mean, she's so stupid, Alex.'

'Sex!' said Alex, a wry grin on his face. 'Raw sex, Hilda! Don't you know that a good one is a silly one!'

Hilda punched him playfully on the arm, and laughed. Alex winced. It was more painful than it should have been. He rubbed his arm, and Hilda looked concerned.

'There's something dreadfully wrong, isn't there? There really is something wrong with you isn't there, Alex?'

'Get up and walk with me for a while,' he said, getting to his feet. They walked along the sand, keeping clear of the breakers that were still coming in. The sea was choppy and grey of aspect, and there was a dark patch of cloud overhead, cutting out the sun.

'It's cancer, Hilda!'

He heard her sudden intake of breath, but didn't look around. He had no intention of becoming emotional now.

'Pancreatic cancer! Old Doc Proust told me in his usual, stuffy way that I should live as if I still have fifty years to go. Silly old bastard!'

'How long have you got?' Hilda's voice betrayed her with a tremor.

'Eight weeks he reckons... give or take six months – *if* I take the palliative care route. Of course that means six months of vomiting and diarrhoea, my hair falling out, my skin turning yellow, and too weak to get out of the wheelchair.'

'Oh, Alex,' Hilda cried out, then covered her face with her hands. 'I'm sorry, I'm so sorry,' she said, and then sank down onto the sand.

'Come on old girl, it's not that bad. We've all got to die one day!'

'Yes... but Alex... forty-three! This is terrible! Can't you get a second opinion?'

Alex just looked at her, pityingly.

'I've got no intention of going into denial, Hilda. I know what I have to do, arrangements are in hand.'

'But that's awful, Alex. You shouldn't have to do that! If you like you can leave all the arrangements to me. I'll sort it out for you.'

Alex looked at her, strangely.

'Oh! The funeral! I wondered what you were talking about for a minute. No, I wasn't talking about my funeral, though all that will be pre-arranged too. I hope you're going to keep this to yourself, Hilda.'

'I promise... not a word!'

'That includes your kids.'

'I know, I promise.'

'And not a word to Joss… especially not a word to Joss! I don't want her to know any more than she knows at this moment.'

'Well, that's a bit hard, Alex. I mean, it's not that I like the woman, but she is your wife after all. She should be fully informed of the situation. That's only fair!'

'Not a word, Hilda,' said Alex, raising his finger in emphasis.

'All right! But that brings a whole new lot of questions to the fore. Like, what's going to happen to us when you're gone? We'll be out on the street. I can't see your widow allowing us to stay on any longer than she has to.'

'No, nor can I,' Alex agreed.

'Well, aren't you going to do anything about it?'

'Am I my brother-in-law's keeper, Hilda? When you married him, you formed an alliance… you two against the world! You rely on him; he relies on you! If he's not up to supporting you and your children in the manner you're accustomed to, get shot of him and marry someone else. It's not my problem!'

'But I'm your sister, Alex, and it's not as if you're hard up! You've got millions! Surely you could make some provision for us in your will, maybe set up a trust account for your nephew and niece, that sort of thing.'

Alex turned to her on the beach, a dangerous look in his eye.

'I could… but I'm not going to. Let me ask you – if the positions were reversed, would you do it for Joss?'

Hilda was silent, and averted her eyes.

'Look at it from my perspective, Hilda. I had to put up with that oaf of a husband of yours lauding it over me for years, with his false bonhomie and his sarcastic criticism. Even so, when he fell on his face, as I knew he would, I didn't rub it in, did I? I offered you a place to tide you over until he got back on his feet. Is he back on his feet – No! Greg's the sort of fellow that will scrounge off anyone if it means he doesn't have to shoulder his own responsibilities. Surely, even you must have realised that by now. The guy's all hot air; all gush and no substance. As long as this house is available to him he'll never strike out on his own, because he knows he doesn't have to. He can drink my wine, raid my refrigerator, enjoy rent-free accommodation in a millionaire's paradise. Why would he want to go back to work, for God's sake? No Hilda, I'll be doing you a favour by leaving you nothing. That way he will have to get back on the job, go out and provide for you, or go down with the ship. Of course, a better scenario would be that you would wake up to him at last and ditch the beggar, find yourself a real partner, one that pulls his weight.'

Hilda pulled out a handkerchief and wiped her eyes.

'You can be really cruel, Alex!'

'Cruel! You don't know cruel! You say why don't I provide for *'my'* nephew and niece, as if they were anything to do with me. Get real, Hilda! You've brought up two of the most appalling, badly behaved, contemptuous little bastards that it's ever been my misfortune to meet. Their manners are disgusting, and they have no respect for person or property. They certainly have no respect for you, or for Greg! I wouldn't give them a dollar between them. You should have thrashed some manners into them while you had the chance, but now it's too late. You're about to launch these two ferals onto an unsuspecting world, where they can cause havoc and grief to everyone they meet, not to mention the pain and suffering they will experience themselves from rejection by their peers, because they are incapable of basic, disciplined, civilised behaviour. No Hilda, no money for them! No money for Greg – especially no money for Greg! He can learn to live with his own mistakes, which means providing the money from the sweat of his own brow to make up for the appalling way in which he's raised those kids… because they're going to give you hell, Hilda! Hell!'

'And what about me, Alex, your own sister! Do I get dragged down as well?'

'You've brought it on yourself, sis. Surely you don't expect your little brother to keep you in the big world out there. You're half of the problem! You should have put your foot down when you had the chance, and stopped him squandering your hard-earned gilt. In a way, you've allowed this situation to happen by being too weak. You know what our father would have said.'

'I'm desperate, Alex. I'm asking for your help. I know you have the money, I just want a one off payment of four hundred thousand dollars to put us back on our feet again, that's all!' She reached out to touch his arm. 'After all, you can't take it with you!'

'Four hundred thousand….' Alex nearly choked. 'Is that right! You'd be surprised what you can do if you try! Your four hundred grand is a pipe dream, Hilda, believe me! But beyond that, I'll tell you what I've put in place. I have a friend who has been put in charge of a trust account. He also has the deeds to a small apartment in the suburbs. On the day that you get your decree absolute from that waster of a husband of yours, he will contact you and allow you to move in, rent-free. The apartment will never be signed into your name, because I have no intention of letting you either sell it, or leave it to those rabid little ferals of yours. But you can use it for as long as you need it. He will also be in charge of a fund of one hundred thousand dollars, which he will dole out to you in cash, in small amounts, as long as not one cent ends up in their pockets. If he discovers that you have been passing the money down the line, the money tree will cease. It's there for you, and you only. And that's my final word!'

'Aren't you going to tell me this friend's name?'

'No, because I want this handled on an informal basis. You won't be able to make it the subject of a court action if you don't know the source of the funds. Then if you don't access them by getting divorced, they will eventually be left to a charity of his choice.'

Hilda soon recovered from her fit of emotion. She now had a hard glint in her eye.

'You really are impossible, Alex. Well, we'll just have to contest your will, that's all!'

'You'll find a clause in there which states that anyone who contests my will shall get nothing! Don't worry, it's watertight. I've checked!'

'You're a bastard, a right bastard, Alex,' Hilda cried, and she turned and ran back up to the house, sobbing for all she was worth.

II

Over the next few days, Crab Island became a hive of activity. Two thirty-foot caravans were towed over the causeway from the mainland and placed in position over near the boatshed. Shortly afterwards Jack Delaney arrived with the driver of a semi-trailer full of materials, all judiciously covered with a tarp. They had to wait four hours for the next tide, and slept uncomfortably in the cabin of the prime mover. It took over a day to unload it, and another day before the tide was right for the semi to return the way it came. Jack's three helpers arrived at different times, one of them bringing a girlfriend along who, the story went, couldn't stand to be away from her man. Alex was rather annoyed about this at first. He didn't want the operation turning into a circus.

'She'll just have to bunk in with the rest of you,' Alex said shortly, when asked what provision was going to be made for the girl's accommodation. 'After all, she wasn't invited here, and you shouldn't have brought her without asking.'

Roddy Donovan was not impressed.

'Well, maybe you can do without me altogether,' he said, petulantly, 'seeing as you're so hard up for accommodation.'

'Maybe we can! You're free to go any time you like. Nobody's holding you here!'

Roddy thought about the promised ten thousand dollars for three weeks work, and rapidly changed his mind. But there was an overflow of bad feeling, nevertheless.

The girl, Tina, bustled her way into one of the caravans and tried to turf the other fellow out, but he was having none of it either.

'Listen here, girl! These caravans have been provided for the workers; that is, two caravans, two men to each caravan. If you want to bunk in here with your boyfriend then I've got no objection. But you're on his bunk, not mine – get it?'

She got it!

Jack soon got the boatshed into shape, and had benches set up for the manufacture of his pyrotechnical extravaganzas. Soon a steady stream of tubes and box-shaped affairs were exiting the boatshed to be stored in the double garage, and in the basement of the house. Jason and Darlene hung about trying to discover what the big secret was, but were barred from the worksite, and also from the storage sites. Joss was going frantic with apprehension.

'Don't you think I deserve to know what's going on in my own house, Alex?'

'Since when was this your house? If you remember rightly, I bought this house while you were away, sunning yourself in Fiji.'

'That's not the point, Alex. What's got into you lately? You're acting really strange, ever since that doctor told you about the cancer.'

'More to the point, Joss... what's got into you! Or should I say who?'

Jocelyn had the grace to blush and retire distractedly from the field. Some of his remarks lately were barbed that way... 'it's as if he *knew*,' she thought to herself.

McRae had thought it prudent to remain in town, for a week at least. The memory of that phone call had not dimmed in his mind, and every day he waited for an irate call from his one client, accusing him of boffing his only client's wife. It was a nerve-wracking week.

Meanwhile Janelle filled in for Jocelyn, locking the office door at lunchtimes and arranging herself invitingly over the coffee table in a tempting array of buttocks and thighs. Whenever McRae dropped his office manner and his trousers to approach her from the rear, she would emit an erotic 'woof-woof', just to stimulate his jaded appetite.

Janelle Marquete was ambitious in her own right. She knew all about McRae's accounting discrepancies, and she knew what he was worth. At twenty-eight, she was sick of bouncing from one man to another, looking for the right mix of charm, staying power and inordinate wealth. Up until now she had only managed to find candidates with two out of three. The missing virtue was usually staying power, either sexual, or that necessary for the long haul of a relationship. She had no intention of marrying just to get divorced again. This meant that he would have to be able to maintain his interest in her, and she in him, for forty years or more. That was hard these days. There were so many other distractions.

But with McRae she could see that a mix of kinky sex, blackmail and the fact that she could be his partner in crime, might just lure him into the matrimonial net. If she could somehow save him from the results of his current folly, perhaps he would begin to appreciate that she offered brains as well as butt.

After getting up off her hands and knees, brushing her teeth in the office washroom, and rearranging her underwear, she went back into the office where McRae was slumped miserably at his desk.

'There's an easy way out of this, Lindsay,' she murmured, stroking the back of his neck. 'I'm surprised you haven't seen it yet. Power of attorney!'

McRae sat bolt upright in his chair, and stared into the distance.

'Power of attorney? Yes! That would solve a lot of problems all right. But how the hell do I get him to sign it over to me?'

Janelle looked down at him, pityingly.

'He's dying, isn't he? That means that over the next few weeks… or months, however long it takes, he's going to get very ill. That means his concentration is going to waver. He's going to be so sick that he won't know what he's signing, from one document to another. All you have to do is hide the document halfway down a pile of genuine documents, and by the time he gets to that, he'll just sign it automatically. I can sign as witness later on. It will be too late by then. If he kicks up a fuss, we'll arrange to get a psychiatrist in to deem him incapable of running his own affairs.'

McRae looked up at her in surprise.

'Do you think a psychiatrist would do that?'

'Of course he would… once you've doped Alex out of his brain with morphine… with maybe a touch of LSD included. You'll come up with something!'

McRae sat back and smiled.

'By God, Janelle, I think you've come up trumps! Once I've got power of attorney I'll be able to cover my tracks. I can lay all sorts of false trails that would point to the fact that Alex was going off the beam for some time before, and that it had only just come to a head after months of bad deals and crazy decisions. They'll never be able to untangle it. And once he's dead, why would they bother? It's not a public company! I could even buy into it as a sleeping partner, and if I end up with fifty one percent of the company, that means we control it. Our friendly bimbo, Jocelyn, wouldn't know one end of a spreadsheet from another.'

'Why bother doing that,' said Janelle, thoughtfully, 'when you can get him to leave you sixty percent in his will? Jocelyn won't make too much of a fuss if she ends up with forty percent of ten million a year.'

McRae was suddenly revitalised. This woman was amazing! He looked at Janelle with new eyes, and she anticipated what was coming. She patted her brunette curls into place, climbed up onto his desk and spread herself out in front of him. When she pulled his head down - for her own gratification this time - she knew that she was the one calling the shots.

Chapter Six

Hilda collared Greg one evening after he came back from a relaxing game of golf.

'It's nice to know that some of us can afford to spend our leisure time out on the golf course,' said Hilda, acidly. 'You leave me to do your dirty work for you, then go off and act as if you haven't got a care in the world.'

Greg deposited Alex's spare clubs in the hall cupboard, and then came back into the guest lounge room. He looked at her quizzically.

'You've spoken to him! Well, how did it go? Get any change out of that miserly brother of yours?'

'No! Did *you* get a job?'

Greg began to bluster.

'Now see here, Hilda, that's no way to go speaking to me! I told you jobs would be few and far between in this hell-hole. Anyway, what's that got to do with your brother and his money?'

'It's got everything to do with him. I spoke to him a couple of days ago, I just didn't tell you. He's not going to give us a cent, Greg, not one cent! He says he can't stand our kids, that they're spoiled brats, and that we should have disciplined them while there was still time. I must say, I'm inclined to agree with him.'

Greg turned on her and sneered.

'Oh, we're back on that, are we? I tell you, Hilda, that smacking a child only leads to violence. I'm not saying the children are perfect, not by any means. They're imperfect, as all humans are imperfect. But I think that you and I knew best what was right for our children when they were small... more so than your childless brother, anyway! What would he know, for god's sake, about bringing up children?'

'He was once a child himself, Greg. He saw the way our father did it.'

'Oh yes, weren't we all! I was a child once, and my drunken brute of a father used to beat the crap out of me every time he got a skinful. The times I've come home to my mother's mince pies...' He turned to her scornfully, and added, 'that was our euphemism for black eyes. *'Mum's got a mince pie'*, we'd shout. *'Look out!'*'

'We're not talking about brutality here, Greg, just the smacks that normal children get to keep them in line. How else do they learn to differentiate between good and bad behaviour.'

'They have it explained to them. You show them reason!'

'Well it didn't work with our two did it? You must admit, Alex's description of them as a couple of ferals wasn't far off the point.'

Greg stuck his nose in the air in disdain.

'Any opinion your brother might have about this family, he can keep to himself. He's not exactly a saint, you know. If I know Alex, he's as shady as they come. Look at those lentils! You can't tell me that he just came along and plucked *'lentils'* out of the air, then invested a million dollars in their futures, just off the cuff. He had inside advice.'

'And doubled his money! You've got to give it to him, Greg, he's far more astute than you or I.'

Greg went red in the face, and barely contained himself.

'You speak for yourself, Hilda. I will not be adversely compared to that prat of a brother of yours, by you or by anyone else. He's just been lucky, that's all! Pure luck!'

'Anyway, I asked him for the four hundred thousand as you said, and he just about laughed in my face. He said not a cent, not for the kids, not for me, and especially not for you. He said you could pay for your own mistakes in the upbringing of the children.'

'Oh God, Hilda! I didn't mean you to come right out and just drop it on him like that. Of course he said no! You were supposed to lead up to it slowly, not slap it in his face like a wet fish. You've got no damned tact! Some of my biggest coups in the insurance game had to be baited for weeks ahead, and then I reeled them in slowly, like a big fat schnapper! You have to alternate threats and promises, but not direct threats, just subtle ones… like things that might just happen, if this or that were to come about. Oh, well…'

Greg picked up the newspaper and flopped into an easy chair, an event that usually signalled the conversation was over. Hilda wasn't going to be so easily put off, however.

'Like him dying suddenly you mean,' she said, sardonically, conveniently forgetting the promise she'd made to Alex on the beach.

'Yes… something like that!' He caught the look on her face. 'Why did you say that? Was something said…'

'He's dying, Greg. He told me himself! I had to promise not to tell either you, or the kids, or Jocelyn, because it appears that he doesn't want her to know any more than she knows already… for whatever purpose he has in mind.'

Greg began to stutter, his face losing its usually rosy glow.

'You're n.not serious! Alex… dying! Of what?'

'It seems he has cancer of the pancreas, and it's inoperable. They've only given him eight weeks, but if I know Alex, he has no intention of losing control of his life at this point in time. I think he's planning to end it early.'

Greg jumped out of his chair in shock.

'What do you mean? Not suicide… By God, Hilda, do you realise what a fix that would put us in. That bimbo will never let us stay on once he's gone.'

'I know all this! That's why I asked him for the money outright. He refused me. I even said we would fight his will, and he said he'd already covered that by inserting a clause that said anyone who contested his will would get nothing.'

Greg dashed his newspaper down and clenched his fists in anger.

'Why, the damned mountebank! He would let his sister be thrown out into the street, and not leave anything to keep body and soul together? The man is an animal!'

'Animal or not, Greg, we've got to make plans. We're obviously wasting our time here, so we're going to have to make a move back to the city and get you a job. If we have to rough it in a flat for a while, then that's what we'll have to do.'

Greg turned green at the thought of that pokey little flat in Enfield, with the children fighting constantly, and the neighbours hanging out over the balcony to accost him every time he put a foot out the door.

'Never! I will never go back to that way of life, Hilda, and neither should you. We're just going to have to work our way through this somehow, try and get our hands on some of that money he's got stashed away. If we can't do it after he dies, then we'll do it before. At any odds, we've at least got to try.'

'Easier said than done,' Hilda replied, frowning. 'We know nothing about his finances, how he controls the various funds coming in, what he's got invested. But there's one person who does know, and that's Lindsay McRae. It wouldn't surprise me if his accountant is running a little scam of his own, now I come to think of it. Have you seen the car he drives?'

'Yes, I have… a little flash, two-seater thing. Must have cost a bomb.'

'And another thing,' said Hilda. 'I don't know how observant you are, but the last time he was up here, Jocelyn seemed to spend a hell of a lot of time in his company. I wasn't around most of the time, but when I was they were usually in the lounge, sitting cosily together, or out walking down along the beach. All very innocent on the surface, but my instincts tell me something's up.'

Greg appeared to come to some conclusion of his own, and drew himself up to his full height.

'You may be right there, my dear. You may just be right. In which case a little friendly persuasion might just put us in possession of the facts of the case. If there is a fiddle going on, Mister McRae will be literally pooping himself when he finds out Alex is on the way out. He'll have to cover his tracks, because an audit will uncover the whole pigsty. I think I'll pay Mister McRae a visit, get him on his own, and then put the fear of god into him.'

Hilda looked at her husband, and suddenly smiled.

'I didn't think I would ever sanction an action against my own brother, but you're right... we have to look out for ourselves! And if Alex isn't going to be around and his money is, well... all's fair in love and war!'

II

After a few days of intense activity with gunpowder and blue touch paper, Alex began to absent himself from direct involvement with 'Operation Fireworks!' The Grotto held a morbid fascination for him, as he had now decided that he was going to instruct his old mate, Jack Delaney, to initially deposit his body in the Grotto after his death, and then to set explosives to collapse the entrance to it forever. It would be his own personal vault, carved out of nature with the stalactites growing in splendour over his dead body for eternity. There would be no need for a headstone. In fact, if he planned it right, he could avoid letting the authorities know the whereabouts of his body, as no doubt they would have objections to a cadaver being placed anywhere but in a properly constituted cemetery.

Alex sat on a ledge in the 'Cathedral' and stared at the ceiling. The reflection from the surface of the water cast moving patterns of light at most times of the day, varying according to the position of the sun. He was watching the patterns change when he heard the sound of someone stumbling through the tunnel, further around the bend. He waited silently, wondering whom it could be that had the impudence to invade his own private sanctum.

Presently he saw the shape of the intruder, outlined against the light coming through from the entrance. It was a young woman, treading warily along the ledge, and trying to avoid falling in the water. She had a big shock of naturally wavy hair, russet coloured, its red lights catching the light behind her and glowing in the dark. She was almost on top of him before she realised she wasn't alone.

'What the blazes do you think you're doing?' said Alex, angrily. It was bad enough having uninvited guests, without them importuning him with their presence.

The girl let out a shriek.

'Oh, God! You scared the daylights out of me! I was just going to squat down and have a pee, if you don't mind. *Now* what am I going to do?'

'*Now*, you can get yourself out of my cave,' said Alex, cantankerously, leaning back against the wall.

'Oh that's right, Mister Grump himself! Just because you've got potloads of money, you think you can talk to people like shit, don't you? Well, it's not your cave... you only have a lend of it. It belongs to the planet, and everyone on it.'

Alex groaned, and put his face in his hands.

'For God's sake, girly, don't give me all that greenie bullshit. I bought this island to get away from people like you!'

'Oh, is that right? Well firstly, my name's not 'girly', and I'm not a girl. I'm a woman, and my name is Tina.'

'I think I know this,' said Alex, wearily.

'Secondly, you can turn your face the other way, because if I don't squat, I'm going to have an accident.'

'This isn't a bloody public lavatory,' said Alex, angrily. 'This place is sacred, or hadn't you noticed the limestone formations in the roof?' He turned his head nevertheless, and she squatted over the edge of the ledge.

'This is very embarrassing for me... don't make it any worse than it is,' the woman replied. She adjusted her shorts, and stood up. 'All right, you can look now. Then you can talk to me as if I was a real human being, not someone you dragged in out of the gutter.'

'What on earth would I want to talk to you for,' said Alex, rebelliously. He was now in a rotten frame of mind, his inner sanctum defiled by the most basic of human needs.

'You come in here, uninvited, pee in the water, and then have the gall to talk to me in terms of someone who wants to save the planet from pollution.'

'Aren't you the original Mister Nice Guy,' said Tina, sitting down on the ledge some five feet away. 'Do you talk to all of your guests like this? I'm surprised that someone hasn't clobbered you!'

'I'm a very private person, and I value my privacy... is there anything wrong in that?'

'Not in itself, no! But there is such a thing as good manners, or so my parents taught me. It doesn't cost anything to be nice to people.'

'I can afford *not* to be nice if I don't want to, and I don't want to,' said Alex.

'No one can afford not to be nice, least of all you! They tell me that you're dying, is that true?' Tina stared at him with all the ingenuousness of the young.

Alex looked at her in shock. He hadn't expected that, not from a total stranger.

'Are you always so brutally frank? You should wear a sash, saying: 'Miss Tact – 2012.''

'There's no time for tact when someone's dying,' Tina retorted. 'You have to make the most of every minute you have left!'

'You sound like my doctor,' said Alex. 'It's easy when it's not happening to you!'

'Oh, don't be such a pain in the butt! I think you should talk about it, get it out of your system. It's obviously eating you up, making you all bitter and twisted. Get it out into the open and squash it… you'll feel better for it.'

Alex looked at her earnestness, her youth, and her beauty for the very first time.

'What is this… are you some sort of weeny psychologist? I can assure you that there is no way to squash what it is that I've got. Yes, I'm going to die! The doctors have given me eight weeks. So what the fuck can you tell me, Tina, to make me feel all warm and cosy about it?'

Alex was in the mood to feel sorry for himself, and there was no way he was going to be talked out of it.

'Anybody would think that you're the only person on the planet that's going to die, as if a cruel fate has picked you out for its special attention. We're all going to die,' said Tina, musingly, 'just at different rates, that's all. Put it this way... at least you know when... you can make plans, tidy things up before you go. *I* could be dead before *you*, under a bus or a truck. I could be attacked and left for dead, or I could pick up a simple virus and be dead in three days.'

'The key word to each statement being 'could',' said Alex. 'There's no 'could' with me! I'm staring the harsh reality in the face. I mean, look at you – how old are you – twenty-three, twenty-four?'

'I'm twenty-six next week,' said Tina. 'I know – I look young for my age.'

'Yes, well... you do actually. But that's beside the point. I've got twenty years on you, I'm forty-three, and it's been a hard twenty years. I wasn't born rich, you know! I had to work hard for what I've got.'

'Who gives a toss about what you've got! None of that matters now. What matters is you, and the way you live out the last few weeks of your life. You can sort out your mistakes, make everything right before you go. Don't you see... this is a golden opportunity to bury your own Karma!'

'I don't quite get what you're talking about,' said Alex, bemused.

'All those bad experiences, the ones you don't like to think about... All the rotten things that you've done in your life! This is your opportunity to put them right! You can leave this place at peace with everyone in it, or you can carry all your misdeeds over into the next life, and have to go through it all again.'

Alex frowned.

'What is this... are you a Buddhist or something?'

'Not exactly! But I do believe in Karma, and I do believe that we have to come back, time and time again, and learn from our mistakes.' Tina smiled at him, and moved in closer. 'This isn't the end, Mister Grump! This is just the beginning. You have a clear and definite choice and, with you, it's urgent! You have your time frame set down for you. Forget about yourself now, and think of other people for a change. Turn your thoughts outwards, and embrace the future.'

Alex stared into the water and shook his head, slowly.

'It must be nice to be young and idealistic. All those years ahead of you, uncluttered, like a nice new exercise book that no one's written in yet. You couldn't possibly see it from my point of view. You're too innocent.'

'Not that innocent,' said Tina, pursing her lips. 'You know absolutely nothing about me, nothing at all!'

'Is there anything to know... at your age, I mean. You're not really old enough to have committed any deadly sins, or even develop character-forming traits. You're idealistic, with a head full of thoughts about the inherent goodness of people, and how to save the planet. I, on the other hand, have long been aware of the inherent rottenness of people, and the fact that the planet's probably not worth saving. We're at opposite ends of ideologically incompatible viewpoints.'

'You like big words, don't you,' said Tina, suddenly grinning in the gloom. Her smile hit Alex like a spotlight in the shadow. She permeated the atmosphere of the grotto with her vitality, and the cave seemed to reflect it around the walls.

She held her arm out in front of her, and nodded to him to look at it. For the first time Alex noticed that every few seconds her hand would give a definite twitch, something she obviously wasn't able to control.

'Do you know what that is, Mister Grump,' she said, staring at her hand.

'No! What... a nervous twitch... a spasm? Maybe it's a muscular problem.'

'It's more serious than that. It's genetic, handed down through my mother. Have you ever heard of St. Vitus Dance?'

Alex felt the hairs on the back of his neck prickle and stand up, as a cold shiver ran along his spine. He looked at Tina in a new light.

'You don't mean Huntingdon's Chorea? You're not serious?'

'Huntingdon's Disease they call it these days. It's not very common, even now. You could call it the aristocrat of diseases, as it only affects the few.'

'Or the disease from hell,' said Alex, pale now in the gloom. 'Are you certain of this? Have you been tested to see if you carry the gene?'

'Yes, I tested positive all right. So you can see, Mister *'Woe-is-me, I'm dying.'* It could be worse... you could be me!'

'I am... really sorry! Really truly sorry,' said Alex, pierced to the core with a new appreciation of his own selfishness. 'I had no idea!'

They sat in silence for a few moments, finding it hard to know where to go from there. Finally, Alex broke the silence.

'And your mother, is she...'

'Full blown I'm afraid. She's strapped to a hospital bed, tied down so she doesn't injure herself. She was reasonably able to manage up to the age of thirty, and then it started. She began to walk clumsily, and knock things over. Then she would go to put her coffee down on a table, misjudge it, and drop it from a few inches above the surface. Of course, the coffee would go everywhere. Within two years she was in a wheelchair, and then the spasms got worse, and the dementia set in. She began to rant and swear uncontrollably at people, now she just flings her arms and legs about in a constant frenzy. She could be like this for another five or six years before her body finally gives out through pure exhaustion. It's disgusting!'

Alex reached out and took Tina's hand. He could feel the tremor every so often run along her arm and into her hand. He gave her a comforting squeeze.

'I thought you were just here with your boyfriend on some mindless jealousy trip. I was told that you couldn't bear to be away from him.'

Tina began to laugh. She clapped her hands in delight.

'Oh, that's a good one. Quite the opposite in fact! He's the jealous one! I have nothing to look forward to, so I pretty well do as I please. I can't have children without there being a fifty percent chance of passing it on, so it stops here. I had myself sterilized last year, when I got the first symptoms.'

'So what are you going to do,' said Alex, posing the unthinkable question.

'I've got it all worked out. When the spasms get bad enough to make me think I'm losing control, I shall take my father's shotgun out into the paddock, and stick the barrel in my mouth. It will be very quick!'

Alex looked at her in shock. That this young, pretty woman should even have to entertain such an idea! It was unbearable!'

'That would be a bit messy, wouldn't it? What's wrong with poison, or slashing your wrists?'

'Nah! Too slow for me.' Tina said, off-handedly. 'I want it to be quick!'

'I'm going out with a bottle of Jim Beam and a hundred aspirin,' Alex said, glumly. 'Not 'til after the fireworks, though! You wait 'til you see this firework display... it will give you something to remember for the rest of your life!'

Tina stood up and peered down into the water.

'How deep is that? Deep enough to swim in?'

'About twelve feet, I think. I've swum in there before. But it's damned cold.'

'Who cares,' she replied, and in a forced mood of gaiety said, 'you coming in? I feel like a swim!'

She then suddenly peeled off her top and her bra, and before Alex could move stepped out of her shorts and pants and stood naked beside him.

'If you can catch me, you can have me,' she said, teasingly, and dived into the water. Alex took ten seconds to make up his mind, then stripped off himself, and dived in after he

Chapter Seven

Jason slouched into Darlene's room and flopped on her bed. She was sitting at the dressing table, trying out a new way of styling her hair, and was not happy to see him. She addressed him through the mirror.

'What are you doing in my room, you little turd? Get out of here or I'll call Greg!'

'And what's he going to do, Darlene? Tell me not to annoy my big sister? You'd better make the most of this room, Darlene, 'cos you won't have it for much longer. I heard Hilda tell the old man we've got to move.'

Darlene half turned in her seat and looked directly at him.

'That's rubbish, and you know it, Jason. We can stay here as long as we like. If you hadn't pulled that stupid stunt with the swimming pool there wouldn't have been any argument.'

Jason affected a look of unconcern. He squinted back at her through his beady eyes.

'Don't believe me then! But it's true. She's talking about going back to a flat, like the one we had in Enfield.'

'Over my dead body,' Darlene snarled, and jumped to her feet to confront him. 'You're just trying to stir me up, Jason! I'm going to call Hilda and tell her what you've been saying.'

'Go for it,' said Jason, collapsing back on the bed. 'But you're going to have to share a room with me again, so you'd better get used to the idea.' He plucked a jar of face cream off her side table, and began to toss it negligently into the air and catch it again.

'Look, put that down you little shit! Stop touching my stuff.'

Jason dropped it back on the table.

'She reckons old Alex is dying, and he's not going to leave her any money. They had an argument about it down on the beach. She reckons he said he wouldn't leave us a dollar between us... I told you he was a prick!'

Darlene straightened up at the word 'dying', and sat down again, her back to the mirror.

'What does she mean, he's dying? Does she mean soon... next week, next month, or what?'

'She reckons the doctor's given him eight weeks, but she thinks he's going to bump himself off before then. I don't give a shit anyway, as long as I get the Jag!'

Darlene curled her nose up in contempt.

'What, *you*... the Jag! Don't make me laugh. If anyone gets that it will be Greg, and that will be a laugh. He'll probably wrap it round the nearest tree.'

'She reckons that we're not going to get anything, so I'm going to steal it the moment he carks it.'

Darlene repeated her nose trick.

'You? Steal a car? You can't even drive, you idiot. You're all talk, Jason! You're a *'gunna'*.'

Jason sat up on the bed, aggrieved. He knew exactly what a *'gunna'* was – somebody who was always 'gunna' do this, or 'gunna' do that, but never actually got around to it.

'I can so drive a car! I've been going out in the paddocks with Geoff Martin and Barry Fidler. There's some old wrecks behind Geoff's father's place, and we go hacking around the paddocks in them. It's great fun!'

'I'll believe it when I see it,' Darlene sniffed. 'You haven't got the guts!'

'I'll bloody show you whether I've got the guts or not,' said Jason, and he got angrily off her bed and stomped out of her room, determined to show her what he was made of.

At the next low tide he was off, over the causeway and wandering through the streets of Meddleton, looking for an easy mark.

Meddleton wasn't a very large town. There was a summer population of 15,000 that dwindled out of season to 8,000 permanents, and these were mostly farmers and fishermen. But there were plenty of cars about at this time of the year, and Jason walked slowly along the kerb, just keeping an eye out for one with a set of keys in the ignition. He soon gave up on the main street – too many people and potential witnesses around. Out in the back streets things began to look more favourable. It was sleepier out here, and folks weren't so careful about their cars. At a quarter to six he saw a blue Falcon XF, with mags, that looked a bit sporty. The keys were in the lock.

He opened the door quietly and climbed in. It was an automatic, so he didn't have to worry about the gears. With a hurried look at the house, he twisted the key in the lock, started it with a growl, and slammed it into drive. The flyscreen door flew open, and an angry young man came running down the garden path as Jason took off. With yells and curses ringing in his ears, Jason put his foot down and careened around the first corner to his right, turned right again and headed off for the highway to Ceduna.

Before he was even out of town he realised he'd made the mistake of not adjusting the seat. He was fairly short, and the owner was considerably taller. That meant that he could barely reach the pedals. He grappled around, trying to find the handle to adjust the seat forward, but was unfamiliar with this particular make of car. He pushed himself forward on the seat and clung desperately onto the steering wheel, his agitation sending the car swerving from side to side along the road until he bounced it off a traffic island, flattened a keep left sign and left a huge dent in the right mudguard and a scrape along two doors and the rear panels. He swung right, a little too hard, and the impetus threw him across the car into the passenger side of the bench seat, while he hung desperately onto the steering wheel. The car bucked, then slowed, and as he slid himself across the seat, and put his foot back onto the accelerator, he sideswiped a yellow Camira that was standing by the kerb.

The sweat was breaking out on his forehead by now, and panic was setting in. Reaching for the seat belt, he buckled himself in, and hoped that would stop him from being thrown around the interior of the car. He got out onto the main highway and saw the sign to Ceduna, and gunned it. By the time the police were in hot pursuit, he was ten kilometres from the town, heading west, and driving like someone who'd had too much to drink.

'It wasn't my fault,' he whined later. 'The seat was too far back, and the pedals were slippery. My feet kept sliding off!'

Twenty kilometers out of Meddleton he saw the patrol car across the road, its blue lights flashing for him to stop. A policeman was standing in front of the car, holding his hand up imperiously and motioning to him to pull over.

Jason froze! All of a sudden, it was as if he'd forgotten how to drive. He didn't put the brake on, because he'd forgotten the car had brakes, and he was only capable of staring, hypnotised, at the police car ahead. There was a resounding crunch as he hit, and the car spun sideways and stopped. Jason felt the blood running out of a gash on his forehead where he had hit the steering wheel, then the door was wrenched open, and a hand reached inside and dragged him out by the collar of his shirt.

'You little prick,' were the only words he remembered being spoken, before he was face down in the gravel, a huge weight on his back, and his hands being cuffed painfully behind him. He woke up in Meddleton hospital.

That evening, Darlene and Hilda faced each other off across the lounge room, while Greg stood back by the door.

'You basically dared him to do it, Darlene. If that's what you said, you dared him! You... *stupid* girl!'

Hilda was angrier than Greg had ever seen her, and he wasn't going to get involved in this catfight.

'Don't you fucking call me stupid,' Darlene screamed back, her fists clenched. 'I just told him he hadn't got the guts, that's all. I'm not responsible for that little turd and what he does. You should have been tougher with him when he was growing up – it's *your* fault, not mine!'

'No Darlene! You're not going to get off that easily this time. You're always goading him, always pushing his buttons to see what will happen. I've watched you doing it. You're a selfish little bitch!'

'Don't you fucking call me selfish. What the fuck have you ever done for us, you silly old bitch? You tell her Greg,' she shouted at her father. 'You tell her what a fucking useless mother she's been all these years.'

Greg waved his hands and shook his head, vehemently. He wasn't getting involved in this. He'd had a basic fear of violence ever since he was a kid, and he avoided potentially violent situations like the plague. He'd never really seen Hilda lose her rag before, and the sight of it frightened him.

'Useless mother, eh! Yes, I was a useless mother, because I didn't do what any halfway decent mother would have done... shut your rotten little mouth up a long time ago!'

Darlene stuck her fingers up in defiance.

'I'd like to see you try, you bitch! I might just shut *yours* up for *you*... I'm not a kid anymore you know!'

'You're not too big to drop, Darlene!'

'Is that right? Well you just try it, you come and try it, that's all, and see what you get.'

The two women flew at each other across the room, and Darlene went for her mother with her nails. Hilda was too solid to be intimidated by this. She seized Darlene by the throat with one hand, drew back her fist and punched her daughter squarely in the mouth. Darlene fell to the floor in shock, blood spurting from her lips and nose, as Hilda looked ruefully down at her own skinned knuckles.

'Now get up and give me another crack at you,' said Hilda, menacingly.

Darlene just let out a high-pitched whine and started to cry. Then she spat her two top teeth out onto the carpet, and went into hysterics.

II

Roddy Donovan was not happy! He was on the prowl around the island, looking for Tina, because for one reason or another she'd been making herself scarce lately, and had hardly spent any time with him at all.

He could understand that in the daytime. She couldn't be hanging around while he was working, mixing up various quantities of gunpowder and cordite, in an environment that would go up like a bomb with the tiniest spark. Tina smoked, and so she couldn't even pop her head around the corner in case she forgot and consigned them all to kingdom come. But after work it was different. She should have been there for him, seeing to his needs. Instead of that she was off somewhere on the island, poking around in areas that had nothing to do with her, and he resented it. In bald terms, he was jealous.

Roddy had been the last of the four men to be hired by Jack Delaney, and he had wondered at the time if Donovan was a wise choice. Roddy had a reputation of being a bit of a hothead, and was always showing up with cuts and bruises, black eyes and split lips to show for the latest run in at the pub, or at the snooker hall. He'd always been a bit gung-ho, even in their army days, and he had never had much luck with the ladies. Once they found out what he was like, they usually left him a 'Dear John', and fled. Delaney had been more than surprised when he'd shown up with this delightful young lady called Tina.

Tina, with her shock of russet hair that billowed out around her face, highlighting those high cheekbones and almond eyes that gave her features such a look of pure class. Her manners weren't so classy, however. She could mix it with the best of them, and often did. But she could also take being beaten in an argument, which was more than Roddy could do, without threatening his opponent with his fists.

Alex hadn't taken to Donovan at all. From their first confrontation over Tina's accommodation, Alex had resolved that if there were any further trouble with him, he would pay him what was owed, and kick him off the island. After his interlude with Tina in the cave, however, he wasn't quite so sure. If he sent Donovan packing, presumably Tina would go with him, and he didn't want her to go.

That day in the cave had been one of the more memorable experiences of his life. When he dived into the water, Tina swam up and wrapped her legs around him, and they both sank slowly to the bottom of the pool, entwined, and in each other's arms. From beneath the water they looked up and could see the lights, reflected on the surface, giving the water a green fluorescence that it didn't have when viewed from above. It was like a wonderland down there, with rocks covered in shellfish of various kinds, and strands of green weed that floated stringily around them in some sort of ballet of the deep. After half a minute they looked into each other's eyes, both seeking the answer to the question uppermost in their minds.

'Shall we surface, or shall we just stay down here and drift slowly out of this life, leaving our dead, naked bodies to be found by those who come afterwards?'

For a few seconds Alex thought that he could stand it, dying down there now, with a beautiful young woman in his arms, his last moments spent with perfection in female form. But when lungs begin to burst for air, the natural reaction of the body at that moment is to live, and they rushed upwards together, breaking the surface and gasping in the pure, clear air of the Grotto.

'God, that was magnificent,' said Tina, laughing now in the thrill of the moment.

Alex felt like he was twenty-five again, floating weightlessly in that medium, his aches and pains having disappeared while he stayed suspended in the water. Tina turned to him and opened herself up to his probing hands, thrusting herself towards him so that they might make love under the water, hidden in the shadows of the natural world. They stayed in the water for ten minutes, finally crawling out, freezing, and collapsed onto the ledge. It was some minutes before they had the strength to overcome natural gravity again, and stand up to put their clothes back on. Then Tina offered her lips to him and he kissed her, and his youth came flooding back to him in a pit of regret, and for the first time in years he felt the hot salt of tears on his cheek.

After that, although they tried not to appear to seek each other out, they stumbled across each other continually in various parts of the island, and spent timeless hours together, discussing all sorts of topics and philosophies bar the one that tied them together in an invisible bond – death!

This particular evening they were sitting down at the old boat dock, dangling their feet in the water and muttering together in desultory tones. One of the reasons they kept their voices down was that they didn't want to be seen there together, and they certainly didn't want to attract other company and destroy the atmosphere of the moment.

'I keep meaning to ask you...' said Alex, proceeding warily. 'The boyfriend, Donovan! I find it a bit hard to understand. He must be, what... forty-one?'

Tina looked at him and smiled.

'Confusing, isn't it? I feel like that myself, sometimes. Of course, I haven't known him that long you know, only three or four months. It's not a grand passion – not for me, anyway. I suppose I was just bored.'

Alex looked at her, a wry look on his face, and shook his head repeatedly.

'Bored? Is that a reason to go out with someone?'

'It is for me! Because of my situation, I feel that it would be cruel to the other party to form long-term relationships, with the inevitable heartache that would result once I hit the hard times. So I make do with liaisons, short term and superficial. If I start getting too close to someone, then I back off at a hundred miles an hour.'

Alex was silent for a moment, staring at the black surface of the water around his feet.

'And what if someone starts to get too close to you, even though you don't feel involved with *them?*'

Tina threw her head back, and laughed.

'You mean you! You're not very subtle, Alex. Well, I don't have to worry about that, do I... because you'll be...' She stopped, and bit her tongue. 'I'm sorry! That must have sounded incredibly callous.'

Alex shrugged. It was only the truth, after all! He remained silent.

'Besides, what makes you think that I don't feel close to you as things stand? Stranger things have happened you know.'

'Because it would go against your principles, and anyway; you might get hurt yourself, and that would be futile, wouldn't it?'

Tina looked at him with a glint of a tear in her eye.

'You can't threaten a drowning man with a bucket of water, Alex!'

She looked away, out to where the moon hung low over the sea.

'What you're saying is that neither of us can feel sorry for ourselves about losing the other, because we're both dying – is that it?'

'That's about it,' said Tina, quickly wiping at her eye. 'You and I both know where we're going. It may not be fair... it may not sit right with us because, let's face it, everyone wants to live! But for whatever reason, you and I have been singled out by a random fate to go through certain experiences. On the plus side, we have a certain knowledge, and we have an approximate timescale. That's more than most people ever get. It means that we can live for every moment we have left... together and singularly, and we will value every moment of every day because we know that every second that passes...' Here she broke down and began to cry. Alex reached over and went to put his arm around her shoulder, when there was a disturbance behind them.

'So that's where you are, Tina! This is a pretty little scene. My girlfriend and my employer, all huddled up in a cosy little *tête à tête*.'

Tina looked up with a start, and hurriedly dried her eyes.

'What has he been saying to you, Tina? Has he been upsetting you?'

Alex spun around and looked up. Donovan was standing menacingly over him with his fists clenched.

'Don't be silly, Roddy! Of course not! We were just talking about things that are a bit emotional, and I was getting a little depressed, that's all.'

'Well, what the hell are you getting emotional with him for? He's just the potty local millionaire! Is that what's going on... money! Jeeze, Tina, I didn't think you'd fall for the old money trick!'

'You're talking rubbish, Roddy. Stop making a fool of yourself and go back to the caravan. I'll be there in a minute.'

Roddy was feeling aggressive. Alex stood up, prepared to defend himself, but Donovan towered over him by a good six inches.

'Do as you've been asked to do,' said Alex. 'We're just finishing a private conversation here.'

'Oh, is that right, Mister Bloody Smart Arse? Nobody tells me to piss off and leave my girlfriend behind! And you,' he indicated Tina; 'you get your arse back to the caravan – now!'

Tina got a sudden glint in her eye. She wasn't used to being spoken to like that.

'Don't you *dare* talk to me like that! I'm not your chattel, and don't you forget it. I don't belong to you, or anybody. I'll come when I'm good and ready!'

Donovan reached out and grabbed her by the hair. He twisted it around and forced her halfway down to her knees, then dragged her past him and gave her a shove in the direction of the caravan.

'Hey...hey! What do you think you're doing,' yelled Alex, trying to pull Donovan off her.

Donovan turned and grabbed Alex by the collar of his shirt.

'You fuckin' lay a hand on me, buddy, and you'd better know what you're letting yourself in for!'

He gave Alex a shove, and Alex staggered, tripped and fell backwards over the side of the landing into the water. He came up spluttering just as Tina brought her foot up and kicked Donovan in the groin. He went down like a sack of potatoes, letting out a howl that alerted Jack Delaney and the others over at their caravans.

Rushing down, the three of them were on him before he had the chance to get up. Between them, they sized the situation up, helped Prittik out of the water and threw Donovan in headfirst.

'Maybe that will calm you down, you bloody redneck,' yelled Delaney. 'You've been bloody asking for it ever since you got here. Well, you're fired!'

Alex said nothing, but cradled his stomach. He felt a shooting pain the like of which he hadn't felt before, and he knew he had to get out of his wet clothes. The last he saw of Tina was her striding away in an ungainly fashion towards the caravan, her head down, and her shoulders heaving with sobs.

Chapter Eight

Jocelyn clattered around the house for days, feeling lost and alone. Alex was totally non-committal on the rare occasions that he spent in the house. He seemed distant, somehow; acted as though she wasn't really there. She thought that maybe he was paying her back for the disinterest she had shown him over the previous eighteen months, when she had acted so bored with his every statement. Then, part of her thought that he had, somehow, overheard her conversation with McRae, but if so, why hadn't he reacted; why hadn't he lost his temper?

Joss was used to less civilised responses. With previous partners, when caught out with other men she had expected, and got, a beating. Alex wasn't like that. She began to feel that she should have appreciated him more. Perhaps her little escapades with his accountant had been foolish and ill advised? It had been exciting at the time, of course, and that was the hallmark of all Jocelyn's affairs. The excitement of the moment! What was the use of being the perfect siren, if you couldn't practice your art?

What was more distressing to her, however, was the lack of a suitable response from McRae. Since that phone call, he had pretty well blocked any communication between them. She would phone, and the voice at the other end would reflect the self-satisfied tones of Janelle.

'No, Mr. McRae is not available at the moment. He's in a meeting with a client, and can't be disturbed. However, I'll tell him you called, and no doubt he will call you back when he has a minute to spare.'

But he hadn't called back. Five phone calls later he still hadn't called back, and Joss began to experience a chill down her spine each time she heard Janelle's voice.

'I'm so sorry, Mrs. Prittik, but he's not feeling the best today, and is asleep at the moment. I think he must have been over exerting himself, because this is very unusual for him, as you know.'

'Well, can't you wake him up – this is urgent!'

'I'm sure it is, Mrs. Prittik. But Mr. McRae gave me very specific instructions not to disturb him. I always follow Mr. McRae's instructions to the 'T'.'

'You tell him that his number one client is not very happy.'

'I'll pass that on. You have a good day!'

Jocelyn almost threw the receiver down at that point. *Still* he didn't call!

The weekend came and went, and Jocelyn watched all the activity going on outside, without having the slightest idea of what Alex was up to. When the semi-trailer arrived, she was almost out of her mind with apprehension. She had never operated well on her own, she always needed a man to prop her up, to give her a sense of identity. The image that she carried of herself was not self-sustaining. It only really came into its own when she lay spread-eagled on a bed, acting out the part that she played so well, and participating in the gratification of the partner of the moment.

Who it was didn't matter! The fact that a man engaged in the sex act with her was experiencing cataclysmic orgasms, was enough to fill in the part of her that seemed so insubstantial when she was facing life alone. Jocelyn didn't fully exist outside the sexual experience, which was why she attempted to fill the gap between copulations with mammoth shopping sprees, the results of which often found their way into the Red Cross bin a week later, when the futility of her purchases became obvious, even to her. During this period of incommunication, therefore, she could feel herself slowly disappearing into the wallpaper, fading gradually away until she began to be afraid to go to sleep, in case she never woke up again.

But when Joss got angry, she also got mean.

'You tell that fuck that he's about to lose his number one client. I want to speak to him… and I want to speak to him *now!*'

This was on the Tuesday morning, a week after he'd told her that he would be up for the weekend, but hadn't showed up.

Janelle smiled to herself, and stole a glance at McRae, who was staring at the phone in her hand with a worried frown.

'Of course, Mrs. Prittik! He's here now. Shall I put him on?' She handed the phone to Linsay.

'Is that you? What do you think you're playing at, keeping me hanging up in the air? I've called you seven times… no eight, this is the eighth!'

'Now calm down Mrs. Prittik,' McRae began. He had to walk the tightrope here. Alex might be listening in.

'Don't you tell me to calm down, Lindsay. And what's with this Mrs. Prittik crap?'

'Err, Jocelyn, Jocelyn... you might be overheard. Please...'

'Oh! So that's what you're worried about. Well don't bother, because he's not here. He's never here these days, he's always out somewhere, and I don't know where most of the time. He doesn't even speak to me any more! Do you know what it's like being cooped up here on your own, for days at a time, with no-one to talk to?'

'I was just trying to protect you, Jocelyn. You wouldn't want him to divorce you, would you?'

'Divorce! He wouldn't dare. The court would give me everything, and he'd be out on his ear.'

'I don't think it works like that, Joss. They don't make orders on good looks!'

'So what? He's dying! But he won't talk to me about it. He hasn't said another word since he first told me about it.'

'You mean since our telephone call? When his voice came in and said he'd recorded the conversation? Wake up Joss, he knows! I'm sure he knows, that's why he's acting like this. I think he wants to catch you out though, make sure and certain of his facts. Then he'll get rid of me and divorce you. And you know what that means; ruin, for the both of us!'

Jocelyn felt a sudden shiver down her spine. McRae sounded convincing! Her anger faded, and she reverted to the helpless little girl that he knew so well.

'But... are you sure? He wouldn't divorce *me*, Windsay... would he? I mean... what am I going to do?' Her voice crept up a register, and he could sense that she was bordering on hysteria.

'I just want you to hang in there, just for another three days. I'll definitely come up there this Friday and suss out the situation. Do you think you can do that, cuddle-pie?'

Reassured by his tone, Jocelyn melted.

'Did you know that he's got four men here, making fireworks? A great big truck came and delivered all this gunpowder and stuff, and these old friends of his are working down in the boatshed making all these bangers and things.'

McRae sat back in stunned silence.

'He's fucking what? Fireworks? No, he never said a bloody thing, Joss. I haven't heard anything.'

'I heard one of the men say it's going to be bigger than the Sydney Olympics, Snookums. A huge display... in about three weeks time! Maybe he's going to blow the island up!'

'God almighty! Look, just keep calm. I will definitely be up there on Friday night, and I'll find out what's going on. When I get there I want you to keep your distance a little bit if he's around. We don't want him to get more suspicious than he already is. And look, if you really need to speak to me from now on, use a public phone in Meddleton. At least that way we can't be overheard – got that!'

'Yes, Snookums! I love you!'

'Love you too, sweetie-pop.'

McRae dropped the phone, and looked at Janelle.

'We've got to go to Crab Island on Friday, I think he's going barmy!'

'We'd better get some documents made out then. I think we'll need them,' said Janelle, thoughtfully. 'But you'd better keep Joss happy when we get there. I'll just look the other way.'

'You're a real trooper,' said Lindsay, grinning in reply.

Despite the fact that she was lonely, Jocelyn did not appreciate the presence of her husband's sister and family at the rear of the house. Hilda was no company for her! Even if Jocelyn had liked other women, which she didn't, Hilda always gave her the feeling that she looked down on her in some way, as if she wasn't good enough to be married to her brother. She had made no attempts to be friendly, and the only time she saw her was when Hilda came through into the main house to borrow something from the larder.

She was always borrowing things, and quite often Joss went to the larder to get something, a new bag of sugar, or a packet of biscuits, only to find that Hilda had been there before her and taken them back to her family at the rear. Nothing made her angrier than to find some commodity missing that she had known was there, only a day or two before. Then she and Alex had to go without until the tide turned, and she could make a special trip to Meddleton to stock up again.

'Your sister's taken the last jar of honey... and the strawberry jam! God, Alex, can't you have a word with her about it. Free rent is one thing, but stealing our food is another.'

'Don't make such a song and dance about it, Joss. It's only food! They're living on a shoestring back there. You

104

should be thankful that we're in the fortunate position that we don't have to borrow off *them*.'

'I'm sure your sister would have something to say about it if the position was reversed, Alex. She gives me the snottiest looks if I even stick my head into their part of the house. She seems to forget that the house belongs to us... all of it, not just the front part. I mean, they're not even paying rent!'

'I'm just helping them out, Joss. It won't be for long. Greg will get himself some work sooner or later, and they'll be able to move out and get their own place again.'

'Well I don't like it,' she pouted. 'Those kids of theirs, they're like animals. They're always screaming at each other and rough-housing and breaking things. It's put me right off having children.'

Alex had looked at her with a glint in his eye.

'You never intended to have children, Joss. It would spoil your figure – remember? I found the pills you'd hidden away when you told me you were really trying!'

Jocelyn darted a guilty look at him and flushed in embarrassment.

'Well, after seeing those two, I'm certainly not going to have any. You should hear the language that comes out of there!'

That had been over eighteen months ago, when they were still on reasonably good terms with each other. But Greg hadn't got a job, and the following summer they'd still been there, much to Jocelyn's disgust. This was the third summer in a row that they'd had to share their summer home. Even

Alex was getting fed up with it, and it showed as he became more irritable, especially with the two teenagers.

Now he was going to die, and they were still there. Jocelyn made a mental note that the moment he was in the ground, she would get an eviction order and turf them out into the street. She wasn't going to put up with them a moment longer than she had to.

More recently she had felt more and more helpless in the situation, and when she went out and found Alex standing over the two teenagers in a deep red swimming pool, while they shouted curses and abuse at him, she felt the whole situation was becoming surreal. It added to her own feelings of insubstantiality.

One night Alex came staggering in, holding his stomach and dripping water all over the carpet. He looked as if he was in agony, and she thought that maybe this was it! He was dying in front of her eyes.

'Get me some of that morphine,' he gasped, as he limped through to the shower, peeled his clothes off and stood under the hot water until he took the chill off his bones. He took two of the pain-killers, hoping that by doing that he would get rid of the pain more quickly.

For someone unused to taking medication of any kind, however, it was a little like over-kill. The pills knocked him out completely, and he woke up the following day at twelve thirty, the pain gone.

He thought back over the events of the previous evening. His first thought was that it was lucky Donovan hadn't thought to punch him in the stomach, because it would probably have killed him on the spot. Then he thought of Tina.

He struggled out of bed, threw on his clothes and walked past Joss in the lounge room, where she was keeping herself occupied with a jigsaw puzzle. She looked up as he pushed past her to the door, and went to speak. But Alex wasn't interested in speaking to Joss. She had pretty well ceased to exist for him. With the limited time he had left he certainly wasn't going to waste it on an unfaithful wife.

Heading over to the boatshed he collared Jack Delaney, who was putting the finishing touches to a triple starburst.

'How are you feeling, Alex? You look a hell of a lot better than you looked last night. Don't worry, Donovan's gone! We packed him off first thing this morning, the moment the tide went out. He had to wade through water for the first thirty yards, nevertheless. He wasn't too happy!'

'It's all right, I don't give two stuffs about Donovan. What happened to Tina? Is she still in the caravan?'

'No, she's gone too. She waited until an hour after Donovan had disappeared, then when she felt it was safe, she took her stuff and walked over to Meddleton.'

'Oh, for chrisesake… did she say where she was going?'

Delaney looked at him in alarm.

'Hey! Steady on! You look as if you're getting a little bit involved there. Forget it, Alex. She's just a kid!'

'She's nearly twenty-six, believe it or not. And I've got to find her, Jack. Believe me, it's important.'

'Well the only way you're going to get over the causeway now is by boat. The tide's almost in.'

'I'll use the dinghy. I haven't started the outboard for a while, I just hope it hasn't seized up.'

Delaney accompanied him across to the causeway, and between them they dragged the dinghy into the water. The motor started on the third pull, and Alex clambered aboard, leaving Jack to stare after him, a puzzled look on his face.

By the time Jack got back to the boatshed, Colin Bartel and Eddie Grainger had returned from the bunker they had been building, down by the waterfront. It was to be one of the staging posts for the firework display, and had to be big enough for one man to be able to walk unseen along the rows of skyrockets to let the bursts off at the right time.

'Where've you been, Jack? We could have done with a bit of help down there with the sleepers.'

'Sorry fellas! I was making starbursts until I got interrupted by the boss. He's taken off after Tina, for some reason or another.'

Colin laughed.

'I know what reason, mate! The same reason Donovan ducked him in the water. Though what he would want to be playing about with Tina for, when he's got a wife like that blonde bombshell in there, I really don't know. She absolutely sizzles with sex, man.'

'Well you better keep your eyes off her, mate. We've got a lot of money riding on this job. I don't want Alex's nose put out of joint.'

An hour later, with Delaney safely back in the shed, and Eddie taking time out to lie down with a crook stomach, Colin decided to chance his arm, and took a pile of newly manufactured fireworks over to the house, to store in the basement. Joss looked up as he came in, and he asked her politely if she would mind opening the door to the basement for him, as he had his arms full.

Joss obliged, and took a second look at this man, noting the broad shoulders and the biceps. She felt an old familiar urge coming over her, so when he dropped a few on the step, and left them to go down the stairs, she gathered them up and followed him down.

'Where would you like me to put them?'

'They seem to be stacking them in the corner over there,' she said, faintly, sensing possibilities in the situation that might dispel an otherwise gloomy afternoon.

As Colin deposited his load in the corner, and began to go through them, Jocelyn slipped and fell on the concrete floor.

'Oh, blast! I think I've twisted my ankle,' she said, remaining seated on the floor. 'Maybe you'd better have a look at it.'

She hoisted her skirt up to her thigh, and Colin thought that maybe she didn't have a very good idea of where exactly her ankle was. He hurried over to her and bent down to help.

'Maybe it's my knee as well,' Jocelyn said, looking him boldly in the eye.

Colin made a careful examination of her ankle, kneading and pressing the bone and rotating her foot gently, then moved his hands up to her knee and began the same manoeuvre. This time her skirt slid back along her thighs, and Colin knew that he was in for a new and unique experience.

'Don't stop there, big boy,' she whispered. 'Keep going! You're doing a good job so far.'

Colin carried her over to an old camp bed in the opposite corner, and continued to do a good job, so much so that Joss felt at one with herself for the first time in weeks.

II

Jason was left to languish in hospital for two days after his mother had paid him an anguished visit on the evening of the accident. He found himself locked in a room with bars at the window, and a bolt on the outside of the door so that, even if he was inclined, he couldn't go anywhere. The police had made it clear to the matron that Jason was under arrest, and was not to be allowed to leave under any circumstances.

He lay in bed, his head swathed in bandages, with a headache that approached migraine proportions. At eleven o'clock on the second night, a face peered through the window of his door that seemed strangely familiar to him. He heard the bolt withdrawn, and the figure ducked inside and shut the door behind him.

'Remember me,' said the guy, and Jason suddenly got a fleeting memory of a flyscreen flying open, and a young man running down the garden path, cursing and swearing, as he accelerated away from the kerb.

'That was my bloody car you wrecked! Do you know how long it took me to rebuild that Ford? How much it cost to respray it? It's written off, did you know that, you little prick!'

Jason began to sit up in panic, but a fist smashed into his face and flattened him back onto the pillow. For three minutes Jason received a hail of punches to the head and body without being able to utter a scream, or utter a sound. One of the first blows had winded him, and he lay there in terror, thinking that this guy was going to kill him where he lay.

As suddenly as it had begun, it finished, and the guy had disappeared before Jason could get his breath back and call for the sister. She took one look at him, and phoned for the police. They took one look at him and decided that he would have much more chance of a full recovery if he were allowed to go home, and then be pulled in front of a juvenile court at a later date.

Greg finally picked him up thirty-six hours later and dragged him home by the scruff of the neck. For once, Jason wasn't in a condition to argue. He slunk through the house, back to his room on strict instructions not to attract Alex's attention.

Darlene pushed her way into his room and sat on the side of his bed.

'Shhee what you causthed.' she lisped, through the huge gap in her top teeth. 'Thass your faulsh, you lissle prick! Hidda bassed my teesh out!'

'If you hadn't dared me,' said Jason, speaking painfully through his swollen lips, 'I wouldn't have done it. It's your fault, really!'

Darlene's eyes bugged out in self-righteous rage. She hit him with his own cricket bat, and broke his nose. Greg only arrived just in time to drag Jason off his toothless daughter, and save her from being further mutilated with a penknife.

That night he locked them both in their rooms, and for the first time began to think that suicide might just be a viable option.

Chapter Nine

Donovan had crawled ashore that morning in a foul mood, forced to leave the island at the insistence of his three erstwhile friends. They had stood menacingly along the shoreline of the island, threatening dire consequences if he should once again cross over that causeway. Delaney promised to forward on such money that was owed to him, and so, fuming at his lost opportunity, Donovan headed for Meddleton.

No sooner did the first hotels open than he was to be found propping up a bar, determined to get stinking rotten drunk. That was his usual answer to the self-inflicted reverses that littered his misguided past. Fall foul of the authorities – go and get drunk! Fall out with his girlfriend – go and get drunk! Lose his money on the Pokies – go and get drunk! It was a recurring theme in a grab-bag of missed opportunities and inter-related temper tantrums. And as usual, Donovan swore revenge!

As his head dropped, and the drink inspired fit of maudlin regret crowded into his overtaxed brain, he began to think of Tina. His beautiful Tina! She had refused to have anything to do with him after that episode with Prittik, wouldn't even talk to him. Couldn't she see that it was only because he loved her that he was driven to such desperate acts? She had chosen the company of another man over him, one that was even dying, for god's sake. How could you have less going for you than that? It was a bloody insult, that's what it was. So, the guy was a millionaire! Big deal! He couldn't take it with him. Or was that the point... maybe she had some idea about benefiting from the poor dope's will?

Donovan slammed his glass down on the bar in anger. It was possible that his uncontrolled behaviour had screwed up a nice little scam that both he and Tina could have benefited from once the old coot was dead. Yes, that was the only rational answer! She'd been angling for his money and he, Donovan, had screwed things up. Suddenly he felt as if he could kick himself.

Why hadn't she warned him? If she'd said something he could have played along, kept out of the way and let her go through her little routine with him, get the sucker hooked. Then they could have laughed about it together, later, and they would have had enough money to set them up nicely. As it was, he had even lost out on the ten thousand dollars he'd been promised for the three weeks this job would take. He was only going to get about fifteen hundred, and that really pissed him off. He ordered another Jack Daniels, and tried to blot his own stupidity out of his mind.

Tina had spent the night in misery. She had crawled into the other caravan, and begged the protection of Eddie Grainger and Jack Delaney, who had readily offered it. She slept in Jack's bunk, while he curled up in his sleeping bag on a bench seat. Neither of them got much sleep.

She lay for a long while, hoping that Alex would materialise from the house and take her in, perhaps offer her a guest room until Donovan cleared the island and she felt safe again. But Alex didn't reappear, and she thought that this was as much due to a sudden lack of interest in her and her affairs as his unfortunate dunking. She thought that he must think her an idiot to be attracted to a caveman like Donovan, when in actual fact she wasn't. It had only started as a drunken tumble with a 'rough', and had only continued due to Donovan's incredible persistence, and her lack of any alternative routine to adhere to in her life. Like the moon at times, she had been *'void of course'* once the gene had been identified in her system.

Nothing seemed worthwhile any more. It spelled the end of ambition, and the end of hope. Her day-to-day existence had become permeated with a sense of futility, as she became more positively aware of the road that she followed, and of the monster that lay in wait for her, the further along that road she travelled. Alex had loomed out of the darkness like the definitive lesson in absolutes – *no matter how dark or gloomy your own situation appears to be, there is always someone worse off than yourself!*

Alex gave her something she had never experienced before, namely someone to feel sorrier for than herself. This alone had allowed her to reassert her natural humour, and adopt the position superior. It allowed her to sympathise, but better again, to empathise! Somewhere in the depths of that emotional tangle they had found common ground, and had made love, as if love was the one thing they were both incapable of bestowing on any creature not cursed with that same knowledge of their own mortality. Tina's long held determination not to become involved had immediately crumbled, and she lay fearfully on her bunk, knowing that she had become attached to Alex via a karmic umbilical chord, which only his death, or hers, could sever.

The following morning she had refused to come out of the caravan on Donovan's urging, and it had taken Eddie, Colin and Jack Delaney to persuade him that she really didn't want to see him. She had watched him make his way over the causeway, and shuddered to think that she could ever have seen anything in such a Neanderthal. Then she had waited for another hour, hoping against hope that Alex would appear to deliver her from her doubts, and ask her to stay. But Alex hadn't appeared, and after an hour had gone by she knew that she would have to take that walk across the causeway soon, or be cut off again by the rising tide.

Her greatest fear was that she would run into Donovan in Meddleton, and be met by maudlin regrets, or by physical violence. He was capable of either or both at the same time. So she made her way to the bus station and ordered her ticket for Port Lincoln, hoping to lie low enough to avoid him until the bus rolled in at three o'clock that afternoon. Then she went into the women's toilets and tidied herself up, after which she sat in a cubicle for three quarters of an hour, hoping that by that time Donovan had already quit town, heading for Adelaide.

Finally, at eleven thirty Tina emerged into the main street, looked cautiously around, and made her way to a small café. She ordered toast and coffee, and sat close to the window, watching the townsfolk going about their daily business. She was beginning to feel a little more secure by now, as Donovan had still not appeared, and she relaxed and enjoyed a second cup of coffee, watching the clock and wondering what she was going to do to fill in the time until the bus left at three.

At twelve twenty she decided that she might as well buy herself a paperback to pass the time, and go and sit on the beach in the shade of one of the eucalypts that grew along the front. She called into a little second-hand bookshop, and picked up a tattered copy of *'The Afterdeath'*, which she had been meaning to read for some time. Then she crossed the road and wandered down to the beach.

The causeway to Crab Island lay a hundred yards to the south, though it presently lay covered by the tide, and the island now *looked* like an island. It had suddenly become part of another world, an impenetrable world of wealth and privilege that she had briefly rubbed shoulders with, but that was now closed to her by more than just three hundred yards of tidal causeway. She sat on the sand and put her bag down beside her, and opened the book.

She had barely settled when a buzzing noise began to irritate her consciousness, like an insistent mosquito. She looked up and over towards the island to see a small rubber dinghy with an outboard, heading toward the shore, pretty well following the line of the now submerged causeway. Her heart skipped a beat, and she squinted at the boat to try and bring it into greater focus. Within half a minute she could make out the occupant. It was Alex!

A great conflict of emotion rose up in her throat, and she found that she was incapable of making a sound. Should she stand up and wave? God, no! Alex was probably making a shopping trip over to the township, possibly running an errand for his employees for some ingredient that they lacked, or had run out of. It was inconceivable that he would be looking for her!

The dinghy ran up onto the sand, and Alex cut the motor. He jumped out, pulled it up out of the water so it wouldn't drift away, and looked wildly around him, up and down the beach. It was his erratic behaviour that first gave Tina hope. He didn't just head off purposefully to the main street. Instead he seemed to scour the beach and the roadway nearby for a sight of something he seemed to expect to be waiting there.

Tentatively, she folded her book and stood up, and Alex caught sight of her and began to run. He waved madly at her as he ran, and was soon either out of breath, or suffering from the stitch, as had to slow down and begin to walk swiftly in her direction, holding his side. She started to walk uncertainly towards him, and then tentatively waved back, hoping that she hadn't misread the signs. When he was ten yards away he began to shake his head at her, and then stopped, to get his breath.

'Thank God for small mercies,' he said, breathlessly. 'I thought I'd lost you forever.'

'What do you mean? I thought you didn't want to see me... I mean, after last night...'

'Oh, fuck last night! Don't worry about that idiot. He's gone now, anyway. Just you worry about us! Tina... I think I love you!'

Tina felt the tears well up behind her eyes, and struggled to stop them running down her cheeks. That would be most undignified.

'I thought we said we weren't going to get involved like that,' she replied.

'Well, I'm afraid I can't help it, Tina... I can only offer you a few weeks, only about two weeks to be exact. But I want to spend them with you! You don't have to love me in return.'

Tina walked up to him and put her arms around his neck.

'I don't have to, Alex. But I think it's too late for that already. I think I love you too.'

Then she burst into tears and hugged him to herself, and he kissed her wildly, like a drowning man, who is clawing his way to the surface and taking in oxygen for the first time. They were so engrossed in each other that they didn't notice the shadow that fell between them on the sand.

'I knew there was something going on between you two... I fucking knew it! You bloody bitch!'

Donovan stood swaying slightly, fighting to maintain his balance between his anger, and twelve shots of Jack Daniels.

II

The Reverend Elder Berry was sitting uncomfortably in the study of his own vicarage, while the Bishop of his diocese sat at *his* desk, and leafed through the quarterly returns of Births, Deaths and Marriages. Bishop Bagwort was an unprepossessing cleric, not known for his humour. His mental scenery was provided by certain passages of the Old Testament that reeked of sulphur and brimstone, Sodom and Gomorrah, and the stoning of the unclean who lay down with the beasts of the field. The twenty first century seemed to have somehow by-passed his attention, as his focus was firmly fixed in the twelfth. The only inventions since that time which, to him, had any merit at all were the cat-o-nine tails, the Iron Maiden, the Rack and Little Devil firelighters, which would probably have been handy in the sixteenth century for igniting the piles of damp firewood to immolate witches.

He was a short, fattish man, with red, jowelly cheeks and a perpetual scowl. He was never seen out of his robes, and as a result was something of a legend in the Anglican Church where even his superiors sought to avoid his churlish gaze.

'I see that Benjamin Astleborough has finally gone to meet his maker,' Bagwort muttered, almost to himself. 'How old was he... eighty-eight... eighty nine?'

The Reverend snapped to attention in his seat, and looked apologetically at his superior.

'Err... ninety-one, actually, your worship! We held the service last month. Delightful man, great loss to the community!'

Bishop Bagwort looked up, over the top of his pince nez.

'You think so, eh? If I know Astleborough, he will be presently sitting in a pile of toad droppings at the seat of his master, the Black Lucifer. Not every incarnation on this earth was provided by God, you know! The Devil also sent his cohorts! I can remember the Astleborough of fifty years ago who served a short term of imprisonment for his unnatural attachment to a chimpanzee. I'm sure God hasn't forgotten him, either!'

The Reverend Berry gulped, and slumped in his seat. These sessions always had a nightmarish quality about them, as his pronouncements about the worth of his parishioners were almost always found to be specious. At such times he felt like sliding under his seat, and falling through a crack in the floorboards.

'Did he leave us anything?'

Bagwort was always interested in the pecuniary aspects of death.

'Yes, I believe he did.' Berry consulted a sheet on his lap. 'Two thousand dollars, your worship! The will hasn't been settled yet, however.'

'No, nor will it be! I hear that his estate has been sequestered by the Taxation Department for some considerable deviations in good accounting procedures. In short, he owes the government seven hundred thousand dollars in back taxes!'

'But... but... I understood his estate to have been worth less than three hundred thousand,' Berry stuttered.

'That is correct,' said the Bishop, and went back to his perusal of the returns.

The Reverend sat motionless, almost holding his breath. He looked at the clock up on the wall and prayed that he be delivered from this inquisition.

'I understand that you paid a visit to Mrs. Bagley-Gore a short while ago, Berry.'

'Yes... that is, she is one of my regular parishioners, and I always visit my regulars at least once a month.'

'Yes, she was telling me,' said the Bishop, not looking up from his reading. 'She also related that little mix-up you had, when you both had the misadventure to attempt to sit on the same divan.'

The Reverend felt his blood turn to ice water in his veins. Surely not! Surely she would have had the good sense not to tell the Bishop!

'What... err... particular mix-up was that, Bishop?'

'The one that found your free hand nestling somewhat intimately between the cheeks of her bottom, Vicar!' Bagwort looked up, and glared at him in disapproval.

'Oh! Yes, that... She actually sat on my hand, your worship. Frightfully embarrassing! I did however, have the palm of my hand turned down towards the cushion, your worship.'

'I'm glad to hear it, Berry. It's not that I'm trying to be picky, you understand, but it is important that as men of the church we are generally believed to be above the lusts of the flesh. Don't,' he continued, meaningfully, 'let it happen... again!'

The Reverend Berry flushed a bright scarlet, and breathed a sigh of relief. At least that was out of the way.

'This entry here... Eleanor Rigby! Not the lady from the satanic chant of the same name by any chance?'

This was Bagwort's only attempt at humour. To him, any vehicle of Rock ' Roll represented a satanic chant, inflicted upon God's children to lead them astray via the artifice of popular culture. The name 'Eleanor Rigby' had obviously impressed itself upon his retentive mind due to the funereal words of the final verse.

'Err, no, your worship. That was Eleanor Rigby of Meddleton East. She only retired here last year, and died three weeks ago.'

'And did *she* leave us anything, vicar?'

'As a matter of fact she did. A block of land that she'd held for years, right behind the church. It would be ideal for a parking lot for parishioners, Bishop.'

'I will put your suggestion to the synod,' he grunted, in a tone that didn't offer a great deal of hope. With land being at such a premium, it was usually sold off to swell the coffers. If the parishioners wanted somewhere to park, they could do it in the street.

'Which brings me to a topic of great portent, Reverend. It has been pointed out to me, forcefully I might add, that we are living in the age of information. The Anglican Church has never put much stock in modern methods up until now, but it appears that we are being outdone in terms of bequests by some of the less orthodox of the churches that have sprung up in recent years. They are using modern technology to track the movement of wealth, from one generation to the next, and in the process have been able to convince large numbers of their flocks to bequeath estates for the benefit of the church. Whole estates, mind you, some of which consist of both property and cash amounting to hundreds of thousands of dollars. When I look at the paltry proceeds that this church manages to collect on a yearly basis – and I am not singling you out, not by any means; this is common across the board for Anglican ministries everywhere – it becomes obvious that we are deficient in our methods. Accordingly, you are to be equipped with the very latest in computer technology, and you will be expected to design a database that will track those local parishioners, and others, who may at some future time be persuaded to leave substantial bequests to the church.'

The Reverend Berry's mouth fell open in shock.

'But... but... I've never used a computer in my life, your worship!'

'All the more reason for you to learn now!'

'B.b.but... I thought I heard your worship say – some time ago now, admittedly – that computers were the devil's workshops! You said they were the moral equivalents of Orangutans... They could remember, but they couldn't form a valid judgement!'

The Bishop scowled at him, over the top of his pince nez.

'True... all true! Unfortunately, this is not my decision. I am comforted by the fact that if we are to use the devil's tools, we at least do so in furthering the work of the church. And that is all I have to say on the matter!'

Bagwort put his head back down, and continued to scrutinise the book in front of him. But something was troubling him, and presently he closed the book, and fixed Berry with his steely eye.

'Talking of such things brings to mind a certain local parishioner, whose husband is, I believe, under sentence of death. Cancer! Do you know of whom I speak?'

'Prittik, your worship! Alex Prittik! His wife is a parishioner of mine, and very generous she is too. She never fails to drop a twenty-dollar note in the offertory.'

'Hmmmm! Admirable, I'm sure. However, I believe her husband, Alex, is a multi-millionaire, who is not so convinced in the liberating properties of the gospel as his wife – would that be correct?'

'A straight-out agnostic, more like it! I've had a terrible time with him. He could afford to pay for the refurbishing of the church organ on his own back, and it wouldn't put a dent in his drinking money. But he refuses to even discuss the matter. He really is a most frustrating man to deal with.'

'Yes,' said Bagwort, 'I'm sure he is! I heard of his situation through a good friend of mine, Dr. Proust. Excellent doctor, Proust! If you should ever require medical attention... there again, you know what I mean,' he tailed off, sounding like a long defunct cigarette commercial. 'But Proust is a good source, Vicar. You should keep him in mind for your database. People like him, in sensitive positions in society; they usually know the right names to pass along, if you know what I mean. You should cultivate him, pay him especial attention. If any of his patients are about to slip out the back way, Proust would know.'

Bagwort cleared his throat.

'Huurrrrummmm! But talking of Prittik... he has millions, I hear! He would be a good starting point for you to practice on... the new art of *'Bequest Intervention'*. See how much of Mr. Prittik's fortune you can peel off from Mrs. Prittik's inheritance! I suggest you get yourself over to his little agnostic establishment, and put pressure on the good Mister Prittik to honour his wife's church with a good, solid bequest in his will. It will stand him in good stead when he is looking at the twin portals of *Pearls* and *Swine*, in deliberating which his immortal soul may enter. You must put our point of view to him most forcibly, Vicar!'

The Reverend Elder Berry almost groaned that he had done as much as mortal man could to separate Alex Prittik from at least some of the filthy lucre that he had amassed, without result, but he forbore to say anything, just in the hopes that the Bishop would soon leave him to his own devices.

'Well, if that's all Vicar, then I must go,' said the Bishop, consulting his watch. As he swept out in stately grace, the reverend noted that his superior was the privileged owner of a *Prittique!*

Chapter Ten

Alex spun on his heel and faced up to Donovan, pushing Tina protectively behind him. Donovan looked down at them both and sneered.

'You think you're up to it, do you? I could tear you both apart with my bare hands! Push off, Prittik, I want to talk to my girl on my own.'

'She's not your girl, Donovan. Now cut out of here or I'll have you arrested.'

'Not before I put your teeth down your throat, you won't.'

Alex blanched. He had never been one for fisticuffs, and this fellow was obviously a street brawler from way back. Tina pushed around the side of him.

'If you don't leave us alone, Roddy, I won't just kick you in the nuts this time, I'll cut them off and shove them down your throat.'

Donovan took a pace backwards.

'But honey… why are you being like this? You know I love you! I just want to talk to you, that's all, away from this jerk-off. We need to talk, honey-bun.'

'Never! Get it through your thick head that I was never *your girl*. Can you get that? I was just having a fling, that's all… now it's over! So piss off and leave me alone!'

Donovan's face went redder than usual, and a vein began to pulse in his forehead.

'Why you fucking bitch! You've just been leading me on!'

'That's right, lover boy. Now take a hike! I have no intention of speaking to you, either now, or at any time in the future.'

'But you said...'

'No, Roddy... I didn't '*said*' anything! I said I'd come along for the ride, if you really wanted me to. But if you remember rightly, I didn't want to come. It was just a bit of a hoot!'

Donovan looked confused and angry at the same time.

'If this is about what happened last night, I can explain all that. I'd had a shit of a day, and then when I went looking for you, I couldn't find you anywhere.'

'So you push Alex off the boat landing, and you rip my hair out by the roots! Good one, Roddy! Go take a good look at yourself in the mirror, and ask yourself why on earth I would ever want to have a relationship with someone like you. You're a bloody idiot!'

'Why you...'

Donovan raised his fist and aimed a blow at Tina's head. She ducked! Alex saw his chance and punched Donovan clean in the nuts, as hard as he could, then they both turned and ran; ran as if the hounds of hell were snapping at their heels. By the time Donovan had achieved a crouching position, doubled over in pain, they were pushing the dinghy out into the water and Alex was desperately trying to start the outboard. After three pulls it finally caught, and they looked back to see Donovan staggering towards them, just thirty yards away, as the little dinghy took off and headed into deeper water.

'I'll fucking get you for this,' he yelled, shaking his fist. 'Don't think this is over, because it's not. I'm gonna get the both of you... Don't turn your backs!'

Tina gave him the finger as they headed back to the island, then turned back to Alex and smiled.

'I didn't think we were going to make it,' she grinned. 'He's bloody mad, that one. I think you'd better employ a couple of armed guards to watch the causeway for when the tide's out. He's just mad enough to come over and start something!'

'Jack Delaney will sort him out, and he knows it.'

Tina looked at the island ahead, and was suddenly apprehensive.

'Well, lover... what about your wife? I don't think she's going to like this, not one little bit.'

'Just give me an hour to sort things out. She can't exactly say much... she's been having it off with my accountant for months.'

Tina looked at him in surprise, and shook her head as if to clear it.

'She's been what? God! You never told me that!'

'No! You're the first person I've told. I haven't even told my sister.'

'No wonder you were upset that day in the cave. Did you know about her before or after you found out you were dying?'

'About an hour or so after! I overheard a phone call she made,' said Alex.

'That must have really cut you up,' said Tina, concerned. 'What are you going to say?'

'I'm going to tell her that I know all about McRae - the accountant – and that she can have him, but that I'll be living with you from now on.'

''Oh-oh! I can see all sorts of complications blowing up over the horizon. Are you sure she won't knife you or something? I think you'd better be on your guard.'

'Don't worry, I will be,' he said, and guided the boat up onto the shore by the causeway.

They walked hand in hand up to the house from the rear, skirted around and went in through a side door. Alex led the way through the house, looking for Joss as he went. There was no sign of her in either the kitchen or the lounge room. He checked the bathroom, the toilet, and their bedroom. Nothing!

It was only the fact that the basement door was ajar that drew his attention to it. He looked at Tina and put his finger to his lips, then slowly opened the door and began to quietly descend the stairs. As he got to the bottom, he could hear the heavy breathing and the violent movement on the camp bed in the corner. They hadn't seen him, so when Alex and Tina stole up behind them, and stood watching the action, Joss got quite a shock.

'Hi Joss,' said Alex, cheerily.

She was bent over the camp bed on her hands and knees, as Colin pumped madly into her from the rear.

'Oh, God! Oh, Jeeze! Get off me,' she squealed as she jumped to cover up the nakedness of her position. Colin fell over sideways and looked apprehensively up at the boss, his manhood subsiding in the shock of the moment.

Joss pulled her skirt down and took up a defensive position on the floor, her arms protecting her face.

'Sorry to disturb you folks, but I just wanted to introduce my new girlfriend.' He stood aside and motioned Tina forward, where they could see her. 'Tina, this is my wife, Joss! Tina will be moving into the master bedroom this afternoon, so when you've finished here, if you can just empty your clothes out of the cupboards and things... Okay Joss?'

He smiled, and waved his hand in salute.

'What the... Alex!' Joss shouted in alarm, suddenly awake to the situation. Alex turned back.

'It's all right, Joss! I know all about you and McRae as well, and I don't mind... Really! He'll be up on the weekend, I understand, so you'd better pick out a rather large room for your stuff, especially if you're going to be entertaining Mister Bartel here as well. Maybe you'd better type out a roster.'

He turned to go up the steps and burst out laughing at the incongruity of it all. Tina was beside herself. By the time they got to the top of the stairs, she could barely walk for laughing.

'God, have you ever seen anything like that in your life. I wish I'd had a camera. It was priceless!'

'Don't worry! Lindsay McRae will be bringing his digital camera up at the weekend. I understand they're into naughty pictures! Maybe if you ask nicely, they'll let you sit in the corner and watch.'

'You mean, I get a watch for Christmas,' Tina squealed in hysterics. 'Don't tell me... it's a *Prittique!*'

They both collapsed laughing on the couch, and it was a good five minutes before they could recover themselves.

Down in the basement, the mood was far more sombre. Joss was being the same old ostrich she'd always been.

'Do you think he really saw anything?' she whispered. 'I mean, I know he saw, but did he see us doing it? I could say that I was just giving you a demonstration about the way people cuddled up in bed, you know, when they call it spoons! I could say you asked me!'

'Are you for real, lady?' Colin pulled his shorts back on, thinking he could wave his ten grand goodbye. 'I think he knows a screw when he sees it!'

Joss jittered on one spot, thinking desperately how she could talk her way out of this one.

'I could say you made me! I could say I was afraid of you because you were so big, and I thought I'd better do as I was told.'

'Are you mad? You're not going to put that one on me. They'll have me up for rape, you crazy bitch!'

'You don't seem to understand. It's my marriage at stake here. All you'll do is a couple of years inside, and I'd make it worth your while. Oh, Pleeease!'

Colin backed away from her, staring at her as if he had suddenly come across a monster he'd never seen before. She was serious!

'Don't you even dare think about it. You were a willing participant, and don't you forget it. You even egged me on! I didn't ask you to pull your skirt up to your waist, and flash your legs at me. You even asked me to massage them, if you remember rightly. I'm only human, you know!'

Joss stamped her feet.

'Oh, don't help then! I don't care anyway. He's dying... he'll be dead before he could even get it into court. I'll inherit everything!'

Colin began to shake his head, slowly.

'I don't think so, somehow. I think you just blew it, lady! He'll be leaving it all to a dog's home after this.'

Joss looked confused for a moment.

'Is that because we were doing it doggie fashion? Why would that make him leave it to a dog's home?'

Colin backed off across the floor, and then took the stairs at a run. No wonder the guy preferred Tina. This bimbo was three sandwiches short of a picnic!

Colin didn't even stop at the top, but went swiftly out the front door, and over to where Jack Delaney was still working away in the boatshed. He'd have to break the news to him, and then hope for the best.

II

Hilda had locked herself in her bedroom for two days after the fight with Darlene. Despite Greg's pleas for her to open the door, she wasn't going to budge. The whole structure on which she had based her world for the past twenty years had crumbled at the foundations, and she no longer knew what to do for the best.

She had believed in family, in love between family members, and in mutual respect. She had believed in hard work and self-discipline. She had believed that with goodwill and determination, the greatest setbacks could be overcome in time. She had believed that with her unfailing support, Greg would eventually get over his blue funk, and go out and get a job. She had believed that Greg had known best in how they should bring up the children, and that by using love, kindness, reason and persuasion they would raise two children to be proud of. She had believed that her children respected her, and that deep down, they even loved her in their own funny way. She had believed that her two children also cared for each other. She had believed that her brother cared for her, cared for her children, and that in time he would overcome his antipathy to Greg. She had believed that by steady application and hard work they would eventually own their own house, and that she wouldn't have to struggle in her old age to make ends meet.

'I must believe in fairies,' she said to her reflection in the bedroom mirror, blurred though it was by the tears that had run through her mascara, and turned her face into a grotesque mask. She watched her own face crumble in the glass, and fell back onto the bed to cry again; to experience another twenty minutes of the deepest misery.

On the evening of the second day she waited until she heard the two children go to their rooms, to be locked in, and then she got up, wiped her eyes, and walked out into the lounge.

Greg came back from his, now, nightly duty of protecting both Jason and Darlene from each other, and saw her standing there.

'Oh, thank goodness, my dear. I've been so worried about you. Sit down! Please sit down and talk to me.'

Hilda looked at this little rotund man, with his thinning hair, and his careworn brow, and tried to remember the man that she had married, all those years ago. The image had gone! She ducked down into her heart-drive, poked around amongst folders and files, flipped through a million familial photographs, burnt now onto a CD-ROM in her brain, and discovered that she could no longer find the folder called, simply, 'Love!'

Love had gone! There were only files called 'misery', 'emptiness', 'rejection', 'aggravation', 'failure', and 'hate!'

'I want a divorce,' she said, blandly.

The words issued from a mouth that she felt she no longer had any control over. She was like someone in a trance, a computer that had been over-driven, and that had blown the CPU. All her systems were closing down! She had wept so much over the previous forty-eight hours that she had wept all the emotion out of her. She was empty, spent, and needed to crawl away into a dark corner where she could nurture herself, rediscover who she was.

Greg looked flabbergasted. If he had expected anything, he hadn't expected this!

'You don't mean that, Hilda! You don't mean that... Tell me that you don't mean that, Hilda,' he begged, and then suddenly the tears were running down his face, and the hard cold shell of Gregory Tressor was melting in the afterglow of a relationship that was beyond saving.

'I do... I most certainly do. Our marriage has become an anathema to me! I feel as if I've been imprisoned in a cage, all my married life. The time has come to walk away! I'm walking away, Greg. I'm leaving!'

Greg put his face into his hands, and openly cried.

Hilda stared at him in curiosity, untouched by her partner's sudden misery. She felt that perhaps there was something wrong with her... her ability to feel had somehow been impaired. Maybe she was just worn out. Her bearings were seized, or the gimbals of her equanimity had toppled, and she now flopped from one disconnected thought to another like a gyroscope that had lost its power.

'But what about the children, Hilda! What about them?'

He looked up at her, pleading, willing her to soften and change her mind.

She licked her lips nervously, and felt a terrible statement rising in her throat.

'I hate them! I really hate them, Greg. You've turned them into monsters, and I hate them! Once I leave here, I never want to see any of you again!'

Greg jumped to his feet in pain and disbelief, and paced backwards and forwards across the lounge room floor.

'You can't mean that! If you leave, the children go with you. They're your children, Hilda. The children's place is with their mother!'

'That's where you're wrong, Greg. They're *your* children! They're certainly not mine. They have none of my attributes, none of my finer feelings, and none of my sympathies. You shaped and formed them! You twisted them into monsters by withholding the discipline they needed to work out their own parameters. They've grown up into hateful, selfish, destructive animals, and it's all your doing.

136

You made me stand back from their upbringing, and watch. I became a spectator in the rearing of my own children. Now look at what you've got! You should be really proud of yourself, Greg. You've managed to turn two swans into a pair of ugly ducklings.'

Greg stopped pacing and stood over her.

'I won't listen to this! I won't! You're deranged, Hilda. I thought so the other night when you punched Darlene in the mouth. What sort of a mother does something like that? You knocked her top teeth out. It's going to cost a fortune to get them fixed, and you've put a wedge between you and your daughter that may last for years.'

'Good! I hope it does! Darlene is a foul-mouthed, small minded, slutty little bitch!'

Greg was totally taken aback. He stood for a moment with his mouth open.

'Did I hear you correctly? Did you call your own daughter a slut, Hilda? Good God woman, what's got into you?'

Hilda shook her head.

'See… you didn't know about the abortion, did you Greg? Your lovely little girl had been playing the town bike since she was fifteen. You know what the town bike is, don't you, Greg! It means everybody's ridden it! And that was true of Darlene. I had to go to Alex last year to borrow the money for Darlene to have an abortion. We couldn't have her father worried about it, could we? We couldn't spoil that pure image that he carries around with him, fondly thinking that it reflects his little girl. Oh no! She had an abortion, Greg. Get that through your thick head!'

Hilda sat staring straight ahead for a moment. Then she said, 'she didn't even know who the father was!'

Greg's legs buckled under him, and he landed on the carpet. He sat there looking confused for a moment, went to speak, but no words would come. Hilda got up and helped him into a chair.

'You might think I'm enjoying this, Greg – but I can assure you, I'm not! The sooner this is over, the sooner we can both get on with the rest of our lives.'

'So you really mean to leave me,' he said, bleakly. His whole world was coming down around his ears. It was hard enough to deal with the hostility Jason and Darlene felt for each other, without this.

'You knew, of course, that Darlene broke Jason's nose with a cricket bat, after I brought him home the other night. She just picked it up and smashed him in the face with it.'

'Probably trying to knock *his* teeth out,' said Hilda, listlessly.

'By the time I got there, Jason was on top of her, punching her into the carpet, and trying to stab her with a penknife.'

'Par for the course,' said Hilda.

She wasn't really interested anymore. If her two children wanted to murder each other, then she felt no responsibility for that. It was Greg's fault, and if he couldn't, or wouldn't see that, then there was nothing she could do about it.

'Don't you care that our children hate each other? After all, it was all because you hit Darlene, and the damage you did!'

Hilda smiled, sardonically.

'How you twist things, Greg! It was because our little arsehole of a son decided to go out and steal some poor innocent young fellow's car. It was because the little idiot wrote it off! I'll say one thing… I'm glad that young man got into that hospital room, and beat the shit out of him! It might just be the making of him. He'll think twice next time, won't he, if he thinks it will end up with a beating.'

Greg shook his head, angrily.

'That fellow will be going to court. That was pure assault, nothing else, and if I have any say in it, he'll be going to jail!'

'Not if I have any say in it, though! I fully intend to go and make a statement in that young man's defence. I will tell the court what a little feral our son has turned out to be, and plead extenuating circumstances on that lad's behalf. He wasn't insured, you know. Unless Jason pays for it, that lad is left with nothing.'

'I don't give a damn! He had no right…'

'No! Jason had no right… No right at all! *You*, who have nothing; *you*, who have squandered everything we've worked for all these years… You'd think that *you* would understand loss! You should be ashamed of yourself, even thinking about defending Jason in court. You should go to that young man on bended knee and apologise… Yes, apologise… for allowing that little feral out onto the street. What's more, if you were any sort of a man, you would arrange to replace his car. That would only be fair and just.'

'We obviously have no common ground on which to base any further relationship,' said Greg, heavily.

'That's right, Greg. No common ground!' She stood up, and turned to go back to the bedroom. 'I'll be leaving first thing in the morning. Please don't attempt to find me. I'll contact you in due course with the divorce papers.'

Greg sat for a good half an hour, staring at the wall. What was he going to do now? What?

Chapter Eleven

Jocelyn remained in the basement for a good twenty minutes, totally deflated. She tried to squeeze out a couple of tears of remorse to decorate her cheeks, but failed miserably. She was panicking, she was apprehensive, but she felt no remorse whatsoever. That Colin had been rather good. She'd enjoyed it! How many times? Three… three times in a row! Jeeze, he had some staying power. No doubt, if they hadn't been interrupted he could have gone twice more.

Jocelyn's measure of a man was how many times a night he could manage to keep it up, and she only respected those who could come back time and time again until she was totally, blissfully worn out. Then she would sleep the sleep of the satisfied, wake up during the night and do it again. It had been a long time since Alex had been that prolific. He'd lost interest after the first eighteen months of their marriage, and was back to once every second or third night. No wonder she needed topping up by any healthy body that happened to be available.

Jocelyn felt quite aggrieved. The least he could have done was warn her by making a noise, or calling out. If he hadn't found her upstairs, and he had called out, she could have been decorously stacking the fireworks with Colin by the time he descended the stairs. No one would have been any the wiser – or so she convinced herself. Jocelyn tended to think that everyone was as naïve as she was, and that a simple subterfuge would pull the wool over anyone's eyes.

She looked at herself in the basement mirror, rubbed at her eyes until they were good and red, as if she'd been crying, and stood back to gauge the effect. Not good enough!

She walked over to the corner, picked up one of the fireworks and broke it open. Then she got some of the gunpowder in her hand, and sniffed it up her nose. Immediately her eyes began to water madly, and her nose began to run, as if she had a bad dose of the flu.

'God!' she thought. 'I must be allergic to this stuff!'

She began to sneeze uncontrollably, and turned to dash up the stairs while the effect was at its worst. Alex was walking between the bedroom and the lounge, dumping large quantities of her clothes on the couch.

'Alex… what are you doing? Those are my best dresses! You can't do that!'

'Just watch me,' said Alex, with a sardonic grimace. 'I told you… it's all over, Joss. I'm with Tina now!'

'No you're not, you're with me,' she cried out, desperately. She ran over and clung onto his arm, tried to pull him down into a chair. Alex firmly pried her fingers off his arm and pushed her away.

'You're not going with that slut!' she yelled, in sudden temper.

'I'll do what I want in my own house. You and I are finished! You finished it, Joss, when you thought you could get off with screwing the accountant.'

Joss sat back and stared at him defiantly.

'Who says I did? I tell you, Alex, he came onto me, and I told him not to be so silly. Get rid of him if you like, it won't worry me!'

Alex thought he'd try a new ploy.

'I've seen the photo's, Joss. You know, the little leg-open ones, with you grinning into the eye of the camera. Tina and I have been going through them on the computer. You're very adventurous, Joss!'

'That's not true… that's not true!' she said, hysterically. 'There aren't any photo's – I don't know what you're talking about.'

Alex stared her down.

'What about the ones on the broomstick, Joss? The ones where you seem to have forgotten to put your knickers on?'

Jocelyn shrieked, then went pale as a ghost, shook her head in horror and buried her face in her hands.

'That bastard… that rotten bastard! He said no one would ever see them but us! I'll kill him! He's humiliated me, Alex! He's taken advantage of me… I shouldn't have been so trusting, Alex,' she wailed, and then turned the tears on for real.

Alex looked down at her in disgust. So it was true, then. She'd mentioned the broomstick in that phone conversation… how long ago now? It seemed forever!

'Just put your stuff in one of the other rooms, Joss. We can sort out all the legal implications later. Right now I want to get Tina settled in. You might as well get used to the fact, because she will be here until I die!'

He was silent for a moment, then added: 'Don't worry, you won't have to wait too long.'

Joss seemed to recover immediately.

'When? How long, Alex, I need to know.'

'Only a matter of weeks, so if you'll just be patient it will soon be over.'

Jocelyn twisted her fingers together and pouted, like a naughty little girl. That was always the prelude to some scheming question that she thought she could disguise as an innocent enquiry.

'So… when are you going to make your will? I'm your wife, Alex, and I deserve to know what's going to happen to me once you're gone.'

Alex acted surprised.

'I thought you knew that already, Joss. McRae will be looking after you, maybe Colin Bartel as well. If you get yourself on down to Hindley Street, it's still not too late to make good money with that body of yours. You should have at least another five years in you before you're all shagged out.'

Joss didn't see the funny side for some reason.

'You've got to leave me your money… that's the law!'

'I don't have to leave you anything, Joss! Not a damned thing. You've committed adultery on more than one occasion! I know the courts don't take that into account these days, but I do! I shall be disposing of all my liquid assets before I die, and giving them to people I trust. The business will be signed over to Tina here, and she will be the recipient of all future royalties on the *Prittique*. Your free ride is over, Joss. I intend to dispose of the properties, and you can go house hunting on your own… with your own money.'

'You can't do that, I won't let you!'

'You can't stop me! Your name isn't on any of the land title documents... I made sure of that when I bought them. And by the way... I've cancelled all your credit cards, so don't try to use them, because that's fraud. If you check the joint account you'll find there's only about a hundred dollars in it. That's because I've moved everything offshore. It's already done, Joss. There's nothing you can do about it!'

Joss went into hysterics on the spot, and Alex walked out and back into the bedroom where he locked the door. He looked at Tina, took a deep breath and fell back on the bed.

'You haven't done all those things, have you,' she whispered.

He shook his head.

'No – of course not! Though I have emptied the account, and I have cancelled her credit cards. I just wanted to put the shits up her. She'll freak now, and I wouldn't want to be in McRae's boots when he rocks up here, expecting his darling Joss to welcome him with open arms. He's in for an almighty shock.'

Tina giggled and lay down next to him, her face next to his.

'You're a real prick, Alex Prittik! I'm glad you're on my side, though.'

They both chuckled behind the locked door, and then made love with wild abandon.

II

Greg had awoken late that morning, too. By the time he rolled off the couch in the guest lounge, Hilda had long gone. She had packed one bag, taken her handbag, her mobile phone, and her savings book, and had crossed the causeway fifteen minutes after Donovan had made his exit.

She, too, had gone to the bus depot, like Tina, and bought a ticket through to Adelaide, though what she was going to do once she got there she had little idea. If the worst came to the worst, she could always go to a Women's Shelter. There was always that option. But she was hoping that there would be enough in her savings account to at least get her into a little flat, so she could go out, and try to find some work.

Hilda had never been work-shy. She had washed dishes in restaurants, scrubbed floors and cleaned out toilets in her younger days. She wasn't too proud to put in a good day's labour for a day's pay. If she had to sell her labour, she would, and the heavy manual work might even act as a palliative, to help calm her ragged emotions, and speed up the healing process.

Hilda noted the bus time, and fretted that she had so long to wait. She didn't want Greg coming over and making a scene, and if the children came with him, she thought she might just have a nervous breakdown. So she lost herself in the shops, and wandered aimlessly around, killing time.

It wasn't until much later, on Middleton Beach, that she saw Tina. She recognised her as that young girl who had caused such a fuss when she had first arrived, because of the accommodation situation. Hilda was a good sixty yards further along the beach, sitting on a bench in the shade of a eucalypt when she spotted her. She had no idea that Tina had formed any sort of link with Alex, because after that unfortunate interview on the beach, she hadn't seen Alex at all. He was just another bitter taste in her mouth, to add to the other bitter tastes that life had dealt her, over the past few years.

It was a great surprise to her, therefore, when she saw Alex come ashore in the dinghy, and for a moment she thought he was looking for *her*! She was soon disabused of that notion, however, when he raced up to Tina on the beach, and they embraced. She sat back in the shadow and watched the whole contretemps with Donovan, and was shocked when Alex punched the other fellow in the testicles. Very shocked! She hadn't thought Alex capable of such a low blow. There again, she looked at the size of the other fellow, took note of his threatening manner, and excused Alex for displaying an instinct for self-preservation.

Donovan had later walked along the beach in her direction, and on recognising her had scowled in her face.

'That brother of yours is gonna get what's coming to him,' he remarked out loud, as he ambled past. 'You tell him from me that he'd better watch his back, because one way or another, he's dead meat!'

Hilda shivered, and turned her face away. Donovan wandered off to the nearest pub, and she didn't see him again before she boarded the bus to Adelaide.

Greg let Darlene and Jason out of their rooms, and in no uncertain terms ordered them into the kitchen, where he sat them at opposite ends of the kitchen table. The table was six feet long, so as long as they remained seated, they at least couldn't belt into each other.

'Right! You're going to put a stop to this nonsense right now, or I'm going to crack a couple of heads!'

They both looked at their father in astonishment. He had never, ever, spoken to them like that. The very idea of him threatening violence was almost laughable.

'Oh yeah, you an' whose army?' Jason muttered, defiantly.

Greg whacked him around the back of the head with his open hand, and Jason looked up at him again, in shock. He went to curse, but thought better of it, and stared down at the table.

'You're notsh going tsu shreassten me,' said Darlene, insolently.

Greg walked over and grabbed her by the collar of her dress, and shook her. Since hearing about the abortion he had dramatically revised his opinion of his favourite child, and was just looking for a good excuse to give her a hiding.

'Don't you dare talk back to me, you little bitch! That's right... I said bitch! If you're going to act like a bitch on heat, that's the way you'll be treated.'

He let her go and moved back to the centre of the table.

'Your mother told me about the abortion! I'm disgusted with you, absolutely disgusted! How any daughter of mine could lower herself... *and* she told me that you didn't even know who the father was! Is that right?'

Darlene stared at him in horror, and her face dissolved into a flood of tears. He knew! That bitch had told him, and she'd promised she never would! Darlene felt betrayed.

'Well it all comes to an end, right now! I've tried to do the right thing by you two all your lives. I've never so much as raised my hand to you, because I remembered what it was like to be on the receiving end when I was young. And believe me, it wasn't pleasant. You're lucky you didn't have *my* father to contend with, because it was never a slap with him, it was always a closed fist. I always said, that if I ever had children, they would never have to put up with what I put up with. But it now looks like I was wrong, because instead of you turning out to be decent, law-abiding human beings, I've managed to turn out a couple of ferals.'

Jason went to say something, but was silenced.

'Don't interrupt! If you've never listened to me before, then by God, you're going to listen to me now, because I'm at the end of my tether, and something's got to give.'

He straightened up, and tried to calm himself.

'You may not be aware of it, but your mother left this morning. She's gone for good! Between you, you've managed to destroy your parent's marriage. How do you feel about that?'

'Rubbish!' muttered Jason. 'It's not our fault. You always blame us for everything.'

'Thassh right! Hidda's a bitssh, an' you're as weak as pissh! I'm glad sheesh gone. Look whast sheesh done to my teesh!'

'What you got, you asked for, Darlene! You went for your mother with your nails, and you got your come-uppence. Don't go crying in your milk because you came off second best. And you, Jason! Stealing someone's property like that, and then wilfully destroying it. In the past I've put your rotten behaviour down to childish pranks, and hi jinks.

But you're an evil little mongrel, aren't you? There's no light in your soul, only darkness.'

'Yeah, yeah, yeah,' said Jason, contemptuously. 'Why don't you go out and get a job, so we can get out of here? Maybe it's because we hate this place!'

'Yessh! Heesh right! I hate thissh place, an' I hate Alecsh! Heesh horrible to ussh! He puthssed me in sthuh sswimming pool!'

'Well, what did you expect, Darlene, after this little idiot, here, threw a red dye bomb in the water? I might not like Alex that much, but really… did you expect him to *thank* you?'

They both glared at each other, at each end of the table, and then glared at their father. Jason fiddled with a paper napkin on the table. He seemed disturbed about his mother leaving.

'Anyway… she'll be back! She won't have anywhere to go out there so she'll come running home,' he said, hopefully. The situation was just beginning to hit him.

'I don't think so,' Greg said, sombrely. 'She's gone for good, all right. She told me before she went that she hated you two, and never wanted to see you again. I would never have believed that a mother could say that of her own children.'

'Well, sshtuff her,' Darlene sneered. 'We don't wanth her back. Who needth her?'

'I do,' said Greg, rounding on his daughter. 'And if you don't, then maybe it's you that should be leaving! If you think you can get along on your own, maybe you should leave, Darlene.'

'Not thill I get my teesh ficthed. No way! You can bloody pay for sshem, too! You sshould have sthopped her from bassing me!'

Greg sat down at the table and put his head in his hands. Hilda had been right. These two were irredeemable.

'Go on, both of you... piss off! You make me sick!'

They both got up and left the table, Jason to dash outside to relative freedom, Darlene to the lounge where she put the television on.

The tide was in, there was an argument going on in the front of the house between Alex and Joss, and Jason was feeling very aggrieved and sorry for himself. He ached all over, and his broken nose - that Darlene had swiped with the cricket bat - was killing him. He wandered around, throwing stones for a while, then walked over to the carport where the Jag was parked.

Jason was fascinated with that Jag! To him, it was the essence of luxury and speed. He had the idea that if Alex died, he could somehow wangle it for himself.

Standing there, it gradually dawned on him how unfair everything was. He'd never get that car! Greg would stop him somehow! His mother had gone, and even though he held her in contempt most of the time, he felt apprehensive now about facing life without her. To have to spend the next year or so, putting up with his father's platitudes, without his mother's moderating influence, fuelled his fraying temper.

He suddenly decided that he wanted to do something outrageous, something demonstrative, like a wolf, baying at the world about how dangerous it was. He walked around to the other side of the Jag, opened the door and got in.

151

It was a minute or so before he realised that Alex had left the keys in the ignition, and the discovery filled him with excitement. What was the worst thing he could do to Alex… and through Alex, to his father?

The answer was obvious – wreck the Jag!

He sat back, his hands on the steering wheel, and savoured the prospect. A hundred and fifty thousand dollars worth of rebuilt, designer car.

It was high tide. If he drove it out of the carport, he still couldn't get it off the island, but he *could* race it around the perimeter of the island along the dirt road, and finally crash it into something pretty solid. But what?

Whatever they were doing down in that boatshed seemed to be pretty important. Everyone had warned him off the place, and those guys were still working in there. Maybe he could kill two birds with one stone. Imagine their faces when an E-type came hurtling through the wall at them! What a lark!

So, he'd get locked in his room… big deal! He'd get another lecture… ho-hum! At least he would have done something to really piss his uncle off, and then, maybe, they would be tossed out on their ear. They could go back to Adelaide, and maybe hook up with his mother again!

Jason reached for the key, and crossed his fingers. He didn't want to get caught now. The moment he turned the key in the ignition the V-12 motor sprang into life. It had a sporty note, and made a hell of a racket under the carport. He threw it into gear and slid out the clutch, and suddenly he was barrelling around in a huge arc in front of the house. He spun out a hundred and eighty degrees, then turned the wheel and headed for the long, straight strip to the causeway. Ramming it through the gears, he was at the beginning of the causeway in seven seconds, and had to spin the wheel to avoid ending up in the water. The car did a neat one-eighty, and ground to a halt.

Jason sat, sweating now, the nose of the Jag pointing back the way he had come. He could see Alex, running from the house and waving his arms madly, trying to catch his attention. Then Greg rushed out… *Good! He'd show them!*

He slapped it back into first, but the car seemed suddenly reluctant to go anywhere. Then a green screen on the dashboard sprang into life, and a map of the island appeared on the screen. There was the sudden crackle of a volume control, then a harsh, metallic voice rang out from a central speaker.

'You have stolen this car! You have ten seconds to get out, or you will be locked in until the police arrive. If you try to over-ride the car's controls, you will receive a severe electric shock. Please take your hands off the steering wheel!'

Jason tried to release the clutch and press down on the accelerator, and the car moved forward ten feet, then stopped. The accelerator felt as if it had been disconnected as the revs died down, and the car just idled. Jason sat there, stubbornly, as both Alex and Greg ran towards him. Alex seemed to be fiddling with his watch. They weren't going to get him now, he thought. Then the doors locked, automatically.

The voice cut in: *'You have failed to carry out my instructions!'*

153

Jason curled his lip, and swore. He slammed the lever into second, pressed on the accelerator, and received a massive shock that threw both of his hands off the wheel. Jason howled in pain, and punched the dashboard. Now he was mad!

On the dashboard, a grid appeared, with a green dot that flipped from left to right across the screen. The inbuilt radar had cut in, and a steady 'beep' accompanied the ninety-degree sweep of the Doppler.

Jason jammed the gear lever back into first and felt the gears mesh, but before he could press down on the accelerator it went to the floor on its own, and the car took off, its wheels spinning. Jason grabbed at the steering wheel in panic. The Jag accelerated so fast that it took his breath away, and he began to realise that he was now at the mercy of the car, rather than the other way around. In seconds he had raced past Alex, and headed south, past the house, and around a sweeping turn towards the beach.

The metallic voice cut in again.

'You have failed to carry out my instructions!' There was a clicking noise, as of the volume turning off. Then it cut in again: *'You have failed to carry out my instructions!'* It was like a broken record!

The Jag threw itself into second, then third, and raced along the narrow dirt road towards the western side of the island. It was steering itself now, the radar blip flashing across the screen.

Following the car, Alex was desperately pressing buttons on his *Prittique.*

154

'Oh, shit! I knew I should have had that tested,' he muttered to himself, and kept running.

Jason tried to grab hold of the steering wheel, but found he didn't have the strength to turn the wheel. He stood on the brake, but the pedal just went down to the floor, offering no resistance. He could see the cliff approaching, and he looked in horror down at the speedometer. It was already reading 70 miles an hour. He let out a squeal of terror as he realised that he had totally lost control. He tried to unlock his side door, but the top of the locking button had disappeared down inside the door panel, and the handle didn't work. He was still pulling on it and standing on the brake when the Jag shot over the cliff, and flew unerringly towards the natural swimming basin in Stingray Cove.

The Jag hit the water nose down, and Jason was thrown forward into the steering wheel, then back into the seat. His eyes wide in pure terror, he watched as the car floated for a moment, bucking wildly in the swell it had created. Then it slowly slid beneath the surface, and drifted down sixteen feet to rest, quietly, on the sandy bottom of the natural swimming basin.

All the electrics switched themselves off, and the sudden silence was deafening. All Jason knew was that he was under water. It was a minute or so before he noticed that a tiny dribble of water was now trickling in around the rubbers by the foot pedals. It was the only part of the car that wasn't a hundred percent watertight. There was air in the car, but for how long was anyone's guess.

'You have failed to carry out my instructions!'

The voice from the dashboard speaker was obviously not connected to the rest of the electrical system, and at sixty second intervals kept on repeating the same sentence.

Jason shrank back in his seat each time it crackled into life, as if he expected the man behind the voice to suddenly materialise beside him, and take his vengeance out on him with his fists.

'I'm sorry, I'm sorry,' he whimpered, but the voice always relayed the same message – *'You have failed to carry out my instructions!'*

Jason looked over at the passenger door, only to find that the lock button on that side had also disappeared, down inside the door panel. He was trapped! All of a sudden he began to scream and cry, yelling for someone to get him out of this silver coffin that he had so stupidly designed for himself. After about ten minutes, he felt the water run into his shoe, and he sat there in horror, watching the water level rise, slowly but inexorably.

Alex and Greg were still running. They had seen the car go over the edge, and Greg was panting as he ran.

'Oh, for God's sake, Alex, can you get him out of that thing. Save him, you've got to save him!'

Alex just grunted and kept running.

At the top of the cliff Alex stopped and looked down. He could see the roof of the car, perfectly situated in the middle of the pool, a swirl of sand just beginning to settle now that the car was still. The doors were shut tight. He looked around and saw people coming from everywhere. Greg was first in line, but behind him was Tina, then Joss from the house, then Darlene. Jack Delaney and Eddie came running from the shed, and even Colin Bartel stuck his head out to see what they were all running for.

Greg arrived next to Alex, and looked down.

'Oh, my god! You've got to get him out of there, Alex. He'll drown!'

Alex looked at Greg, pointedly.

'Don't you mean that *you've* got to get him out, Greg? He's yours, after all! He shouldn't have stolen my car.'

'But I can't swim! You can't just leave him there, man! That's murder!'

'Suicide, more like! He did it to himself, Greg, it's not my problem!'

Jack Delaney ran up and grasped the situation in a flash. Greg turned to him.

'My son's in there! For pity's sake, can you get him out for me? He's going to drown.'

Delaney shook his head, and pursed his lips.

'It's not going to be so easy as that, mate. Look what's coming!'

Greg looked back down, and saw a shape approaching the edge of the basin. It was just a dark shape at first, but then it swam over the edge and obscured their view of the roof of the car, As it slowly sank down into its usual resting place, Greg finally made out what it was.

'A Ray! A bloody great stingray, Alex,' said Jack.

As they watched, the giant body obscured the top of the car completely, and the tail flicked from side to side behind it. Measuring over twelve feet from tip to tail, with wings about eight feet wide, on finding itself suddenly come to rest on the roof of the car the wings folded down, and then wrapped themselves tightly against the doors. Once it had positioned itself, there it stayed!

Down inside the Jag, Jason saw the shadow first, and thought that the people above had launched a rescue operation. He breathed a sigh of relief, and tried to look up to see what was happening outside his would-be coffin. Then the wings of the ray flattened against the windows.

It took Jason a moment to realise what it was that held the car in its grip, and then, when he did, the icy tentacles of terror seemed to wrap themselves around his throat. The shock was so great that he immediately, and to his great chagrin, wet his pants.

Chapter Twelve

The funeral was held three days later, with Greg half-collapsing as he left the church. Hilda kept her distance from him, and left the church dry-eyed. She walked almost as if she were in a trance, supported by Alex on one side and Tina on the other. Darlene sat at the back, dressed in black, and scowled through the entire thing. She hadn't wanted to go, but had been threatened that if she didn't, she would no longer be welcome at her father's house. Joss had decided not to go, though she *had* gone out and treated herself to a new black outfit the day before, courtesy of Alex's credit card. No doubt, it would come in handy for when Alex departed the planet, she told herself, and she took especial pleasure in the fact that he had, unwittingly, bought it for his own funeral. The three workers had stayed on the job, and now had banks and banks of fireworks set up in bunkers, and ready to go.

The Reverend Elder Berry had conducted the service, and had dug deep into his caché of platitudes, some of which had not entirely gone down well with the congregation.

'Boy, born of woman, has only a short time to live,' he intoned, which seemed rather self-evident if he could still be described as a boy. 'In the midst of life, we are in death,' also didn't go down well with Tina and Alex, who thought that he might have been having a personal dig at them. Otherwise, his 'this young lad, whose vast potential will now only be the subject of conjecture, ended his life suddenly, before he had the opportunity to show the world what special talents he possessed.'

'Not soon enough,' whispered Alex to Tina, reflecting ruefully on the $20,000 worth of water damage to his car's electrics, and the inevitable corrosion to the bodywork after being submerged in salt water for four and a half hours.

'Don't be awful,' Tina whispered back, frowning. She had known nothing of Jason until his last, mad dash for the cliff. She was also fair-minded enough to give everyone the benefit of the doubt.

Not so Bishop Bagwort when he heard the news.

'So, the little reptile has finally conscripted himself to Lucifer's Army,' was his verdict. The blue Falcon that Jason had originally stolen had belonged to his brother-in-law's nephew, who was at present on remand for aggravated assault of a minor. 'I trust that you threw a little sulphur onto the coffin, Vicar, and perhaps a pinch of brimstone. He's going to need it where he's going.'

'At least it was quick, dear,' said Mrs Bagley-Gore, who had been filling in for the organist. She didn't know that such a platitude was totally out of place to a man who had stood by helplessly for four hours, while valiant attempts were made to release his son from the submerged vehicle, especially when it had been noted that the boy was still alive two hours after the accident. It took another half-hour after that before the cabin finally filled up with water, the vehicle was so airtight. When this was pointed out to Mrs Bagley-Gore, she was quite dismayed.

'Oh no, I didn't mean *that!*' she said, aghast. 'I was talking about the service!'

160

Alex had stood helplessly on the top of the cliff, madly trying to work out what had gone wrong. He had programmed the car himself, and it was supposed to deliver the message, then lock the doors for non-compliance, administer a shock from the steering wheel and shut the motor down. The car, in actual fact, courtesy of the fact that the alarm was a sealed unit, delivered the message sixty times an hour for four hours and thirteen minutes, even though the other electrics had all cut out. Even when the dash was under water, Jason could hear the speaker burbling: *'Vlue blaf valed do blarry owd bly ibludshuds!*

When the end came, with Jason's broken nose pressed hard up against the roof lining of the car, his last thought may well have been – *'Thank fuck! I won't have to listen to that anymore!'*

Nobody but Alex was aware of the car's pre-programming, and under the circumstances he thought it prudent to let the police believe that Jason had just stolen the car, then through inexperience, driven it over the cliff. Anything else could have led to legal complications.

The huge stingray had proved to be not the only problem. After forty-five minutes, it too may have tired of the metallic voice vibrating through its delicate tissues, because it finally took off with a great flap of its wings. However, those up above were no nearer to a solution because they really needed a crane, and there wasn't one on the island. What's more, they wouldn't be able to procure one until the tide went out, and that wasn't due for some three and a half hours.

After the departure of the stingray, there were attempts made to dive down and open the door from the outside. Tina went down, and so did Darlene, to Greg's great surprise. She was a fair swimmer, with a remarkable ability to hold her breath for over three minutes. But after it was noted that Darlene spent her time down there making rude faces at Jason through the windscreen, it was decided that the mental torment this must be causing to the trapped boy was more harmful than helpful.

Tina spent her time down there trying to get Jason to pass the keys out of the window of the Jag, so she could unlock the door from the outside. But the windows had been converted to electric, and the power to them was out. It didn't occur to Jason to try and break the windows, as that would have let the water in, and so, eventually, he drowned.

It was all very sad for everyone, except those that knew him, with the exception of his father who was genuinely broken up over the event. Hilda was located via her mobile phone, and took the news with equanimity.

'I should have known he wouldn't be able to resist the Jaguar,' she said. She got back on the bus and came straight back to Crab Island, and Alex put her up in one of the spare rooms until the funeral.

She kept to her room, despite the pleas of both Greg and Darlene. Some little switch in her mind had turned off all family affiliations, and she could now only see her erstwhile loved ones as hostile strangers.

Alex could see the way the wind was blowing, and relented in as much as he gave Hilda a key to a home unit in Blackwood, with the address clearly inscribed on the key ring. He also scribbled out an account number, and sealed it in an envelope with a plastic card and a password. He didn't tell her that the account contained $150,000. He thought he'd leave her to find that out for herself. Hilda hid the items in her bag, saying not a word, either in thanks or in recrimination. Shortly after the funeral she once more crossed the causeway, and took the bus to Adelaide. She would never return.

Greg, on the other hand, was left a total shambles of a personality. For the first time, Alex actually felt sorry for him, and refrained from suggesting that now Hilda was gone, perhaps it would be a good time for him and Darlene to go as well. Instead, he tried to give the desolate father space and time enough to recover from his grief. He avoided running into him around the island, and Darlene sat glued to the television set, ignoring him also.

'Don't you think that we should do something to get Greg out of himself,' Tina whispered one night. They lay together in the main bedroom, the blinds open and the stars shining in at the window.

'He's going to have to work it out for himself, Tina. I am not my brother-in-law's keeper! Let's face it… I've never liked the guy, and he's never liked me. It was only his attachment to Hilda that got him across my doorstep in the first place.'

Tina lay back on the pillow, a beam of moonlight on her face.

'Do you remember what I said in the cave that day, Alex? About Karma! I said that this was your one big chance to make everything right before you go off on the next stage of your journey. This is your one chance to bury this life's Karma forever!'

Alex stirred next to her, rolled over and stroked her cheek.

'Why is it that you have the ability to make me feel like the lowest sort of toad, Tina? You always make me feel guilty!'

'Perhaps that's my mission in life,' she smiled. 'Maybe I was sent here to be your conscience! Don't you see, that doing good for others makes your own soul free and happy? It's all about service to others, Alex! And you're in the perfect position to do something about it.'

'How do you mean?'

'Well, you're rich! You can make the problems of other people... not go away, exactly... but seem far less troubling than they are. For instance, you could pay to get Darlene's teeth fixed. What would it cost... a thousand dollars? What's that to you? But for a young girl of her age to go through life with a gap like that in her teeth, well, it strikes at the very core of her own self-worth.'

Alex pulled a face, and nodded.

'Do you even know what that little cow is like? Have you any conception...'

Tina put her finger over his lips.

'Judge not, lest ye be judged, Alex!'

He was silent for a moment, made to say something else, and then sighed.

'All right! You've got it! Make her an appointment at the dentist's tomorrow, and tell him I want a first class job, no cutting corners.'

'What am I now, your secretary?' Tina laughed.

'Your suggestion, you can do the dirty work. I just delegate. Fair enough?'

'Fair enough,' she laughed. 'Now, what about Greg?'

The plan they concocted to liberate Greg from his misery was never put into effect, because the following morning Darlene found her father had hanged himself in the bathroom, by the cord of his dressing gown. He had left a note on the bureau in his room, which stated in part:

'…you can only be wrong for so long in this life, before the condition becomes congenital, and the future stretches before you as an unbroken plain of mistakes, wrong decisions and uninterrupted misery. What makes it harder to bear is when you still cannot shake the belief that you were right all along.

Tell Hilda that despite all else, despite anything she may feel to the contrary, I did love her. My greatest crime was in not knowing how to show it.

Darlene went into hysterics, and had to be committed to a psychiatric hospital in Adelaide to prevent her from doing herself an injury. Alex arranged for her teeth to be fixed while she was still there, and when she left, she disappeared into the stew of Adelaide's backstreets, and was never heard from again.

Lindsay McRae and Janelle arrived in the middle of the commotion caused by Greg's suicide. There was a police car parked at the house, and an ambulance there, ready to take Greg's body back to the morgue. Everyone was so distracted that their presence was scarcely noticed for the first half-hour, and when it was Alex just said, distractedly, 'find yourself a spare room, Janelle. Lindsay, you'll be sharing with Joss, second door on the left down there. You'll have to excuse us for a bit, we've had a family tragedy here this morning.'

In the background they could hear Darlene's shrieks and howls of disbelief, and they watched as she was sedated and put into the ambulance, along with the body of her father.

'Nasty business, sir,' said the policeman to Alex.

'Yes, yes, very unfortunate! He'd just lost his son, officer. He left a note... I think Tina's got it. Tina,' he yelled, 'could you give the officer the note that Greg left. I think he'll be needing it for the coroner's court.'

'I appreciate your cooperation, sir. We'll get out of your way as soon as we have photo's of the scene.'

The policeman was the same one that had attended on a previous occasion, to caution Jason about knocking a woman over on the pavement. He motioned Alex aside.

'I hardly like to raise this, just at this moment, sir, but the car... the one that was pulled out of the sea the other day, with the lad in it.'

'Yes?'

'I couldn't help noticing that it was out of registration, sir!'

Alex swung around and looked helplessly at his persecutor.

'Oh, for god's sake,' he said. 'Are you for real?'

'Very serious offence! I'd like to take a lenient view, but the registration had expired three days before the lad did his swan song over the cliff.'

'So?'

'I'm going to have to book you for that one! After all, the boy did drive it on a properly constituted road, even though it was a dirt road, in the State of South Australia, while being an unlicensed driver, and in an unregistered vehicle.'

'Yes… well that was him, not me!'

'Nevertheless!' said the officer, as he wrote out the ticket. 'If you had reported it stolen, then you would be off the hook.'

'I hardly had time in the three and a half minutes between the time he took it, and the time he went over the cliff,' Alex retorted, sarcastically. 'Why don't you book his father at the same time, for allowing his son to go around stealing other people's cars!'

'Well that would be difficult, sir, seeing as the gentleman is dead.'

'So why should I wear it?'

'Because it's your car, sir, and even though the lad only drove it around the island, and – yes, I know it's privately owned – but he put other pedestrians lives at stake. They are protected by the same laws on Crab Island as those people in Meddleton back there.' He handed Alex the ticket. 'You shouldn't have left the keys in the car, sir,' he said, as an afterthought. 'When you finally secede from the Commonwealth of Australia, sir, and set up your own puppet regime, I shall be glad to ignore any misdemeanours committed on foreign soil.'

Alex noted that he was grinning as he walked back to the squad car.

'He's fucking got it in for me,' he observed to Tina.

Joss was sitting on her bed, with her arms crossed, when McRae entered the room with his suitcase.

'And who told you to come in here,' she said, obviously very ticked off.

'Hey, it's me honey! Alex said I'd be sharing this room with you... what's going on, has he flipped his lid or something?'

'That's his way of saying you can have me, Lindsay. He's given me to you, like some cabbage patch doll. He said you have to look after me from now on.'

McRae looked somewhat taken aback. Janelle, behind him, looked shell-shocked.

'What the hell's he talking about?' said Janelle.

McRae was more to the point.

' What's been going on here, Jocelyn – the place is a madhouse!'

'Alex has left me! If you must know, he's been looking at the pictures you took of me – the one's with the broomstick, Asshole! How could you do this to me, Lindsay,' she burst out, crying.

168

'What pictures? He hasn't had access to any pictures, Joss. They're all at home, safe!'

'How did he know about the broomstick then? He must have seen them!'

'No, the phone call! You mentioned it on that phone call, remember! It was just a calculated guess on his part. He's been having you on, Joss.'

'I hope you two don't mind, but I'd like to find out where *I'm* staying,' said Janelle, a touch of tedium in her voice.

'You can go out in the caravan. That's right! The one closest to the house! There's a spare bunk, you can use that,' said Joss, dismissively. She was in no mood for any more of Janelle's infernal *'I'm so sorry, but Mr. McRae isn't available just now'* put-offs. The further away she could stick her, the better.

Janelle backed out of the room with a final - *'Lindsay!* I need to talk to you!' Then Joss slammed the door in her face.

After the police and ambulance had gone, Alex walked outside with Tina and they headed for the boatshed. He was feeling nervous, apprehensive, even frightened at the turn of events, and his pallor had taken on a greyish look.

'Are you sure you're all right, Alex,' Tina said, hurrying along beside him. 'You look awful!'

'How awful does it have to get, Tina? Of course I look awful! With all the things that have happened around here lately, I'm in danger of forgetting that I'm a dying man. Why did he have to do it... why?'

Tina shook her head, sadly, and they both came to a halt in the shadow of the caravan. There was a bench seat beside it, and they both sat down, Alex with his head in his hands.

'Maybe it was just too much for him to take. Life can be like that, Alex.'

'You can't tell me that he loved that little shit! Jason treated him with contempt! You should have heard some of the things he used to call him when Greg wasn't around.'

'But is that really the point, Alex?'

Tina held Alex's hand, and patted it, comfortingly.

'If not, what is?' said Alex.

'You've never… and I'm not being funny here, Alex, but it's true… you've never been a father, have you?'

Alex shook her off, impatiently.

'What the blazes has that got to do with anything? You either like someone, or you don't! They either like you, or they don't! It's cut and dried.'

'A father's love isn't cut and dried, Alex. That boy was an extension of Greg himself. In a way you could say that Jason was Greg's only hope for immortality. It would have been Jason that carried his name down to the next generation, Jason that kept his gene pool alive. Greg might not have liked Jason very much, but I'm more than sure that he loved him. It was probably hidden for much of the time, but deep down, Greg was proud that he had a son; and he himself said that he tried to bring the children up without the violence that *his* father had shown to him. Darlene might well have been his little girl, his favourite, but Jason was his hope for the future. No doubt he thought that once Jason had got over his silly, teenage stage, he would turn into a fine young man, one that he could have a laugh and a joke with, take to the pub and have a drink with. Greg probably looked forward to the day when he and Jason could just be *friends*, Alex. Then he had to stand on a cliff-top and watch those hopes and dreams gradually disappear. That, on top of losing the woman that he loved was just too much to bear.'

Alex shook his head, exasperated, and ruffled up his hair.

'You give the man a depth he just didn't possess, Tina! I think of Greg, and I can't see the loving father, any more than I can see the great lover. He was stunted and cold, and boorish and arrogant.'

'He might have been all those things on the surface, Alex, but underneath... what man knows the depths of another? I think his note said it all. *'My greatest crime was in not knowing how to show it!'*"

'Well thanks, Tina! Now I feel fucking terrible! You really have that affect on me.'

'If you'd like me to leave...'

Alex turned to her and grabbed for her hand.

'You dare leave me... just you dare!'

That sat silently for a while, and after a few moments turned to each other and kissed. Then, without warning, Alex was racked by a sudden pain in the abdomen that bent him in half. The sweat broke out on his forehead, and he gritted his teeth.

'It's getting worse, Tina. God, that's painful. If I had to put up with that level of pain on a constant basis, I think I'd go mad.'

'I think you'd better take a painkiller. Here, I've got some in my coat.'

'No, not now! I need my wits about me just now. I'm surrounded by a pack of freaks who are all after one thing, my money. I need to make my arrangements, so that I can control what happens to everything, once I'm gone.'

'You're not thinking of going just yet, are you, Alex.'

'Next Saturday! That's when we're having the great firework display, Tina. You can say that I'm going to go out with a bang.' He attempted to laugh, but was overtaken by another spasm. 'Get me down to the boatshed,' he whispered, through his grated teeth. 'I need to give Jack his final instructions.'

As they walked away, Janelle took her ear from the window in the caravan, and sat up straight. She had a look of satisfaction on her face. Now that she knew the time, she and McRae could begin to plan.

Chapter Thirteen

Doctor Proust was not having a good day. Some of the specimens he'd sent off to the lab for testing had been spoiled by a clumsy cleaner, and that meant that three patients would have to submit to giving samples all over again. For someone as precise as Proust believed himself to be, it was a disaster. Their clumsiness reflected on him, and he had just finished chewing them out over the phone. Now his secretary would have to schedule new appointments.

'Margaret,' he called out, over the intercom. 'Could you please come in here for a minute.'

Margaret was a no-nonsense woman of forty-five, who also prided herself on her efficiency. She was not going to be pleased.

'Yes, Doctor,' she said, notepad in hand.

'I need you to schedule three new appointments, for Arthur Cox, Jane Reed and, let me see… Oh, that's right, Alan Kneebone. The lab has spoiled their samples! We're going to have to do it all over again.'

Margaret let out a long sigh of disapproval.

'I swear, Doctor, I don't know what's going on over there. Jan from the clinic was telling me that they'd messed up a whole pile of their samples just the other week.'

'Well, they're blaming it on the cleaning woman, said she knocked them over. But I would have thought that they would have been under lock and key at that time of night.'

'Just an excuse if you ask me,' Margaret sniffed. 'We can always start sending our samples to the new bio-lab at Port Lincoln, if you prefer.'

Proust shook his head.

'No... we'll persevere for a while. I've known Ed Peabody since we were students together. I've always supported him. I'll have a quiet word, and maybe he can find out which member of his staff is not up to scratch. Knowing Ed, they won't last five minutes once he finds out,' Proust chuckled. 'Which reminds me... is that it for the morning? I've managed to tee up a round of golf this afternoon, as long as I can get clear of this place without too many dramas.'

'Only one to see, Doctor! A Mister Privet! He's out in the waiting room, and he doesn't look well at all.'

'Oh, yes! You'd better send him in... and then I'm going, Margaret, come hell or high water.'

Margaret withdrew, and told Al Privet he could go in.

'Come in, sit down Al! How's that ulcer of yours.'

Proust looked up from his desk at the patient, and was alarmed at what he saw. Al had gone quite yellow, totally jaundiced by the look of him. He was sitting very carefully in his seat as if the slightest movement afforded him pain.

'I don't know, Doc. Those tablets you gave me don't seem to be doing a blind bit of good. I keep taking Aspirin for the pain, but it doesn't do much.'

'You look quite jaundiced to me,' Proust muttered, pulling out the patient's notes. In his scribbled hand he read bismuth subcitrate, 107.7mg 4 times/day, tetracycline 500mg 4x, and metronidazole 400mg 3x. Nothing wrong with that!

'I better have a good look at you, Al. Take your shirt off, will you?'

Five minutes later Proust's door opened and he walked out to talk to his secretary.

'Margaret! I want you to arrange for Mister Privet to be admitted to Meddleton General immediately. Mark him to be seen by Doctor Hennessy. I want a second opinion, and you'd better mark that 'Urgent.''

'Yes, Doctor.' Margaret got on the phone, straight away.

Once Privet had left, Proust sat at his desk for a while, a puzzled look on his face. God, he'd deteriorated fast. He'd only seen him a fortnight ago, and the man, then, looked relatively healthy. It was only a duodenal ulcer, for god's sake, and he'd given him the specified medication

Acting on a whim, he went to his filing cabinet and riffled through his patient's files. Finding the one he was looking for, he took it back to his desk and then phoned the lab.

'Give me Ed Peabody, please... no, I want Ed! Yes it is important. Tell him it's Proust!'

After a few minutes, Ed came to the phone, and Proust launched into his old friend without so much as a hello.

'What the hell's going on over there, Ed? I'm getting samples spoiled, and maybe even worse. Who's the new member over there that's screwing up.'

'We've only got two new personnel, June Davies on secretarial, and Kee Sun on filing and general clean-up duties.'

'Kee Sun... what's that... Chinese?'

175

'Korean! Nice little thing she is, very willing and always likes to keep busy.'

'Yes, but how efficient is she, Ed? Is she behind these screw-ups?'

'She's got a bit of a language problem, but she picks things up fast. I did have to talk to her the other week about throwing out some moulds. She thought it was cat food gone rotten or something.' Ed laughed. 'Quite funny when you think about it.'

Proust drew a nervous finger across his brow.

'I can't afford to have a sense of humour in this business, Ed, and neither can you. Can she read? English, I mean.'

'Oh, passable, passable! She has a bit of trouble with pronunciation. It must be hard for them. But I think she's taking a night course in English at the T.A.F.E. College. She's certainly willing to learn.'

'You know and I know that, sometimes, willing isn't good enough! Do you think I could talk to her?'

'Sure, I'll put her on.'

Proust waited for a good half minute, and then a very hesitant Kee Sun came on the line.

'Yess please! Kee Sun here.'

'Kee Sun, this is Doctor Proust. I need to ask you some questions. Do you understand?'

'Questions! Yes, that okay.'

'Do you remember filing the results for an Alan Privet a couple of weeks ago?'

'A Lun Pivik? Yes! I remember A Lun.'

'What did you do with his test results?'

'I put in folder… Pivik! I remember!'

'And do you remember, about the same time, the tests for an Alex Prittik?'

'A Lex Pittiv. Yes, I remember. I put in folder.'

'Not Pittiv, Kee Sun. Prittik! Prittik!'

Lee Sun laughed, nervously.

'Purr…i…tt…iv! Yes, I remember.'

'Say Privet and Prittik together, Lee Sun. It's important!'

'Pivvret and Pittrick. Pivvrik and Pitriv. That okay?'

'No,' Proust snapped. 'Put Ed back on!'

'What is this, Porky?' said Peabody, reverting to Proust's College nickname.

'We're in deep shit, Peabody! Your girl can't tell the difference between Privet and Prittik! She bunged the results in the wrong folders. I've been treating Alan Privet for a duodenal ulcer, and if my hunch is correct, the poor bastard has got pancreatic cancer! On the other hand, I've told one of the State's wealthy, that he's got eight weeks to live – on a duodenal ulcer!'

'Oh, for chrisesake! You're not serious!'

'You can bet your six figure superannuation I'm serious! And that's just what it might cost us both if this gets to court. This is negligence of the first order, Ed! You've dropped me right in it. And even though Privet hasn't got two bob to scratch himself, Prittik is loaded. He's got the money to pay the top barristers if he decides to get on our case!'

'What are you going to do? I'll be ruined! Every doctor in the area will send there stuff elsewhere if this gets out. If you've ever been my friend…'

'Okay, calm down! I'm not going to blow the whistle on you. But you've got to get rid of that girl, that Kee Sun!'

'Consider it done. She no longer works here!'

'Secondly, you have to keep *your* mouth shut! If I'm going to go in to bat for you, I don't want to be scuppered by something you might inadvertently let out. There's the A.M.A. to think about.'

'Don't worry about me... I've got even more to lose than you!'

'I think I'll get an old friend of mine to intervene for me, a gentleman of the cloth. He's very diplomatic, and has a way of twisting things around so they sound quite innocuous. He can let Prittik know, in due course, that the condition wasn't as bad as we first thought. He's not going to die after all! But I'll have to figure out how to change his medicine, get him onto the ulcer cure. If I'd had the correct information, he could have been cured by now.'

'Look,' said Ed, 'I'm really, terribly sorry about all this. I owe you one! I'll make sure nothing like this ever happens again.'

'You'd better Ed, because I'm not going to ruin my professional reputation covering for you, not a second time, anyway. I'll let you know what happens.'

With that, Proust hung up.

He didn't get his game of golf that afternoon. Instead he sought out his old friend, Bishop Bagwort, who was soaking his bunions in a bucket of hot water, liberally sprinkled with sulphur.

II

Janelle caught up with McRae as he was lying on the beach with Joss, pandering to her battered ego. He soon had her purring like a kitten, and promised her that when Alex was out of the way, the two of them would take a world cruise, on the proceeds of the *Prittique* and other little investments that Alex didn't know about.

'Just you and me, doll! We'll be able to go where we like, whenever we like. Life will be one big party.'

Joss pouted at him in return.

'What if I decide to keep it all to myself, Windsay? Maybe I won't need you! With all that money I could have anyone I liked,' she purred, lying back on the sand.

'But you couldn't have so much fun with anyone else,' McRae replied, tickling her stomach. 'You know how much you like our little rendezvous!'

It was at that moment that Janelle appeared, standing over them like the efficient secretary.

'I hate to disturb you two, but there is work to be done, Mister McRae,' she said, sweetly. 'I have a whole stack of papers for you to sign, and it's time you hooked onto the Exchange in New York to check prices.'

Joss groaned, and McRae rolled over and stood up.

'She's right, babe. I've got to go and make you even more money than you've already got. That's what I get paid for. Keep a warm spot on the sand, and I'll be back as quick as I can.'

As soon as they were out of earshot, Janelle started.

'I didn't work out this master plan so you could loaf about all day with your bimbo pet,' she snapped, as they approached the caravan. 'I mean enough's enough! It's bad enough that you're sharing the same room, without me having to watch you rolling around with her on the beach.'

'Look Janelle, I didn't think it was going to work out like this either,' he whispered, trying to keep it between themselves. 'I can't work out why Alex hasn't fired me already. He knows that Joss and I have had a thing going, and it doesn't seem to bother him. It's like water off a duck's back! I don't know about you, but I feel distinctly uncomfortable about it. It's like the calm before the storm, if you know what I mean. I'm just waiting for the volcano to erupt.'

They entered the caravan and shut the door behind them. Janelle ushered him into a seat, then sat opposite.

'I brought you here, because I've got some information, and time's getting short. We've only got until Saturday to work things out, and then the shit will hit the fan.'

'What do you mean? We've got plenty of time!'

'Don't be so cocksure of yourself. It just happens that Alex and his girlfriend stopped outside the caravan a while ago and sat talking. He seemed to be in a lot of pain. Anyway, the gist of the conversation was that he intends to top himself on Saturday, just about the time of that giant firework display he's been planning. He said he intends to go out with a bang.'

'Good lord,' said McRae. 'What's he going to do, blow himself up?'

'No, silly,' Janelle said, 'he just meant it metaphorically. The important thing is that he intends to do it on Saturday night, which doesn't leave us a lot of time. We have to get his signature on that document before that, and then you'll have to work fast, shuffling assets around. You'll have to set up a paper trail that no one will be able to follow. Can you do it?'

'Once I've got his signature, I can do anything,' McRae said, grinning at her. 'I'm a whiz on the International Money Markets.'

'Well you'd better start right now, because a sudden flurry of activity on the day before he dies would look mighty fishy. At least we've got a few days to show some intense activity in the *Prittique* camp before he goes. That might show that the balance of his mind was disturbed.'

'I'll use the mobile to hook onto the net,' he said, 'and shift a few stocks.' He opened up the laptop that Janelle had brought along, and plugged it in. Then he set up the mobile, and dialled up his server.

'What about this will,' he said.

'I've typed it out on a will form, leaving you sixty percent of the company, and Joss forty percent. I thought it best to leave all real property to Joss. That will stop people being suspicious. All you have to do is get him to sign it. We can fill in the witnesses later.'

'Oh, is that all?' said McRae, pulling a face. 'I'm glad you think that's the easy part.'

'If necessary, we'll wait until the middle of the firework display, and grab him then, when he's three parts gone. I've pre-dated it three weeks, so they won't be able to challenge it on the grounds of sanity.'

'You're a real smart chick,' said McRae, appreciatively, studying the screen.

'Yes, I am, and don't you forget it,' Janelle replied, a note of acerbity in her voice. 'I'm only putting up with this relationship of yours, with Joss, as a Machiavellian measure,' she said. 'But don't think that you can carry it on, afterwards. If you do, I shall see you ruined... totally ruined,' she added, just in case he was in any doubt about the matter.

III

When Alex got as far as the boatshed, he stopped outside for a moment.

'You don't mind if I go in on my own, do you,' he said to Tina. 'It's just that Jack's an old mate, and I wouldn't mind chatting a bit about old times... you know, the army days.'

'Oh, I don't know, Alex Prittik! You're a pretty shady character! You could be cooking up anything in there,' Tina laughed at him.

'Go on,' he said, smacking her bottom, playfully. 'Get out of it!'

He went in alone. Jack was masked and gloved, with a leather apron protecting his chest. He was grinding chemicals down into a fine powder in a ball mill. When Alex came in, Jack put his hand up as if to say, keep back. It was a dangerous operation, and it would take only the slightest miscalculation for the boatshed to go up in a fireball.

Jack switched the motor off, waited until it stopped and then began to peel his gloves and mask off.

'What's up, Alex? It's bloody dangerous in here at the moment, you should stay away.'

'I need to go over some of the fine details of what I want to happen on Saturday night. Just you and me,' he said, indicating Eddie at the other end of the shed.

'All right, we'll get out of here, and walk,' said Jack. 'I could do with a breather anyway. I'd forgotten how tedious it was, you know. People don't realise how much effort goes into a ten second starburst.'

'No, I'm sure they don't, Jack. Let's head for the Cove.'

They walked quietly along the edge of the dirt road that only days before, Jason had taken at speed. The same road that Greg had puffed and panted along, trying to save his son. Now they were both gone, as was Hilda! As was Darlene!

'You know, Jack… in a funny kind of way, I'm not going to be all that sorry to leave this planet,' said Alex.

'Oh yes, life's a bitch, and then you die – eh?'

Alex smiled at him.

'Yeah – if you put it like that! Or how about - *'death is nature's way of telling you to slow down!'*

They grinned at each other. The old army camaraderie was still there.

'No – but seriously! Life's a bit of a shit, over all. A week ago there was another family living in this house, my sister's. In a matter of days, that entire family disintegrated, blew apart like a spinning top that suddenly lost its centre of gravity. The son's dead, the father's dead, the daughter's in an institution and my sister has been psychologically scarred for life.'

'It wasn't your doing though, Alex.'

'That's not the point! I could have done more for them – as Tina has so succinctly pointed out. In retrospect, the only reason I didn't was because I was being petty and small-minded, remembering slights and insults from the past. It was like getting my own back, making them suffer the dreadful unwholesomeness of my charity. I made them feel worthless, Jack! I made them live from day to day in the full glare of my success. It must have been like rubbing salt into the wounds.'

'You're getting terribly maudlin in your old age, Alex. What happened to the old *'fuck 'em all, I'm gonna take on the world if I have to,'* Alex?'

Alex smiled.

'That was the old Alex, the unsuccessful Alex. Money makes you arrogant, Jack. It gives you a whole new perspective on things. It lifts you up out of the shitty streets, and elevates you. Before you know it, you're looking down on people. And what makes it worse is, you can never get back again. Once you've experienced the view from that height, you thirst after it, you become hooked on it! No wonder Christ said that it was easier for a camel to pass through the eye of a needle, than for a rich man to enter the kingdom of heaven. I know why, now. It's all about humility!'

They walked a way in silence. When they came to the cliff, Alex led him around and down the side of the cliff to the ledge face, and they carefully made their way around to the mouth of the Grotto. There they stopped.

'In there, Jack, is where I want my body to lie. No coffins for me, no cremations, just a gradual dissolution of the individual elements of the body back into nature, where I came from. Have you seen this before?'

Jack shook his head.

'No, didn't know it was here!'

'Come inside… you don't mind getting your feet a little wet, do you?'

'No mate, they probably need a good wash anyway,' Jack laughed.

He followed Alex along the tunnel and through into the main chamber. The beams of light from the sun reflected off the surface of the water, and lit up the stalactites in the roof of the 'cathedral'.

'Well, I'll be blowed! Jeeze mate, I can see why you'd want to end up here. It's bloody magnificent, isn't it?'

'It certainly is, Jack. Magnificent! …and melancholy, and awe-inspiring, and holy! That's how I think of it. It's like an ancient place of worship.'

'So what do you want me to do?'

'Well, if I die while I'm still up top, I want you to cart me down here, and drop me in the middle of that pool there. It doesn't matter if I float for a while, though I'd like to float on my back if that's at all possible. So I'm looking upwards, you know!'

'Yeah, mate. I think I can arrange that.'

'Then I want you to blow the entrance. Topple the bloody thing, make it into a sealed tomb, Jack. I don't want anyone else coming in here once I've gone. This will be my last resting place.'

'What do you mean… blow it up? What with, black powder? Have you any idea how much black powder it would take to blow that entrance?'

'No, that's why *you're* here! You're the expert. That's what I hired you for!'

'I thought you hired me to put on a gigantic fireworks display!'

'That's just a blind, Jack. The fireworks will mask the real explosion. People will think it was just a super large cracker. Not too many know of this cave, and once it's over, no one will know of it.'

'I see! Well, old mate, for sixty thousand dollars, I guess you're the one calling the shots. But I can't do it with black powder. I might be able to do something with a bit of dynamite, and maybe some fertilizer and diesel. I could blow up the Bank of England with that!'

'It's up to you how you do it. You've got an open cheque book for materials. But you'd better get them in quick, because time's getting short, old friend. You've got until Saturday!'

Jack looked at him and shook his head, slowly.

'You always did expect the bloody impossible,' he said.

Chapter Fourteen

The solicitor arrived early, on the Thursday morning after ten. He was on his way to a holiday in the west, and didn't want to be held up any longer than was necessary. He drove across to the island in his four-wheel drive while there was still a foot of water over the far side of the causeway. It gave him no problems, and he pulled up alongside the house and jumped out, taking his briefcase with him.

Janelle was out and about, and looked at the newcomer with ill-disguised curiosity. It was up to her to keep an eye on the pulse of the place, and she knew it. McRae went around with his head full of figures, both numerical and female, and was usually lost to his immediate surroundings.

The newcomer was smartly dressed in a city suit, dark skinned and shorter than average, but with a purposeful look about him. She figured him for a doctor or a lawyer, or at least a professional man. He reeked of money, too, which was always a fragrance that Janelle's delicate olfactory membrane could detect at a hundred paces. She could only speculate at this stage, however, as he shortly disappeared inside, and was conducted to Alex's private study.

'Good to see you, John,' said Alex, showing him to a seat on the other side of the desk. 'Have a good trip?'

'Not bad! The Pajero makes for easy driving,' said John Kushelew, opening his briefcase. 'Now – why the sudden summons, Alex?'

'Didn't I tell you? Oh, probably not… I wasn't thinking too clearly at the time. I'd only just had the news, and it tends to throw you at first.'

Kushelew shook his head as if to clear it.

'Do you mind starting at the beginning, Alex. I haven't the faintest idea what you're talking about.'

'Sorry, John! I'm so caught up in the situation myself that I tend to forget that there's a whole world out there that doesn't know about my own personal trauma.' Alex laughed, self-deprecatingly. 'I'm dying, John! Cancer of the pancreas! I was given eight weeks to live about three weeks ago. So I need to make a new will.'

John sat as if pole-axed. His hand, holding the new will form was left suspended in the air.

'God, Alex, I don't know what to say.'

'Goodbye, is usually the appropriate word,' said Alex, with a wry smile.

'How can you make light of it, Alex? If that were me…'

'Yeah, but it's not, is it? It's me! I'm learning to adjust to the idea. So now, about this new will…'

'That's what I don't understand, Alex. You have a perfectly good will already drawn up. Why do you need to change it?'

'Because circumstances change, John! They've certainly changed around here. I've decided to make my will a bit of a lottery. I'll show you what I mean as we go along.'

I'm not quite sure I follow you.'

Alex looked at him over the desk, and grinned.

'You will! It will all become crystal clear to you in time. First of all, that whole bit about the wife goes! Joss and I are separated, and I have no reason to feel grateful to her for sleeping with the accountant...'

John raised an eyebrow.

'... and the handyman...'

John raised the other eyebrow. Alex was tempted to keep on going, to see what he'd do next, but he seemed to have run out of eyebrows.

'...and I have a new love in my life as well! The only problem with her is that she's dying, too. Not at the same rate as me, fortunately. She'll be around for a few years yet. But she has an incurable disease, called Huntingdon's Disease. Ever hear of it?'

'St. Vitus Dance,' mumbled the solicitor. This was getting weird!

'So – first up, I, Alexander Raymond Prittik, being of sound mind, do hereby etcetera etcetera, you know the lingo! One! I leave to Tina... err... Tina? Hell, isn't that funny? You know, I don't even know her surname, would you believe that?'

He got up and went to the door, as John stared after him, the expression on his face saying – *yes, I would believe that, Alex!'*

'Tina,' Alex called out. Tina appeared in the doorway. She moved in close, and they whispered together. Then Alex nodded, looked at her in shock, closed the door and sat down again.

'Archangel! Would you believe *that!* Fucking Archangel! What a name for a surname, eh?'

'And singularly apt, by the look of things around here,' said John.

'Yes... I can't get over that. She *said* she was sent here to be my conscience!'

John made a play of looking at his watch. He didn't want to get behind schedule.

'Oh, yes, sorry John! Just getting a bit sidetracked. So where were we... Tina! To Tina Archangel I leave the sum of one million dollars, to be used by her to pursue a cure for Huntingdon's Disease, or, if not a cure, a medical procedure to minimise the effects, if such a procedure should exist. Otherwise to be used for her own use and benefit absolutely.'

John scribbled the bequest out on a spare sheet of paper. He would be able to type it onto the will form later.

'Now we come to the interesting bit. Quote: As it has been determined that I am dying of an incurable cancer, and that if allowed to follow its usual course to the final days, I would be in much pain, and probably under the influence of mind-altering drugs, I have decided, contrary to the laws of this State of South Australia, to end my life on the night of Saturday through Sunday morning, December 8th/9th, 2012. I do this in full knowledge of the gravity of this action, and wish to make it clear that this was my wish, and that no other person is, or will be, party to my decision to end my life. I make this decision as a rational human being, in order to assert control over the time of my dying, as I have asserted control over all other aspects of my life to this point.'

'My God, Alex,' John spluttered. 'You can't be serious! I can't write this... I'm a solicitor, for goodness sake. I'd be disbarred, maybe even go to jail!'

'Don't worry, I don't need you to sign it. I just need you to write it in legalese, so the will can't be contested in court once I'm gone. You give me the rough draft, I'll write it in my own handwriting and get it witnessed by a couple of strangers. Then I'll send it to you in a sealed envelope – not to be opened until my death! You will be able to claim total ignorance of the contents.'

'Even so...' John muttered. It didn't sit well on his conscience.

'It's worth five thousand dollars to you, John, right here, right now – in cash!'

Alex opened a drawer and pulled a bundle of notes out from his desk. He began to count it out in hundred dollar bills. Magically, John Kushelew's conscience was suddenly overwhelmed and wrestled to the ground by that driving instinct of all solicitors – greed!

'Oh well, if you're sure...' he mumbled, loosening his collar. It seemed to be getting hot in there.

'Now, on to the next bit! The income from *Unique Prittique* is to be used to set up a foundation, to provide worthy inventors with grants to enable them to design and complete their inventions - if considered worthy of such by a Board of Commissioners, who will be appointed. One perpetual member of the board shall be my sister, Hilda Tressor, at a fixed retainer of one hundred thousand dollars per year. On no account is Mister Lindsay McRae or Miss Janelle Marquete, or Mrs. Jocelyn Prittik, individually or in concert, to be allowed to serve on the said Board, or to be employed in any capacity by the Foundation. All real property in my name is to be sold off, and the sum realised added to the residue of my estate. All stocks, shares and bonds are to be liquidated, and the sum realised added to the residue of my estate From the resulting total, one tenth is to go to my sister, Hilda Tressor, for her own use and benefit absolutely.'

Alex waited until the solicitor had stopped writing, leaned back in his chair and said, 'you ready for the next bit?'

John nodded. He felt that nothing would surprise him now. He was wrong!

'This is where we spice it up a little, John. This is where we throw the ravening pack into confusion.'

John looked up at him with a nervous smile. What was next?

'With regard to the residue of the estate not already covered by bequests, I wish the following – that should I die between 12 midnight on Saturday, December the 8th, and 12.30 a.m., on Sunday, December 9th, 2012, one hundred thousand dollars will be left to St. Paul's Anglican Church, Middleton, for the express purpose of repairing the church organ. The remainder of the estate will pass to Lindsay McRae, on the condition that a complete audit of the books shows up no discrepancy in his favour during the preceding twelve months. Otherwise, that portion will be left to Tina Archangel.'

John almost choked, but continued writing.

'I don't know if this is quite legal, Alex. You can't specify a time of death, and then link it to your bequests. It's a bit like making a circus out of the law.'

'The law *is* a circus, John. You should know that! You're part of it, after all.'

Alex gave him a wry smile. John looked confused, but said nothing.

'Next! Should I die between 12.31 a.m. and 1.00 a.m. on Sunday, December 9th, 2012, one hundred thousand dollars will be left to Bishop Bagwort, for his use and benefit absolutely. The remainder of the estate will pass to Mrs. Jocelyn Prittik, on the condition that it may not be disproved in a court of law that she has remained faithful to her marriage vows over the previous twelve months. Otherwise, that portion will be left to Jack Delaney, for his use and benefit absolutely.'

The solicitor kept on writing, beads of sweat now standing out on his forehead.

'Next! Should I die between 1.01 a.m. and 1.30 a.m. on Sunday, December 9th, 2012, one hundred thousand dollars will be left to the Reverend Elder Berry, for his use and benefit absolutely. The remainder of the estate will be left to Doctor Charles Proust, one hundred thousand dollars of which for his own use, and the remainder to re-equip the Meddleton General Hospital with general medical requirements, on the condition that Doctor Proust has never been found guilty of an act of medical negligence. Otherwise, that portion will be left to Hilda Tressor.'

'This is getting horribly complicated, Alex,' said John.

'But that's what you like, you legal beagles! You love pontificating over minute details. That's how you manage to command such exorbitant fees, John!'

The solicitor managed a 'Hurrumpph!' but otherwise kept his peace.

'Next! Should I die between 1.31 a.m. and 2.00 a.m. on Sunday, December the 9th, 2012, one hundred thousand dollars will be left to Janelle Marquete, for her use and benefit absolutely. The remainder of the estate will pass to St. Peter's Roman Catholic Church, Meddleton. Next!' he continued, without pause. 'If I should die between 2.01 a.m. and 2.30 a.m. on Sunday, December the 9th, 2012, one hundred thousand dollars will be left to Lindsay McRae, for his use and benefit absolutely, on condition that he marries the widow, Jocelyn Prittik, and remains with her for a period of not less than five years. The remainder of the estate will pass to Jack Delaney.'

'How long are you going to go on with this,' said the solicitor, exasperated.

'As long as it takes me to die, John! What are you worried about? This is a lawyers' picnic. No doubt you can quibble about this in the courts for the next five years, and make a nice little pile of counting money out of it.'

John looked up and flashed what could have been a grimace.

'Next, and lucky last I might say. If I should die after 2.31 a.m. on Sunday, December the 9th, 2012, one hundred thousand dollars will be left to St. Paul's Anglican Church, Meddleton. The remainder of the estate will be divided equally between Hilda Tressor, Tina Archangel and Jack Delaney, for their use and benefit absolutely. That's it!'

Alex got up.

'Oh, one last thing! Should anybody contest this will and its provisions, then that person shall get nothing! There's a computer and printer over there. If you would type it out, please, and print it on the will form, and on a separate piece of paper, then post the copy up on the living room wall, where everyone can see it. I'll get the original signed later, and post it to you. Thanks John. I'll leave the money on the desk for when you've finished. Have a good holiday.'

Then he went in search of Tina.

II

Lindsay McRae went looking for Joss, and found her in the bedroom, packing his things up, and throwing them into his suitcase. She didn't look up, but tossed the suitcase out through the door, almost hitting him in the process.

'Whoa there, Joss! What's going on? Are you in one of your moods? Have I done something... or what?'

He stopped helplessly when she refused to answer him. Taking him by the elbow, she led him out into the lounge room and pointed out a notice on the wall, held in place by a piece of sticky tape.

'Read that, Lindsay! That's what my lovely husband is going to do to us.'

McRae stood and studied the document. He wasn't the only one, either. Janelle came in looking for him, and stood at his shoulder. After she read it she was shocked.

'What the hell is he playing at?'

'I don't care, to tell you the truth. I got two mentions! How many did you get... on yeah. Just one!'

'Screw you and your two mentions. What about the conditions, you idiot!'

'What conditions... oh... yeah! Shit!'

Joss looked at them both angrily, as if they had somehow written this thing together, and then stomped off back to her bedroom. She wasn't as slow as McRae.

'You can't come in,' she said later, when he came back along the passage, and knocked on her door.

'But where am I supposed to go?' he said, puzzled.

'Anywhere but with me! And if anyone asks, nothing happened,' she hissed at him, through the closed door.

McRae went out to the caravan, and accosted Janelle.

'What's going on around here, Janelle? Joss says I can't stay in that room anymore. Can I bunk in here with you?'

'No, you can't you idiot! Didn't you read that thing? So much for us writing his will for him. Fat chance of that now! Everybody's reading it. Soon the whole town will know the contents.'

'But why can't I bunk in with you?'

'Because there's no room for a start! And secondly, because I don't want people to think we're associated in any way outside of work. I could do with that $100,000. It would make my life so much easier.'

'But I thought you were working with me. Why settle for $100,000 when if I inherit, we can get the lot?'

'Because you couldn't stand up to an audit, that's why. You'd end up in jail, and that Tina would get the loot. Can't you see, the only way we're going to get anything out of this without a lot of conditions attached is if I get that $100,000. If you get it, on that later time, you'll have to marry Joss.

What's more, you'll have to stay married for five years before you get your hands on the money. With me there's no conditions, except that he has to die between 1.31 and 2.00am.'

'So you're going out on your own, now! God, Janelle, I didn't think you'd fall for that one. He's trying to come between us! It's as plain as the nose on your face.'

'Let's put it this way, Lindsay. A bird in the hand is worth two in the bush, especially when it's Jocelyn's bush!'

'But there's no saying that he's going to die at that time! If he dies between 12.31 and 1.00 am Joss gets it, all to herself.'

'Well maybe you'd better stick with her then, Lindsay, but what makes you think that someone's not going to blow the whistle on *her?* I bet you're not the only one that's crawled into her bed lately.'

'No... well there is that,' McRae conceded. 'She did mention something about a bloke called Colin... something about how big he was. I think she was just trying to give me the shits!'

'There you are then. The little virgin won't be able to claim, either. Let's face it, Lindsay, you're stuffed, either way.'

'The question is, where am I going to sleep,' he hissed at her, totally out of control by now.

'That's your problem, lover boy. Go and find yourself a spare room somewhere. There must be a stack of them in that house.'

McRae finally bit the bullet and approached Alex.

'I say, Alex. If you've got a bit of time, I think we should talk, get some of the financials out of the way.'

'Sure, Lindsay! Sorry I've been so preoccupied. What with Greg's suicide and my own personal worries, I've been neglecting the business side of things a bit, haven't I? Come into the study and sit down.'

Once inside, Alex poured them both a drink.

'How're the investments holding up? Don't tell me you've lost another $100,000 on the market,' he said, wagging his finger playfully.

'No, Alex! As a matter of fact we just made $240,000 in the last twenty four hours, when I dumped your gold stocks and bought zinc.'

'That was a clever move, Lindsay. I can see now why I hired you in the first place. You have great tenacity, incredible staying power. And to top it off, you don't fold under stress. You have a hide like a rhinoceros, Lindsay, a very important attribute for someone as thick and as dependable as you.'

Lindsay looked at him suspiciously. Was that a crack, or by thick did he mean that they stood together, solid, impenetrable?

'Anyway, there's a lot of correspondence for you to sign, Alex, and I thought we could get that over first. There's quite a pile... it might take quite a time to read it all so I've been over it all beforehand. It's all kosher... you can just stick your moniker on the bottom.'

'You really take the pain out of making money, Lindsay,' Alex said, as he began to flick through the pile in front of him, barely looking as he went. He signed each sheet with a flourish, until he got three sheets from the bottom, then he pulled one out and put it aside. Finishing off, he gave Lindsay the pile back, and slid the odd sheet into his desk drawer.

'Err…' said Lindsay, making stabbing motions in the air towards the sheet he'd hidden away.

'Oh, that one's not important, Lindsay. I'll look at it later. In the meantime, I hope you enjoy your stay here. We've got a great fireworks display coming up on Saturday night.'

'Yes, so I understand, Alex.'

'Yes, you and Joss should really enjoy it. It should go on for hours… it better, anyway. It cost me an arm and leg,' he laughed.

'Err Alex! I wanted to talk to you about this Joss thing. There was nothing in it, you know, absolutely nothing!'

'That's what they all say, Lindsay. All twenty-three of them!' Alex said, jocularly. 'Don't worry man! You can pinch my wife, and you can rifle my bank accounts… just don't step on my blue suede shoes, eh?'

'No, Alex! I really must insist. Joss means nothing to me. We never did it… or anything… what you think we did!' McRae sounded rather desperate.

'No, sure! Don't worry, Janelle can't overhear us in here. I don't mind if you like bagging two at the same time, Lindsay. That's a young man's prerogative. I'd do it myself if I was your age.'

'Janelle's just my secretary, Alex. You have some very strange ideas…'

'No... you have some strange predilections, Lindsay. Like broomsticks!'

Lindsay turned perceptibly green.

'Oh well, I can see I can't convince you, so I'll stop trying,' he laughed, nervously. 'Look Alex, Joss has kicked me out of that room. Would you have another room somewhere I could...'

'Sure! No worries. Go down the end of that main corridor, there's a little room on the left. Just a bit of junk in there, but you should be able to make use of it for a couple of days, anyway. Use it... it's yours!'

Later on, Lindsay found that the room Alex was referring to was a glorified broom closet.

Chapter Fifteen

The Reverend Elder Berry called that afternoon. He had been watching from afar all the activity going on between the island and the mainland, the arrival of the semi-trailer, and people coming and going in what seemed a constant hive of activity. He had officiated at the funeral of Jason Tressor, and now it looked as if he would be officiating at the funeral of his father as well, which was being held up somewhat by ongoing police enquiries and the coroner's court. Then the Bishop had laid the heavy responsibility on him of acquiring some sort of bequest from Alex Prittik's will before he died. He shuddered at the thought of having to face Alex yet again, and argue through the relative merits of the Anglican Church versus the Catholics. Knowing Alex, he would be just as likely to throw Buddha into the stew as well, not to mention Mohammed and Krishna. But he had received his orders, and as a humble servant of the church, who was he to dispute the Bishop?

As he trudged ashore with muddy boots, he noticed that people generally didn't seem all that happy to see him. McRae scowled at his salutation, and Janelle tossed her head in the air, and basically ignored him. The only response he got was from Joss, who leapt out of her chair and rushed over to let him in.

'Oh, your worshipfulness,' she cried out in surprise. 'It's so good to see you, your honour. Come in, we need to talk about things.'

'Reverend will do... err... Jocelyn. You be giving me a fat head if you keep on giving me titles I'm not entitled to. Hah!' he simpered. 'Rather good that, eh? *Titles* I'm not *entitled* to! I'll have to work that into a sermon somehow,' he muttered.

'Sit down, your godliness,' Joss went on, as if she hadn't listened to a word he'd said. 'Would you like a cup of tea, vicarage? A nice cup of tea with some sugar to build up your energy.'

The Vicar looked at her, a puzzled look on his face. What on earth was she talking about – sugar – build up his energy?'

'It's a long walk over that causeway, isn't it? You must be tired.'

'Oh! Yes, well... yes, thank you Joss. I could do with a nice cup of tea.'

Joss bustled off to the kitchen, making sure to jiggle the appropriate parts as she went past. It was second nature to her to remind everyone she talked to that she was a woman, a very desirable woman in fact, with an excess of sexually tempting flesh in the correct proportions in the right places. From the vicar to the postman, her name was a byword in Meddleton.

While she was gone, the vicar got to his feet and strolled aimlessly around the room. He stared out of the front window, and saw Alex and Tina heading for the beach. Eddie Grainger was carrying some large containers into the boatshed and Colin Bartel was slouching by one of the caravans, watching Alex's progress with undue interest.

Shortly, Berry tired of the scene, and turned to wander around the room. In his reverie, something quite inappropriate to the setting caught his eye. It was a sheet of paper, attached to the wall by a piece of ugly sticky tape. Natural curiosity got the better of him, and he walked over to read what great pronouncement it had to make.

After reading the first few lines, he looked around guiltily, just to make sure that Joss wasn't on her way back. Then he read the rest of it. By the time that Joss returned holding a tray bearing two cups of tea, the reverend was almost a gibbering wreck.

'What on earth... is that a joke, Joss? Who put that up there? I see my name is mentioned... I, well... I would never...'

'Sit down, father, that's exactly what I wanted to talk to you about. It's terrible, isn't it? How could he do this to me,' she suddenly wailed, and almost dropped the tray on the coffee table.

The Vicar rushed over to give her a steadying hand.

'There, there.... Sit down my dear. I want you to tell me all about it, everything! We must get to the bottom of this.'

'He's left me, your goodness! Left me, his wife, and is carrying on with that tart, Tina. He's even thrown me out of our own bedroom, would you believe. He's accused me of, err... flirting... yes, flirting with the accountant – as if I would ever be stupid enough to do something like that, your reverence.'

As she spoke she was bent forward in front of him, and her breasts tried to force their way out of their tiny enclosures. The sight actually hurt his eyes.

'Yes, sit down, Joss. Sit down! That's better. Yes, well, he obviously feels that he has a grievance, Jocelyn, otherwise he wouldn't have gone to such extremes.'

'But he can't do that, can he, not without proof! He hasn't got any proof, or anything!'

The vicar was getting impatient.

'Yes... no! No, I don't think so! But what about that... over there... on the wall? Is that his will, or has he just put that up as a joke... a very tasteless joke, I might add,' he said, putting his nose in the air.

'No, it's not a joke, your grace. He means it! He's taking away my rightful inheritance, and giving it all to some goofy inventors! Then he says that to get what's rightfully mine, I have to prove I've been faithful to him for the past twelve months. It's so unfair! I mean, a year's such a long time, isn't it, rector? I mean, anything can happen in a year.'

'And no doubt, it usually does,' thought the vicar, but kept that gem to himself.

'Why has he put my name in there, Joss? Do you think he's had a change of heart at last. Oh glory be! In one part I see he's left a hundred thousand dollars to the church organ fund. I think that's marvellous. And to leave *me* a hundred thousand dollars, for my own use, absolutely... well I could kiss the man, I really could!'

'It's not that straightforward, your Eldership. If you look closely, you'll see that you only get that money if he dies between, let's see...' She got up and went over to the taped sheet, carefully detaching it from the wall. She was reading it as she sat down again. '…a minute past one and one thirty on December the 10th. The church organ fund only gets it if he dies between midnight and twelve thirty, and the church itself only gets the money if he dies after two thirty one on the morning of Sunday, December the 10th. You can't *all* get the same money!'

'Let me see that,' said the vicar, snatching at the sheet. 'My God… oops… sorry lord! But you're right, Jocelyn. Why, the man's a complete mountebank. It's like he'll be sitting up there laughing at us all as we attempt to decipher his will. I must say, to lift someone's hopes like that, and then to dash them to the ground… it's… it's *evil*, that's what it is!'

'He's even mentioned your superior eminence, Father. Look, Bishop Bagwort! He's not going to like that!'

The Reverend Berry failed to reply. He had a sneaking suspicion that the Bishop might not be above the temptations afforded by a slice of secular wealth, to the tune of $100,000. The vicar instantly conjured up a mental image of his superior, sitting with his feet in a silver bucket to pamper his weary bunions, and to his surprise he felt suddenly envious.

'When does it go to Bagwort?' he screeched, then scoured the sheet in front of him. 'Oh, yes… if Alex dies between twelve thirty one and one o'clock. Well! Wouldn't that be a travesty of justice!' he exclaimed, outraged. 'The difference between the Organ Fund and the Bishop could very well come down to Alex hanging on for an extra minute after twelve thirty. The whole idea is preposterous!'

'Or it could be between the Bishop and you at the other end of the half-hour,' suggested Jocelyn. 'Now do you see? Isn't he an awful man?'

'Awful!' reiterated the vicar. 'Awful, and… the very Devil, in fact! It's almost as if he's trying to tempt one of us to kill him, during the half hour that would benefit that person the most. Oh lord, deliver us from the temptations of this evil man,' he uttered soulfully, gazing up at the ceiling. Then he crossed himself. 'Get thee behind me, Satan,' he muttered.

Jocelyn sat with a fierce light in her eyes.

'I never thought of that! That *is* what he seems to be doing, isn't it, your holiness? And I suppose, if that's what he wants, then it wouldn't be so wrong to…'

'Don't even think about it, my child,' said the reverend, stabbing his hand towards her in a moment of rare integrity. He looked down to find his fingers lodged deep inside her cleavage. She looked down also, and wiggled her breasts so he could release his fingers more easily.

'I seem to be in the habit of making these *faux pas,* don't I, my dear,' he said, embarrassed.

'Oh, I don't mind, Father, I really don't. If your eminence is ever in need of…'

'Don't, my child! The very thought is almost more than I can bear.'

'…another cup of tea, I was going to say,' said Joss, smiling at his confusion.

'Oh, no! That is, thank you very much for your hospitality, Jocelyn, but no thanks! I need to re-evaluate my position in the scheme of things. Do you think it would be possible to obtain a copy of this document… err… so I can peruse it at will, so to speak. Hah! Peruse the *will* at *will!* Another one! I shall have to remember that one,' he muttered to himself.

'I'll copy it on the fax machine,' she said, obligingly. 'I suppose you'll want to show it to the Bishop!'

The reverend was not at all sure whether or not he wanted to show it to the Bishop, because he could see all sorts of complications arising from the revelations contained in this document. But he went along.

'Yes… of course! Bishop Bagwort will be most anxious to press our case against St. Peter's,' he said, lamely.

Joss handed him the copy, and stuck the original back on the wall.

'Do you want to see Alex,' she said. 'He's down the beach, with that little tart. But I could get him for you if you like.'

'No, not at the moment, Joss! I need to study this first before I am sure enough of my facts. I don't want to go half-hearted into a discussion of this magnitude. We'll leave sleeping dogs lie at the moment,' he replied, meaningfully.

He beamed at her and winked, and a very sly wink it was, she thought. She wrinkled up her brow, perturbed. How on earth had *he* got to know about the doggie in the basement?

The world was a great and continuing mystery to Jocelyn. The way people must talk about every little thing that went on! No wonder she couldn't keep a secret!

II

The interview that Doctor Proust had concluded with Bishop Bagwort had been somewhat embarrassing. Though old friends, it was always difficult conducting a discussion where there was any question of ethics involved, especially where there was a hint of wrongdoing. Proust knew that he would have to walk gingerly on the thin fabric of the Bishop's tolerance, and yet he could see no other way around the problem without the possibility of a general scandal erupting.

Bagwort sat like an uncompromising toad, hunched over in his chair with his feet in a bucket. He still wore his robes of munificence, for he had a fear of people seeing him in ordinary attire, where they might make a judgement of him in accordance with his short, fat frame, his prominent jowls, and his steely grey eyes under beetling brows. Bishop Bagwort in a suit would be a caricature.

'Hello Harold, good of you to see me at such short notice,' said Proust, on his entry. He took in the gloom of his surroundings, and felt a slight chill creep over his soul.

'Hello Charles… sit yourself down! I won't get up. As you can see, I'm somewhat inconvenienced at the moment with the travails of the flesh. Even the servants of the church have to suffer from the dissolution of the body as the spirit grows more feeble. Bunions, you know. They give me gyp!'

Proust peered into the murky bucket at Bagwort's feet, and delicately sniffed the air.

'What have you got in there, Harold, Epsom Salts?'

'No - Sulphur! At times like these I often take a punt on both horses, if you know what I mean!' He looked briefly upwards from under his eyebrows, as if to be more precise might involve his immortal soul in some deadly conundrum. 'What brings the eminent Doctor out to see me on such a lovely afternoon, when no doubt you'd rather be amputating gangrenous toes, or snipping off some bloated appendix?'

Proust laughed.

'Life generally isn't so much fun as all that, Harold. We sometimes have to buckle down and attend to the more serious aspects of modern life, like belting a little white pill around eighteen holes. That's where you find out whether or not you can cut the mustard.'

Bagwort almost forgot himself, and smiled.

'I've never had the pleasure myself. It always seemed to me to be a rather futile pastime, knocking little balls into little holes, then picking them out again. A bit like Catholics going to the confessional every Sunday, so they can go out and repeat their admitted felonies every Monday.'

It was Proust's turn to smile, though he forbore to comment on Bagwort's contention as he had little or no belief or interest in the foibles of religion. As a result, he always felt he was on unsure ground whenever jousting with a cleric.

'I'm here to talk about a joint acquaintance of ours, and if I betray the doctor's vow of patient confidentiality, I'm sure you will understand that I do it only on the grounds of your exalted position in the church, in the knowledge that whatever I say will go no further than these four walls.'

Proust looked at Bagwort meaningfully, and received the nodded assurance.

'No doubt you have a very good reason for any confidences you might be forced to utter, Charles, and as one professional man to another I can guarantee that the matter will be dealt with most circumspectly.'

The doctor breathed a sigh of relief.

'Well it's like this, Harold. I believe that I have already mentioned the circumstances surrounding a Mister Alex Prittik, who graces us yearly with his presence at Crab Island?'

Bagwort sat up straight in his chair. This might be interesting!

'Yes, you did mention something of the sort... nothing that might not be picked up in general gossip about the fellow, however. Do go on.'

'Well, as you are aware, I diagnosed him as suffering from pancreatic cancer, some three weeks ago now. I felt that there was no point in equivocating about the matter, so I led straight from the shoulder. I gave him eight weeks!'

'And very commendable, I'm sure. All men should be given the opportunity, before that dark gate of oblivion opens up before them, to make peace with their maker. Such is only fair.'

'My thoughts, entirely,' Proust continued. 'Unfortunately, in this particular case, complications have arisen which require a delicate touch to restore equilibrium. I immediately thought of you, naturally, as being a past master of the art of diplomacy. Perhaps you could bring about a result which would appease all parties.'

'I take it that your diagnosis left something to be desired,' said Bagwort, perceptively. Proust shot him a quick glance. The man was quick, incredibly insightful. No wonder he was a Bishop.

'You would be correct. Due to circumstances beyond my control, certain tests that were carried out - the results of which were the basis of the diagnosis - have now been found to be erroneous. To put matters in a nutshell, without naming names, a certain filing clerk without a good knowledge of the English language, contrived to place the results of two different patients into each other's folders. Both patients were accordingly misdiagnosed, and one of these has now been admitted to the local hospital without any chance of recovery. The other patient is Mister Prittik.'

'And the diagnosis was... of this other patient, now known to be Prittik?'

Proust shook his head in an extreme of embarrassment. It was like wrenching his heart out from his body on a sharp skewer to divulge information like this, but it must be done.

'Duodenal ulcer!'

The words dropped sharply into that silent air, and Bagwort held his breath for a long minute, savouring the moment. Then he began to chuckle, a rasping, grinding sound from deep inside his chest, like an old motor that hadn't been started up for over twenty years.

'You gave the poor sap eight weeks to live... on a duodenal ulcer?'

Bagwort suddenly gave out a huge bellow of a laugh, and Proust almost jumped out of his seat. He'd never heard him laugh before.

'Oh, my, that's a good one, Charles! You've got yourself into a right little predicament, haven't you? I can see why you came to consult me. It must be something approaching the doctor's worst nightmare, medical negligence with ramifications far in excess of the original gaffe. His team of solicitors would make mincemeat of you in court, Charles. Not that they're going to, because between us we shall effect a solution to this little contretemps that will soothe Mister Prittik's aggrieved soul.'

'Do you really think you can do anything to help, Harold,' said Proust, now white and sweating, with his original fears coalesced, and immanent with the portent of doom.

'Don't you worry your head about it, Charles. I shall use my influence with our local vicar here, who is an intimate of the lady of the house. He is well intentioned, and I believe a popular figure there. He visits often. Between us we will find a way to let Mister Prittik off the hook of his imminent demise, and in the process we may even do some good for ourselves. We have a church organ in the town that is in great need of repair, and I have a feeling that if this thing is handled properly, we may be able to bend Mister Prittik's arm to his cheque book. Let us hope so, anyway. The bearer of good tidings should always hope for some slight reward for his efforts, especially if it means that the community benefits.'

Proust breathed a sigh of relief.

'Thank god... err... goodness for you, Bishop. I knew I could rely on you. It... err... shouldn't be necessary to involve the vicar in the details of this little problem, should it? The less people know...'

'I understand entirely, Doctor! You have my word.'

Proust would not have been as happy and relieved if he had been a party to the Bishop's thoughts after he had left.

'That's all very well, but what the blazes do you say in cases like this,' thought Bagwort, frowning. 'Maybe young Berry might have a better idea. He knows the Prittik's on a familiar level. Local knowledge is always best!'

Proust would have been even more distressed if he had known what the Reverend Berry was carrying around in his pocket at that very minute. A mighty battle was going on between the vicar's conscience, and the vicar's unacknowledged lust for personal wealth. Lust presently had the upper hand, but the awful possibility of being discovered to have kept such an earth-shattering revelation to himself had raised the image of a rampaging Bishop Bagwort into the forefront of his mind, and the thought terrified him. Should he, shouldn't he? It was a riddle that only he could answer.

Chapter Sixteen

At eleven o'clock on the Friday morning, Alex sat on the ledge at Stingray Cove, looking out over the natural swimming basin that he had formerly loved so much. He reflected on the fact that it now conjured up a totally different association in his mind than it did in previous times, when it had just been a glorious swimming hole for the family. Now it was sullied and spoiled, and had a dour aspect to it that had only now become apparent. All he could see in his mind's eye was the roof of his own E-type Jag, where the car had sat on the bottom, slowly filling up with water. He thought of Jason, trapped and terrified, as the water slowly rose up in the cabin, and the futile efforts of those who dived down to attempt to rescue him, once the stingray had gone.

'Stupid!' he spat out to himself, 'Stupid! Stupid! Stupid!' – as if the reiteration of that one word could wash away all the pain and heartache that had ensued for his sister, Hilda.

When Greg died at his own hand, some days later, Alex had phoned Hilda at her new home, dreading her response, but she had remained very quiet as he told her of the circumstances of Greg's death. He had faltered to a stop, feeling her pain through the line, but unable to reach out to her, or to comfort her in her distress. Before he could even beg the question, she said, 'I won't be coming to the funeral, Alex. I don't think I could bear it!' There was a long silence, then she said, 'I'm afraid that if I let go now, I'll never be able to find my way back.' Then she hung up.

Tina came sliding down the path to their favourite spot, and he didn't even look up as she sat down beside him. She followed his eyes out to the pool, and divined what it was that was tearing him apart inside.

'There was nothing you could do, you know. It's no good blaming yourself!'

He looked around at her in surprise.

'I don't blame myself! That's the problem! If I could afford the luxury of that, I would probably feel much better about myself. The fact is, Tina, that I don't seem capable of *feeling*, one way or the other! I can identify with Hilda's pain, I can sympathise with Greg, even. Thanks to you, I don't feel any great antipathy towards Darlene. But that little shit, Jason... I can't forgive him for what he did to everyone else, and I can't feel sorry for him. He got his just desserts! Whether he got them last week, or next year, or in ten years time, the end result would always have been the same for him. He was on a collision course with disaster, and I think that, in some strange way, he knew it.'

Alex suddenly suffered a coughing fit, and the pain in his midriff overwhelmed him. Suddenly he could taste blood in his mouth. He groaned, and rolled over sideways on the ledge, clutching at his stomach. Tina got up in panic and moved around so she could put her arms around him.

'I'll give you some painkillers, Alex. No, don't fob me off, you've got to take them!'

Alex succumbed, and tried to swallow the two little pills she proffered. It took about ten minutes for the pain to subside, by which time he had broken out in a sweat, and was deathly pale. Once he'd recovered, he took her by the hand and began to lead her into their Grotto.

'Take a good look at it, Tina. It might be for the last time!'

She followed him into the cave, looking at him, questioningly. They walked through the shallow water, along the tunnel and around into the 'Cathedral'.

'What did you mean by that, Alex? It might be the last time?'

Alex led her over to the ledge where they had both sat on their first meeting in the cave. He patted her hand, and they sat down.

'After tomorrow… I may be here, but you never will again, Tina. I've told Jack to blow the entrance… you know, with explosives! It will become sealed off, a tomb! My tomb!'

He looked around at her, and saw she had tears in her eyes.

'What makes you think I don't want to come with you, Alex? We could both go together. After all… after you've gone, what's left for me?'

Alex put his arm around her shoulder, and gave her a squeeze.

'You don't mean that, Tina! The sun will still come up for you on Sunday morning, and the birds will still sing in the trees. The sea will be just as blue, and you…' he stroked her cheek, 'you will be just as beautiful as you are right now! Just know that if there were any way around this, any other choice, I would take it. But I'm a rank coward, Tina, where it comes to physical pain, and having had a few tastes of what it will be like over the past few days, then I know in myself that I can't face it! I just want you to know that I love you, girl... more than I've ever loved anyone in my life.'

'Well if you love me, let me go with you,' she snuffled. 'I'm just the same as you, Alex. I can't face it either! The thought of being strapped to a bed, having no control over my bodily functions, throwing my legs and arms around like some maniac, screaming abuse at everyone in my dementia... what sort of a future is that to look forward to? We could die in each other's arms, Alex, and then afterwards, if there is another world to go to, we'll be together! We won't have to spend thousands of years looking for each other in a hundred different lifetimes, only to miss each other by a generation.'

'I will never leave you, Tina. I may not be there for you physically, but I will always be there in spirit. Anyway...' he continued, as if trying to break the spell, 'I've made provision for you in my will.'

'I know that, I saw it on the wall! I don't want your money, Alex! I want you! A million dollars is nothing without you to share what's left of my life!'

'Oh, Tina,' Alex sighed, shaking his head. 'What sort of demonic fate does this to people, who love each other as much as this? I love you so much, it hurts!'

'So do I,' she cried, giving in to the emotion of the moment.

They clung to each other in the gloom, as if those few moments were the only ones they had left. It was as if the forces of an implacable nature were determined to tear them apart.

'I want you to fly to America, and hunt out a cure for that disease. They're making great strides in medicine these days, and the cutting edge seems to be in the U.S. With any luck they'll have come up with something, even if it's only something to alleviate the symptoms.'

'And if not?' said Tina, petulantly.

'Don't be like that,' said Alex, patting her knee. 'If not, well, make sure you have a ball spending the million dollars. Live life to the full... and think of me from time to time,' he added, sadly. 'I'll still be here, looking up at the stalactites!'

Tina cuddled into him and held on until she thought her heart would burst.

II

Bishop Bagwort received his invitation to the firework display on the Friday morning. At the same moment, the Reverend Elder Berry received his. Doctor Proust received his later in the afternoon. On the island it was Tina's job to hand out invitations to everyone, including McRae and Janelle Marquete, Jack Delaney and the other workers, and Joss herself who was now being treated as an outsider.

Hilda had been invited by phone, but on hearing Alex's voice had swiftly hung up. She was determined to isolate herself from all family, and start her life afresh. The fact that she had found herself the owner of a unit in Blackwood, with access to $150,000 in a savings account, had not slipped her attention. But as she considered that to be only her due anyway, she felt that she had no reason to feel grateful for her brother's generosity, or to express thanks. She had already decided that she would never return to Crab Island.

On Bishop Bagwort receiving his invitation, he immediately recalled Proust's visit, and phoned the good reverend.

'Reverend Berry! Something has recently come to my notice with regard to Mrs. Prittik's husband, and I would like you to call around to discuss the matter.'

The reverend's legs turned to jelly on the spot. He'd found out! The Bishop knew! How was he going to explain the fact that he'd had details of this will for twenty-four hours, and had still not informed the Bishop that he was named in parts of it?

The vicar sank into a chair, his mouth opening and closing like a goldfish.

'Er, yes, your worship, straight away! I can explain everything if you'll… oh, no sir, not over the phone! You're absolutely right, your worship. In confidence… yes… Of great importance! Yes, I do know this, sir… Certainly! I'll be around to see you shortly.'

The reverend dropped the phone and went into a dance of despair around the room. He hopped up and down on the spot, cursing his own intransigence.

'Oh lord, lord, lord! I am but a poor servant, and the beguiling chains of untrammelled wealth are at my throat. Forgive me my moment of weakness and doubt. Free me from this lust for worldly gain, and help me to withstand your Bishop's righteous anger and glowering discontent!'

He hurried out and muttered his penances all along the road, casting his eyes up to the heavens at frequent intervals to check for unheralded lightning bolts. The sky was perfectly clear, except for one dense black, threatening cloud, situated directly above the Bishop's residence. As the reverend beat on the old brass doorknocker, the cloud opened up, and it began to rain.

'Come in, Reverend…'

The Bishop's voice echoed along the passages in the gloom, and Reverend Berry went haltingly through into the front room, where the Bishop sat in state upon a large, carved, eighteenth century chair that he had once bought at a garage sale for fifty cents.

Bagwort was holding a sheet of paper in his hand, and on seeing this, the vicar's legs buckled under him and he fell into an armchair.

'I can explain everything, your worship. I was waiting for the best moment to approach you, your eminence, you being so frightfully busy with your pastoral duties and Bishop's returns, I…'

'What on earth are you babbling about, vicar? I called you in specifically to discuss this parishioner of yours, Prittik! Well, not the parishioner exactly, but the parishioner's husband, whom, as we all know, is dying of cancer.'

'Exactly, your worship! Exactly my point! So that will of his…' Here the reverend waved madly at the piece of paper in the Bishop's hand, 'that will of his is truly blasphemous and… *evil*… and…'

'What the blazes!' said the Bishop, looking down at the neatly printed sheet. 'This is an invitation for me to attend a grand fireworks display over at Crab Island tomorrow night. What's this about a will?'

The reverend sank back into his seat, suddenly deflated. The fireworks display? He'd had an invitation to that himself, just that afternoon!

'Oh... yes, the fireworks! True, your worship, I too have been invited! I believe it will be a most impressive event.'

'The will, Berry!'

Pecuniary detail was the Bishop's forté. The Bishop's eyes fixed on the vicar's throat and seemed to drill into his very soul. Berry imagined he saw a few tufts of smoke appear, and curl from Bagwort's eyebrows.

'I was going to tell you all along, your worship! I only found out yesterday myself, and I was shocked, sir, shocked and horrified. I mean, it was almost like the temptation, your worship, during our lord's forty days in the wilderness...'

'Cut to the chase, vicar! My temper is rather short today, and I don't know when it might flare out... *and consume the hapless denizens of the immediate neighbourhood! The will!*'

The reverend reached hurriedly into his pocket and pulled out the vastly mauled copy that he had read and re-read on countless occasions since the previous day. He walked over to the Bishop and thrust it at him, then retired to his chair.

Bagwort sat slumped over the sheet for some minutes. After reading it through once, he then read it through again.

'Remarkable!' he muttered, his left eyebrow going up one notch. 'Of all the...' was the next unfinished utterance. He tempered these with - 'Infamous!'... 'St. Peter's... by all

221

the foul fiends in hell!'… 'Over my dead body!'… 'Incredible!'… and - 'The man is beyond salvation!'

Eventually, Bagwort looked up, a grim and determined expression on his face.

'So this is the sort of man he is! He plays fast and loose with other people's hopes and expectations, and then dashes them into the dirt! He juggles the church organ fund between the Catholics and his accountant's secretary! He has the audacity to include you, vicar, in his demented plan to dangle his devil's shekels before everyone's avaricious eyes, even after he has tempted God's wrath by unlawfully taking his own life.'

'And I see he has even included you, Bishop, in his demented plan,' said the vicar, eagerly. 'It's almost as if – as I said to Mrs. Prittik – he's tempting one of the provisional beneficiaries to commit murder at a specified time, so that they might benefit from his will!'

Bagwort nodded, thoughtfully, and continued to nod.

'I'm tempted to agree with you, vicar! The man is obviously of the Devil's party, and is determined to invoke a mad scramble after his filthy lucre, creating havoc amongst the souls of good men. What is written on this page is sufficient to seduce a Christian man from the straight and narrow, and tempt him to commit an act that would cost him his everlasting soul.'

Behind Bagwort's impassive countenance ran a myriad of thoughts, all of which ran counter to the strong, protestant ethic and Christian morality that the Bishop had, all his life, striven to defend and protect.

Prittik had left him, Bagwort, a hundred thousand dollars! But only if he died between 12.31 and 1.00am on Sunday morning! Bagwort knew only too well that, left to the divine masterplan, Prittik would still be alive, though not necessarily well, on the Monday morning following. He would also be alive a year, and possibly ten, fifteen, twenty years after that again! He only had a duodenal ulcer, after all, and eventually he would discover that fact, and get the appropriate treatment.

But Prittik, it was now revealed, had decided on the evidence currently available to him, to commit suicide. This was against God's commandments and against secular law. But that meant nothing! If a man was determined to commit suicide, then commit suicide he would, and there was nothing that the lord above, or the church, or the secular authorities could do about it.

It was this fact that was what was putting the Bishop into a bind. Given the contents of Prittik's will, and his own private knowledge about the truth of the case, could a decision by him to do precisely nothing to influence events, one way or the other, be construed as morally neutral?

Given the obviously evil slant of this document, designed to tempt his fellow men to intercede and pre-determine the time of Prittik's death, coupled with the fabulous wealth of the man – *and everyone knew that fabulous wealth was only gained by being linked to the devil's party* – was it a morally neutral act, or could it even be a morally Christian act to let the man continue on his course of self destruction, thus freeing the world of yet another of Lucifer's cohorts?

Behind this furious spate of rationalisation, a squeaky little voice in the Bishop's subconscious mind was metaphorically yapping at him somewhere inside his forehead, and attempting to get his attention. Despite being drowned out, the squeaky little voice kept yelping something about it being his Christian duty to save Prittik from himself, to notify him of the misdiagnosis and give him the opportunity to heal himself. By thus doing, so said the squeaky, Bagwort would be saving Prittik from the deadly sin of suicide. Only then could he claim to have committed a truly Christian act.

From somewhere in the depths of Bagworts phlegmatic soul, an unfamiliar voice rose up in his mind and uttered just one, booming word.

'Bo.o.o.ring!'

Bagwort came to, realising that the vicar was still sitting there in an agonised expectation of a final dismissal. There was a decision to make, and Bagwort's own words to his old friend, Charlie Proust, came to mind.

'*...between us, we shall effect a solution to this little contretemps that will soothe Mister Prittik's aggrieved soul!*'

'You wanted to talk to me about Mister Prittik,' prompted the vicar. Now that the misunderstanding over the will was dealt with, he suddenly realised that they had not yet dealt with the reason for his summons.

'Yes, vicar! You have done well! If you don't mind, I would like to hang on to this copy of the will for a while, to study its deeper implications. The church is mentioned in a number of places, and so are the Catholics. I need to ponder it at length!'

'Yes, but… what was it exactly that you wanted to talk to me about, Bishop?'

Bagwort snapped back to the question in hand. Should he tell the vicar to go and diplomatically inform Prittik that his life was not in danger? The Bishop's course lay somewhere between his own worldly aspirations and his spiritual salvation! He decided to take a middle course, one that would cover his bet on both horses!'

'Well, I've decided that Mister Prittik is cured! Yes, that's what you can tell him! Tell Mister Prittik that he need not worry, that Bishop Bagwort has the entire thing in hand, and that he is now out of danger and clear of the cancer!'

The reverend looked at him in undisguised awe. He had no idea that his superior had such a pull in the halls of the almighty. He shook his head in admiration.

'Oh thank you, thank you, your worship! I'm sure he will be delighted.'

Bagwort turned to him before he went.

'You could also suggest to him that as a mark of gratitude, he should donate the money to fix the church organ!'

'I certainly will,' said the vicar, his chest swelling with pride. To know that he had access to an intermediary with God had suddenly made his entire career worthwhile. Berry resolved to tell Prittik on the morrow, in good time before the fireworks display.

Bagwort watched him go from behind the heavy drapes, and chuckled to himself. If Prittik believed that a Bishop could just pronounce a man cured, as if by a miracle, then he was a bigger fool than the vicar! Bagwort's own prognosis was that Prittik would look at the vicar in disgust, tap his forehead silently to his friends, and then carry on as he already intended, and commit suicide. But he was careful not to let that thought intrude into his conscious mind. He felt that, overall, he'd covered his tracks well.

Chapter Seventeen

When Janelle went through the pile of signed documents that McRae brought back from his visit to Alex, she was furious. The deed of power of attorney was not in the pile. She went through the pile again, in case she had missed it, while McRae stood agonisingly on one foot, wondering how to break it to her.

'Where is it, Lindsay? For god's sake, where's the bloody deed?'

'Well, honey, it's like this...'

'Don't you honey me! Our entire future is at stake. You can't re-write the will because he's made it public, but we might be able to salvage something if you only had that deed. So where is it?'

'It's in his desk drawer,' McRae conceded, miserably. 'I don't know how he did it, because he didn't even read it. I'm sure of that because I was sitting right in front of him, watching him as he signed. He just turned up the bottom quarter of each document as he came to it, and signed... until he got to the deed.'

'What did he do then,' she snarled at him. God, the man was infuriating!

McRae just shrugged, and looked a little lost.

'He pulled it out and sat it apart, on the desk. He still didn't read it. Then he put it in the top drawer. When I sort of pointed it out, he said not to worry about it. It wasn't important, and he'd read it later.'

'You're not serious! Oooh! Oh God!' Janelle sat down heavily, as if her legs had collapsed beneath her. 'We're dead! If he reads that, we're dead! Not only will he sack you, and that means me, as well, if it comes to that. But he might get the auditors in, and that would mean jail... for you, anyway! I'd just plead total ignorance. I didn't know what you were up to, did I?'

'You're not going to pike out on me now are you, Janelle? I'm relying on you! After all, this was all your idea, this power of attorney thing.'

'You're not going to drag me down with you, Lindsay. I'm not going to spend my life with a loser!'

Lindsay suddenly took stock, and looked at her in a new light.

'What makes you think I had any intention of including you in my future plans,' he retorted. 'I've got Joss, and I think she's a better bet than you to come out of this covered in roses.'

'Well, that's it, then! You can get out of here this minute. You've made a bad choice, Lindsay, as you'll find out. Better a woman with brains than a thick, rich bimbo any day. You just watch your back, because you've made a bad enemy today.'

McRae found himself being bundled unceremoniously out of the caravan, the door slammed in his face. He stood for a moment, staring at the door, then turned and walked off muttering to himself.

Alex was in the house when he returned, so he resolved to keep a low profile for a while. It was the following day,

Friday, before he felt the way was clear to reconnoitre the place, and try to reclaim the missing deed.

Joss was in her bedroom, alone, practising to be the faithful wife. She sat in front of her mirror and tried out the various faces that she thought might influence the judge, in the event that she might have to prove herself innocent of wrongdoing. Alex and Tina were over at the cliff. Janelle was locked in her caravan, still furious at the latest turn of events, and the workers were still working.

Alex never kept his study locked, so, plucking up the courage, McRae finally made his way to the study and tried the door handle. No problem! He went in and shut the door behind him. It was the work of a minute to get behind Alex's desk, open the drawer and remove the loose sheet that Alex had confiscated the day before. Without even looking at it, he shoved it under his shirt and closed the drawer, being careful to wipe his prints off the handle. He was just about to leave when a voice boomed out from the corner.

'Intruder! Stop where you are! Replace the stolen object and leave this room immediately! Your action has been captured on film.'

McRae froze on the spot. He looked guiltily around the room and then spotted the mini-cam, up in the corner by the ceiling. It was pointed directly at him.

'Another of Alex's blasted gadgets!' thought McRae. Alex was right into that sort of thing, anything electronic or electro-mechanical. He must spend his life trying to scare the shit out of people! McRae gave the camera the finger, then looked around for the tape machine. It was in the bottom drawer of the desk. He opened it up, and pulled out the videotape, replacing it with a blank one. Then he conveniently forgot to turn the machine back on again.

Looking around to make sure nothing else was disturbed, he quietly left the room, pulling the door shut behind him.

He had spent a bad night after the argument with Janelle. Stuck in his broom closet, with scarcely room to move, he had spent a few hours on the internet, shuffling shares from one company to another, then adding his fee to the broker's for his service. Then he would sell, and buy Alex's original shares back again. Sometimes he won, sometimes he lost! At the moment he was on a winning streak, and after two hours of this type of activity, Alex was showing a healthy profit of $70,000. But the stakes had been high. To do that, McRae had shifted over seven million dollars around the world and back again, and moves like that could sometimes be costly. He had also generated a stack of paperwork that Alex would eventually have to sign.

But now, armed with the deed, he thought that perhaps both he and Janelle had been a trifle hasty the day before, and he walked over to the caravan and beat on the door.

'Go away,' she said, before he'd even spoken a word.

'Come on, Janelle... don't be silly! We've had a tiff, that's all. And you'll be pleased to know,' here he looked around to make sure there was no one else in earshot, 'I've got the paper... the deed!'

There was the sound of a bolt being drawn back, and Janelle appeared in the doorway.

'Well, come in, stupid! If you've got the deed we might still be in with a chance.'

He pulled it out from beneath his shirt, and Janelle almost snatched it off him, and laid it on the table. Even a cursory glance told them that it was all over then.

Alex had drawn two pictures, caricatures of McRae and Janelle, accentuating their dominant features as the best cartoonists do. McRae's nose had taken over his face, and he had been paired with Mickey Mouse ears, while Janelle's figure was dwarfed by her breasts and backside. Under each, respectively he had written, *'Mickey Moose'*, and *'Minnie the Moocher.'*

In the body of the document he had signed as *Alex Practical*, and Tina had witnessed his signature as *Tina Terrifical*. The game was up! Along the bottom he had written – *'Nice Try!'*

II

Doctor Proust returned to his surgery, a look of apprehension on his face. He had been called over to the hospital at midday, to see his patient, Alan Privet. When he arrived, he was met by a very teary Mrs. Privet, who wanted to know how come her husband had been allowed to expire with just a duodenal ulcer to his credit. It seemed that Mister Privet had given up the ghost as Doctor Proust walked the two hundred yards between his surgery, and the hospital.

Proust had managed to fob her off by saying that he really wouldn't have any answers for her until an autopsy had been performed to establish the cause of her husband's death.

Doctor Hennessy poked his head into the corridor while this was going on, to see what the fuss was about. When he saw Proust with Mrs. Privet, he divined immediately the cause, and flashed Proust a look of sympathy. That diagnosis had been an almighty cock-up, but it happened sometimes, as Hennessy knew only too well. He caught Proust's eye and raised one eyebrow, as if to say: *'rather you than me, sport!'* If that was intended to make Proust feel better, the intention fell short of the result. It just made Proust feel more exposed.

Back at the surgery he sat moodily in his office, staring through the window at the gardens outside, and across at the buildings on the other side of the green. The weather was most peculiar at the moment, he noted, especially for summertime. The sun shone brightly on his little patch of garden, but over the way, at the Bishop's house, it appeared to be raining.

Proust got up, and out of curiosity crossed to the window. With blue sky all around, there was just one little black cloud, right over the top of Bagwort's residence, and it was literally teeming down. The strangest thing, however, was that it stopped at his gate. It was just as if this cloud had homed in on the Bishop, and was trying to flood him out without affecting the houses on either side. As he watched, Proust jumped as a lightning bolt suddenly shot out of the cloud and earthed itself on the Bishop's chimney. There was an explosion that rocked the neighbourhood, and Bagwort's chimney toppled slowly off the roof and landed in his front garden. Most peculiar!

The doctor sat down again and dialled the Bishop's number. It was a few moments before it was answered.

'Bagwort here!'

'Hi Harold! Are you having a bit of inclement weather over your way?'

'What do you mean… there's a hell of a storm going on! I can barely hear myself think with the noise on the roof. How's your place holding up?'

'Lovely and sunny over here, Bishop! From where I'm standing, it looks like Huey is sending it down just for you, this time.'

'What do you mean by that?'

'If you'd like to stroll out to your front gate, you'll find the pavement outside your place is dry,' said Proust. 'Most remarkable thing I've ever seen!'

'Just hold on a minute,' said Bagwort, and put the phone down. Proust saw him come hurrying out of his front door, holding an umbrella over his head, and make for the front gate. He watched as Bagwort came out into the street, put his umbrella down, and look around him in disbelief. Then he went back in, and picked up the phone.

'You're right, Charles! It's unbelievable!'

'Anyway, Harold! What's the story on Prittik? That's what I really phoned for.'

'You're in a bit of a hurry, aren't you, Charles? You've barely given me time to ponder the matter!'

'It's becoming more and more urgent all the time, Harold. Alan Privet died just half an hour ago in Meddleton General!'

There was a sudden silence at the other end of the phone, then a thump. It sounded like the Bishop had dropped something.

'Are you still there, Harold?'

'Yes… oh yes… sorry about that. No, well about your little problem! I've already primed up the vicar, and he will be straightening the whole thing out tomorrow.'

'Oh, that's good. I'm relieved.'

'I told you I'd fix it, Charles!'

'Yes, you did. It's just that this Privet's death has thrown me somewhat. I want the whole thing cleared up.'

'Leave it with me, doctor,' said Bagwort, and then he hung up.

Once off the phone, the Bishop did a quick tour of the house, checking for water damage. In the main lounge he found, to his dismay, a stream of water running down the now defunct chimney, and forming an evil green puddle in the middle of his Persian rug. Over the next few hours this would grow a fungus so horrible that, rather than clean the rug the Bishop rolled it up and put it out for the rubbish man. As he did so, he looked up.

'I get the message, Father! Forgive me for being tempted, even as you were tempted in the wilderness… But it's all fixed now! I've sent your humble servant, Vicar Berry, to straighten things out!'

Even as he turned to go back into the house, the little squeaky voice in his forehead was attempting to make itself heard, while the other, deep booming voice was drowning it out, humming 'Eleanor Rigby!'

Meanwhile, over at the doctor's surgery, Margaret was handing Proust the afternoon mail. There were seven bills, which he threw aside, and one anonymous looking envelope,

234

which he opened. It was an invitation to attend a fireworks display at Crab Island on the following day. It read as follows:

Alex Prittik of Crab Island
cordially invites you and your partner to the
GRAND FIREWORK DISPLAY
OF THE CENTURY.
to be held on Crab Island on the evening of December 8th, 2012
and commencing at 11.30pm.
The evening has been arranged so that the display will take over three hours,
with breaks in-between to allow you to sample
the finest of Break-Mast Bay's Seafoods,
and South Australia's famous Barossa Valley Wines.
Access via the causeway at low tide: - 8.45pm Saturday 8th December 2012
Return via Mr. Jacobs' boat, who will make several ferrying trips from
3.15am Sunday 9th December 2012.

Firework Display courtesy of *Unique Prittique Ltd.*
Catered by Courtwald's Catering Service, Meddleton.

The doctor sat musing over the invitation for a while, then called his secretary, Margaret, over the intercom.

'Margaret, could you come in here for a moment, please.'

When Margaret appeared, notebook in hand, he showed her the invitation.

'How would you like to accompany me to a *Grand Firework Display* tomorrow night? It does say – 'and partner!''

Margaret flushed slightly. Her employer was single, so it was not unusual for him to require a partner for certain events. This was the first time he'd asked her, however.

'I'd love to go... it looks as if it would be really interesting!'

'That's settled then. We'll go over at low tide... about a quarter to nine. It's going to be a late night... Jacobs is ferrying everyone back starting at 3.15 on Sunday morning.'

'I could stand a late night,' said Margaret, after due consideration. 'It's about time something exciting happened around here!'

Proust pulled a pad out and scribbled a prescription, then handed it to her.

'Could you go to the chemist and get him to supply these, thanks. That way I'll kill two birds with one stone.'

Margaret took the scrip, and turned to leave. She noticed in passing that it was a prescription for the drugs usually prescribed for patients suffering from a duodenal ulcer.

III

By Friday evening, Joss had just about had enough of playing the virtuous housewife, and her jaw was aching from the millions of faces she had practised in the mirror. She ventured out from her room to see if there was any action to be found around the place, and found the house to be surprisingly empty. Alex and Tina were nowhere to be found, neither was McRae. He was actually over in the caravan with Janelle, and they were concocting their own version of pin the tail on the donkey while Colin Bartel kicked his heels outside, locked out of his own caravan.

Joss went back to her room and removed her underwear, then donned the most seductive of mini-skirts, and a brief tube of material that was intended to maintain the minimum standards of decency. Then she went out into the cool, evening air, and walking past Colin, smiled at him sweetly.

'Hello, Mister Muscles! Can't you get into your caravan?'

'No, it's been taken over by those bloody accountants. They said they've got some private figures to go over.'

Joss knew exactly what the private figures were, and one of them was Janelle's. McRae was no doubt going over it right now, with a fine tooth comb.

'I'm going for a walk… if you're interested!'

Colin looked at her uncertainly.

'Not if you're going to yell *'rape'*, at the drop of a hat.'

'Of course not, silly man! It's all over with Alex and me, anyway. I'm looking for a loose end to tie up for a few hours.'

'I'm at a loose end,' Colin grinned.

'Well, can I borrow it, do you think,' she replied, then giggled.

They were going to go off for a walk down the beach, but then Joss changed her mind. She led him over towards the boatshed.

'I want you to show me what you've been doing all this time. What's in there?'

Colin shook his head, fiercely.

'No, you don't want to go in there. It's dangerous!'

'I don't care. I want to see what you do!'

Reluctantly, Colin took her into the boatshed, after first ascertaining that neither Jack nor Eddie would be around to disturb them. They were in the other caravan, cooking their tea. Colin shut the door behind them and turned on the light.

'Now, for god's sake, don't touch anything, because some of these ingredients are really volatile,' he said.

'Volatile!' Joss repeated, rolling her tongue around the word. 'Volatile! That's what I am when I get mad. Alex is going to find out just how volatile I am, tomorrow.'

'What do you mean by that,' said Colin, alarmed.

'You'll find out... all in good time! What are these, over here?'

'They're casings for fireworks. That's what we compress the powder into so it won't just go off with a bang. If you compress it enough it just burns steadily. That's how rockets are made, and starbursts, and fizzers. All sorts of different effects you can get, depending on what you mix in with the powder.'

'And what's that thing?'

'That's a ball mill. The roller spins at high speed, and grinds the black powder down to the texture you want. It can be coarse, or it can be fine, for different types of fireworks. You have to be very careful what you put in it, because the wrong powder will explode, and take you with it. That's why we wear these heavy leather gloves and aprons, and those masks over there to protect our eyes. Then we usually stand behind a small shield so that if there is an explosion, it's directed away from us.'

'Say, this is fascinating, isn't it,' said Joss. She could see all sorts of possibilities with this stuff. 'What are those canisters over there?'

'That's pure black powder. They're just the drums it comes in.' He watched where her attention strayed to next, and said, 'that's a jig. We use it to ram the powder down tight in the casing. We can put about five tons of pressure on the casing to make the firework perform the way we want it to.'

Joss looked around at the shelves of chemicals and the bags of various charcoals and metal powders, and turned back to him.

'Make me a banger, a big one! A super banger.' She looked up at him, excitement in her eyes.

'What for... I mean, how big? A super banger?'

'Yes, a super one! I want a banger that will scare the living daylights out of that bitch Tina!'

'You've got to be careful with these things, Joss. They're not toys, you know!'

'I know that,' she said, as if that was self-evident.

'If you're not careful, you could kill someone – or at the least, maim them. I can't tell you how many people have blown a finger or a hand off, just playing about with explosives.'

'You haven't!' she pouted. 'Go on, just one... one *huge* banger!'

'Only if you tell me what you're going to do with it,' he said, finally.

'I'm going to let it off behind her when she's watching the fireworks tomorrow night.'

'Okay, but no closer than ten feet – okay!'

'Okay, I agree. Ten feet!'

For the next twenty minutes Joss watched Colin closely as he packed a half-inch casing, set up the blue touch paper and sealed it for her.

'That doesn't look very big... will it make much of a bang,' she said, finally.

'You'd better believe it, lady. And you'd better make sure you're at least ten feet away when it goes off, or it might take an eye out.'

'What about those casings over there? What would they do?'

Colin laughed. She was pointing at some two-inch casings for star shells.

'That would take your arse off at fifty feet,' he chuckled. 'Stick to the one I made you.'

They left the shed and went walking along the beach. Finally, in a sheltered spot near some undergrowth, she got down on her hands and knees and said, teasingly, 'here doggy, good doggy,' as she lifted her skirt up her back.

Chapter Eighteen

Early in the afternoon of Saturday the 8th, Alex met the caterers, and told them where to erect their marquees for the big occasion. Once that was all settled, he went on a tour of the various bunkers where the successive groups of fireworks were to be ignited. Jack gave him a rundown on the various sequences, and finally they made their way down to the rock ledge, and around to the mouth of the cave.

Jack had been busy. All around the mouth of the cave Alex could see where Jack had drilled into the rock, and set the charges. There was a long cable stretching from the main charge, and this would be attached to a detonator later on in the evening. Most of the other charges were self-detonating, and would go up with the first explosion. Other charges had been set inside the cave, extending ten to fifteen feet along the tunnel.

'It's a bloody shame, this,' said Jack. 'It's a beautiful cave, Alex! Are you sure you want to close it off forever?'

'Every man has the right to a tomb, Jack! Mine's just a bit fancier than most because I've had the foresight to pick it out. If you had the money, wouldn't you like one like this?'

'When I'm gone, mate, I'm gone! I don't care if they drop me on a rubbish tip in a plastic bag. After all, you won't be able to see any of this once you're gone.'

Alex punched him playfully on the shoulder.

241

'Where's your spirit of romance, Jack? I'd like Tina to think of me lying back and staring at that cathedral ceiling for eternity. There's worse things to look at!'

'Well, I don't intend dying for a while, so it doesn't affect me,' said Jack, glumly. 'But I must admit I feel sorry for you, Alex. I don't know how you can keep so calm about the whole thing.'

'I don't need anyone's pity, Jack,' Alex snapped. 'Just make sure you cart my body down here the moment I'm gone, and then blow that entrance. Coincide it with the last burst of fireworks if you can. I hope you've got this all timed out so that the display continues until at least two thirty?'

'It will be over by about a quarter to three by my calculations,' Jack replied. He was quiet for a moment, then made to speak, but shook his head and relapsed into silence again.

'What's up? What were you going to say?'

Jack looked uncomfortable.

'Oh, nothing much! It's just the guys... you know! They're getting a bit fractious. They want to know when they're going to get paid!'

Alex grinned.

'Right now, my boy! Come back to the house, and I'll fix the lot up, here and now.'

Back in his office, Alex went to the wall safe and pulled out bundles of notes, all tied up with elastic bands. He threw them on the desk, and then began to count them out.

'I had yours bundled in $5,000 lots, and the other guys in $1,000 lots. So there's twelve big fat bundles for you, and ten thin bundles for each of your two mates. Take note that I haven't deducted anything for Colin's knee trembler, so he can count himself lucky. And here's fifteen hundred for your looney friend, Donovan. It's more than he deserves!'

'I'll see he gets it,' said Jack, beaming from ear to ear as he scooped up the money. It was more money than he'd ever seen in his life.

'Enjoy it, my friend. You've earned it.'

Once Jack had gone, Alex hunted Tina up. She was cooking them some late lunch, but Alex wasn't in the mood to eat. His stomach felt raw, and he now had the taste of blood almost constantly in his mouth.

'I'm bleeding from both ends, Tina,' he whispered, as they locked themselves in the bedroom for one last hour together. They made love slowly and painfully, and at the end Tina fell back exhausted, and cried. They slept until seven o'clock, and only ventured out when the sun was low in the sky. They walked over to the cliff and watched their last sunset together, then returned to the house when it became dark.

People were starting to walk across the causeway in answer to the invitations they'd received. Some were Jocelyn's fellow parishioners, some were business acquaintances of Alex. Most of them intended to stay for the fireworks, get a free feed, and take the boat back at 3.15 the following morning. A few of the younger, more adventurous ones had asked, and received, permission to spend the night on the beach.

The caterers were just beginning to get into full swing with their choice samplings of Calamari, Prawns, Crabmeat and Crayfish platters. Most of the visitors headed for them first, and then went off to the wine tent where they could sample a hundred and fifty different wines from Chardonnays to Moselles, from Semillons to Shiraz's. For those not into seafoods there were two barbecue areas, one supplying steaks and chops and the other a sausage sizzle. The marquees had coloured lights strung between them, so the whole effect was that of a funfair, without the rides.

By ten o'clock a lot of people were sitting on the beach, on blankets they'd brought along, and they were just quietly talking amongst themselves, and waiting for the fireworks to begin. Others were still arriving, at the tail end of the tide.

Watching the procession from the far shore was a figure not sympathetic to Alex Prittik, or his new love. Roddy Donovan sat on a bench at Meddleton Beach, drinking from the neck of a bottle of Jack Daniels. He was waiting until the procession had dwindled to a trickle, so he could slope over there and make himself scarce in the crowd. He watched as the Reverend Berry headed for the island, followed some minutes later by Bishop Bagwort in his robes.

'What a weirdo,' he thought.

The moment he saw the white water start to appear around the far end of the causeway, he made his move. He cantered across in the darkness, and then made his way around the eastern side, away from the house and down onto a rough piece of the island's coast where no one ever went. He could remain well hidden there until he was ready. He sat there in the darkness and smiled to himself. This was going to be worth it!

II

The Vicar was in a bit of a state. He had decided to have a nap that afternoon, meaning to get up again at six, have tea, and get over to the island as soon as possible to alert Alex about his changed circumstances. Instead, he had slept in until almost nine, and was one of the last to cross the causeway before the tide began to sweep in.

On getting to the island, he made his way to the house, in an attempt to find Jocelyn. It would probably be better if he spoke to her; after all, most of his contact had been through Joss, and she would know the best way to break it to him.

Joss was off somewhere in the crowd. It took him over half an hour to find her, and when he did she was in the company of Colin Bartel, a great strapping fellow who would probably get in the way.

'Excuse me, Joss,' said the vicar, 'but is there somewhere we can talk. It's rather urgent!'

'Not now, your reverence,' she gushed. 'We're trying out all this delicious seafood... very bad for the figure, I'm sure,' she giggled, 'but it's fun, anyway!'

'No, you don't understand! I must speak with you... now! It's really very important!'

'Oh, just relax, your vicarship! It can't be as bad as all that! If it's about going to heaven...'

'No, Joss! You must listen to me. It's about Alex!'

Joss immediately pricked up her ears.

'What about Alex? *He's* not going to heaven! I know where *he's* going, and it's *not* heaven, I can tell you that,' she said, with emphasis.

'No, Joss, you're right. He's not going anywhere! The Bishop has cured him!'

Joss looked somewhat taken aback.

'What do you mean... the *Bishop* has cured him? What can a Bishop do about cancer?'

The reverend looked and pointed upwards at the same time. Joss looked up.

'I can't see anything. They haven't started yet, have they?'

'Not the fireworks... *God!*'

Joss let out a shriek, and dropped her plate.

'*He's* not here, is he?' She turned and pushed Colin away from her, and looked up apprehensively. 'I didn't do it!' she said, quaveringly. 'Honest, your Overlordship!'

'No... the *Bishop* intervened... he got *God* to cure *Alex!*' the vicar whispered, desperately. He didn't want everyone in the vicinity to hear in case they thought he was crazy. He suddenly realised how it sounded, and he was becoming embarrassed.

'So, Alex is cured, you say. He's not going to die after all.'

'That's the gist of it.'

Berry heaved a sigh of relief. She'd finally got the message.

'And the Bishop did this by talking to God!'

'That's right!'

'Well, no one told Alex. He's going to kill himself tonight, anyway!'

The reverend broke out in a sweat.

'But that's exactly why I'm telling you, Joss. You have to get to him and tell him not to do it. There's no need, now!'

Joss looked at the vicar and began to pout.

'But I don't know whether I want to, your eminence. He's been so mean to me... I don't even care if he *does* kill himself. As long as I get his money, that is!'

The vicar shook his head in horror.

'Oh, Jocelyn! That's a terrible, sinful thing to say. To put his money before his life...'

'If you're nice to me, vicarage, I'll even pay for the church organ if I inherit all his money. How's that?'

'I can see I'll have to see Mister Prittik himself. Where would I find him?'

Joss shrugged. He could be anywhere as far as she knew.

The reverend took off through the crowd, asking at intervals if anyone had seen their host. No one had. He saw the Bishop over at the barbecue, fishing out a couple of well-done steaks, and put his head down so he wouldn't be spotted. If he failed in this mission, he would be finished. He'd never live it down!

Alex and Tina didn't put in an appearance until just after eleven. They put their seats out facing the beach, on the small lawn at the south side of the house. Alex was looking very drawn. He had a bottle of Jim beam in his hand, and was measuring it out into a glass. The vicar found him just before the fireworks started.

As the reverend approached, Alex took a drink, and doubled over as it hit his gut. Tina had been crying, and was now sitting dejectedly beside him, powerless to stop him killing himself with spirits.

'Oh, thank God I've caught you! You must stop that… you're cured, Mister Prittik. I saw the Bishop yesterday, and he told me that he had the matter well in hand. You're cured, there's no reason to go through with this crazy plan of yours any more.'

Alex grimaced, and looked up at him through bloodshot eyes.

'What's the fellow babbling about, Tina?'

Tina looked up and saw the white collar, and looked at him in surprise.

'He says you're cured, Alex. The Bishop has cured you or something. Are you sure…' she said to the vicar, who was standing, hanging over them like a friendly vulture.

'Yes, yes, quite sure. Mister Prittik is cured! The Bishop asked me to relay the message on to you, so you wouldn't go ahead with this crazy scheme of yours. He has interceded… you know… with *him* up there!'

'I see,' said Prittik, already under the weather. 'He's had a word in the big fellow's ear, and he's agreed to cure me… just like that!'

'Yes… just like that,' said the reverend, eagerly. 'God works wonders, Mister Prittik, and it looks as if he's come in to bat for you on this occasion.'

'Well, ain't that jolly!' said Alex, taking a big swig out of the bottle. He grimaced as it went down. The pain followed. 'It's a miracle,' he gasped, when the pain had subsided.

'It surely is… a miracle! You should say hallelujah, Mister Prittik, because God is on your side.'

'Hallelujah!' said Alex, now beginning to look drunk. 'Hallelujah! And what else did God tell the Bishop?'

'Just that your cancer had been disposed of! But... the Bishop did happened to mention that you should think very strongly about showing your appreciation by donating the money to repair the church organ!'

'Hah!' said Alex. 'I knew there was a catch! The old church organ trick! Then once I pay for the organ, no doubt the Bishop will find out it was all a big mistake, and that I still have cancer after all. What a crock of shit!'

Tina shoved Alex hard, and remonstrated with him.

'Don't say things like that Alex. The vicar is here to help you!'

'The vicar is here to help himself I think,' said Alex, blearily.

At that moment, four rockets shot up into the sky and showered golden rain over the sea. There was a loud Oooohhh from the crowd, and a large Aaaaahhhh, when they went out. It was impossible to talk after that, as the sound of Catherine wheels and whiz-bangs and rockets filled the air, and the sky lit up with Jack Delaney's artistry.

The crowd now gathered round, and the vicar was jostled from his spot. Alex took another swig from the bottle, and suddenly brought it all up again, along with a mouthful of blood. Tina snatched the bottle out of his hand.

'I'm not going to let you do this to yourself!' she cried out. 'It's one think to die of cancer, it's another to do what you're doing... it's disgusting!'

A handful of jumping jacks were suddenly released in their area, and people were squealing and jumping out of the way as they exploded, jumping this way and that through the crowd. A series of star shells threw shrieking balls of gunpowder out to sea, where they exploded into golden bursts or red balls, which in turn blew out into yellow sparks. The noise was incredible.

Colin Bartel had left Joss by this time to attend to his job down in one of the bunkers. Eddie was controlling another one, and Jack was co-ordinating the whole via mobile-radio. Joss had been getting stuck into the Chateau au vin, and was slightly the worse for wear. By midnight, she was at a bit of a loss, and went looking for Alex and Tina, over by the house. Their chairs were empty. At the first break Tina had dragged Alex to his feet and made him go inside and soak his head. She hated drunks, and Alex was well on his way to becoming drunk. Joss kept wandering, and ended down on the beach.

'What if what the vicar said was true, Alex,' said Tina, clutching at straws. 'What if you really are cured?'

'What if crocodiles wore pig-skin boots,' mumbled Alex, his head over the sink. 'What if God was a giant artichoke?'

'Don't be facetious,' Tina retorted, angrily. 'I've seen Doctor Proust out in the crowd. I'm going to find him and ask if it's possible his diagnosis could be wrong.'

Alex stood up, and chuckled.

'What? Old Prousty? He's *never* wrong! If *he* was wrong, the world would spin off its axis and disappear into a black hole. No – I've got cancer all right. I can feel it! Why do you think I keep bringing up blood... not to mention the other end?'

'Maybe you've torn the lining of your stomach. It's not unheard of! Maybe it's something else?'

'Maybe I've gone rusty? Maybe it's foot and mouth disease? Maybe maybe is perhaps – perchance?'

'If you don't stop making sick jokes, Alex Prittik, I swear I'll leave! This is serious!'

'I *know* how serious it is, Tina,' said Alex, staring into her face. 'I'm fucking dying! *That's* serious!'

Tina glared at him, annoyed, then turned on her heel and walked out. Alex didn't follow quickly enough, and by the time he went out the door, she had been swallowed up by the crowd.

Janelle had been wandering aimlessly around with Lindsay. She was determined that McRae wasn't going to get the opportunity to pull any stunts before 1.31am, at which time she would be in line for the $100,000. They both spotted Alex at the same time. It was 12.20am.

'There he is, Janelle. Hell, he looks like shit! Maybe I can knock him out before 12.30, and the money will be mine.'

McRae steered her towards Alex, who was standing on the doorstep peering wildly around for Tina.

'You just keep away from him, Lindsay. If he's going to die before 12.30, then let him do it on his own. He doesn't need any help from you!'

'Aah, honey! Just a little nudge in the gut with my elbow… nobody would notice in this crowd. He'd probably bleed to death on the spot.'

'You so much as touch him and I'll see you in prison, Lindsay! I mean it.'

'Okay… okay,' he said, hands raised in surrender. 'I suppose you think you're going to have a go at him after 1.30? Well, what's sauce for the goose is sauce for the gander, doll!'

Janelle curled her lip at him, and dragged him off in the other direction.

A series of rockets howled their way into the sky and attracted everyone's attention. There was a rattle of starbursts, then a whole line of golden rain flared up along the front. Bishop Bagwort found himself standing behind the Reverend Elder Berry, and tapped him on the shoulder.

The reverend looked awkward and nervous.

'Nice display, Vicar! Have you tried the steaks and the Jacobs Creek? Magnifico!' The Bishop blew a kiss in the air. 'Did you manage to get a message to Prittik… about his cancer,' he yelled, over the noise of the fireworks.

The vicar hung his head, and looked miserable.

'I tried, your worship. I told his wife, but she is now estranged from him, and didn't want to know. So I approached him direct. To be quite honest, I think he thought I was barking mad! I would suggest that you approach him yourself, your worship, or he will almost certainly do himself an injury.'

Bagwort smiled grimly.

'Have faith, my son! The lord works in mysterious ways.' Then he disappeared into the crowd.

At ten to one, Tina finally managed to track Doctor Proust down in the crowd. Margaret had wandered off on her own, so he was standing by the wine tent, sipping on a Chardonnay.

'Oh, Doctor... there you are! I've been looking for you everywhere. I need to talk to you about Alex's condition! It's terribly important.'

She dragged him over to the house, and ushered him in by the side door. Once the door closed behind them, there was relative silence. Proust was on his guard.

'Well, you know, young lady, I really can't discuss a patient of mine with you, or his treatment. Doctor/Patient confidentiality you know!'

'You'd better discuss it with me, doctor, or you're going to have a dead patient on your hands.' Tina was determined.

Proust laughed, deprecatingly.

'Now, now... don't you think you should leave medicine to the professionals?'

As if in answer, Tina walked over to the wall and peeled off the copy of Alex's will. She walked back and thrust it in the doctor's face.

'Read that, if you don't believe me. That's his will! In that, Alex announces his intention to kill himself... tonight! ... to avoid facing the pain that he expects to be in at the end! He's already bleeding from both ends, doctor. He thinks he's dying! But the Vicar came up with some ga-ga story tonight that the Bishop had decreed that he was cured. Can you believe that?'

Proust went a deathly pale, one; from reading Alex's declaration, and two; on hearing the way the Bishop had dealt with his request.

'What exactly did the vicar say, my dear,' he said, trying to hide his perturbation.

'He said that the Bishop had asked God to intercede, and that the situation was in hand. The Bishop had pronounced that Alex was cured of the cancer.'

'Oh ,for goodness sake,' said Proust, shaking his head. He continued to read the contents of the will, then stopped, suddenly, and turned to Tina.

'What's this? I see my name is mentioned here!'

'Yeah, that's just Alex's little joke. If he dies between 1.01 and 1.30am today, you will inherit the residue of his estate – but only if you have never been found guilty of medical negligence!'

Proust was staggered.

'Preposterous!' he exploded. 'Absolutely preposterous! I have never been so much as up on the charge…' He stopped. That may well be true to the present moment, but in fact he *was* guilty of medical negligence, in the case of Alan Privet, who had just died, and he would soon be implicated again in the case of Alex Prittik, if he died, as he intended to do this night. It was a conundrum.

Proust turned back to the will.

'*…remainder of the estate will be left to Doctor Charles Proust, one hundred thousand dollars of which for his own use, and the remainder to re-equip the Middleton General Hospital with general medical requirements, on the condition that…* '

Tina paced back and forth impatiently. Proust cleared his throat.

'Err… if you don't mind me asking, this 'remainder' of the estate… How much are we talking about here?'

Tina pulled a face. This man was impossible!

'About twenty million, maybe twenty three!'

'Dollars?' said Proust, his jaw hanging open. This put a totally new slant on things! That new X-ray equipment… the CAT-Scan… trolleys and trolleys of heartbeat monitors and blood pressure equipment! Bedpans by the hundreds, and perhaps, three or four new nurses so they could open Ward IIIG up again! The possibilities were endless. Proust looked at his watch. It was 1.04am.

'Do you think it possible that Alex does not, in fact, have cancer, doctor? Could he have been cured, as the Bishop says he was?'

Proust could feel the three medicines in his pocket that he had specifically requested Margaret to pick up. He had expected the vicar to have convinced Prittik by now, and his intention was to have passed the medicine along. He turned to Tina, and hesitated.

'Do you think the Bishop could have cured him, doctor?' she repeated.

Proust swallowed twice, then slowly shook his head.

'I don't think so, young lady! In fact, I very much doubt it!' he said.

Chapter Nineteen

Tina went looking for Alex during a break in the fireworks, when everyone clustered into little groups and talked animatedly to each other. This was a great show, wasn't it? - This Alex Prittik must be some sort of millionaire to put a show like this on. - Who was he? - Oh, some entrepreneur or other. - I think he's something to do with the movies! – No, he's a famous inventor! Haven't you ever heard of the *Prittique?*

They were the types of conversations going on as Tina made her way through the crowd. When she couldn't see him after fifteen minutes of solid search, she burst into tears, and found herself face to face with Bishop Bagwort. He had a glass of Shiraz in one hand, and a sausage dog in the other. The Bishop's capacity for sustenance was boundless.

'Now what's this, my dear? Tears on a night like tonight? You young things should be enjoying yourselves on these occasions. It's not often that we get a slap-up spread like this in Meddleton!'

'I'm looking for Alex… he seems to have disappeared. I think he might already be dead,' she sobbed. 'Are you the Bishop that said Alex had been cured by God?'

'Well, I…' Bagwort took a step backwards. He hadn't realised that his duplicity would rear up so unexpectedly in the form of a beautiful young woman. This had not been in the script.

'I… didn't exactly say it like that,' he prevaricated.

Tina suddenly recovered, and snapped at him.

'What do you mean… what *is* all this double talk? Can't I get a reasonable answer to a reasonable question tonight? I asked a simple question, I just want a simple answer! Does Alex Prittik still have cancer, or does he not?'

The Bishop looked hurriedly at his watch. It was 1.35am.

'Did you say he has disappeared?' said the Bishop. His brow clouded over! If Prittik should be found dead in the next twenty-five minutes, St. Peter's Roman Catholic Church would benefit, and that would stick in Bagwort's craw. On the other hand, if he could delay the discovery of Prittik's body until after 2.31, St. Paul's Anglican Church would at least get $100,000 – an amount not to be sniffed at!

Tina was still waiting for an answer.

'Why don't we go for a bit of a wander? We might spot him together,' said Bagwort, leading her away from the scene. He thought that probably the last place a man with a chronic ulcer would be hanging out would be the food stalls, so he led Tina in that direction.

'You still haven't answered my question, Bishop! Did you or did you not send the vicar over to tell Alex that his cancer was cured?'

Bagwort put his glass down and grabbed himself another sausage. His ingenuity was beginning to run rather low.

'Well… I *did*… but there's rather more to the story than that. Why don't you ask his doctor, Doctor Proust? He's around here somewhere, I've spotted him a couple of times.'

'I asked his doctor, and he told me he couldn't violate his doctor/patient confidentiality,' said Tina, losing her temper now.

The Bishop's hand halted halfway to his mouth. He looked surprised.

'*He wouldn't tell...* what time was this?' said Bagwort, munching fiercely on the sausage. This was a fine thing... getting Bagwort to do his dirty work, and then refusing to come clean when directly challenged... That wasn't sporting!

'It was about... five past one. Why?'

'The Bishop nodded fiercely. Now he knew! Bagwort carried Prittik's will around in his head, and he knew about the significance of 1.01 to 1.30 as far as Proust was concerned. Why, the slimy dog!

Tina looked at him speculatively.

'*He* asked me that! What the time was! What's so significant about....' She turned on Bagwort and seized him by his eminent collar. 'If you and he are together in something, just because of this blasted will, I'll write to the Pope!'

Bagwort looked relieved. Tina did a double take!

'I'll write to the Cardinal... I'll write to the Archbishop – yes, the Archbishop!' Finally she'd hit the nail on the head. Bagwort swallowed his next sausage whole.

'My dear young lady, there's no need for that. Your Mister Prittik is perfectly fine and well, except for a rather nasty duodenal ulcer. If he approaches Doctor Proust, I'm sure he would be more than happy to prescribe the correct medication for him.'

Tina let him go, and stood back, incredulous. Then she turned and began to run, back towards the beach. She had to find him now, had to!

The next group of fireworks were just beginning to whiz-bang their way through the air as Tina got down to the old boat dock. She hoped that from there she would be able to see far enough along the beach to pick him out. He had to be somewhere. She spotted Jack Delaney trudging along, talking into his little walkie-talkie radio, and she rushed up and collared him, inadvertently ruining the sequence of a line of star shells that were the current focus of attention.

'Not now, Tina! Can't you see I'm busy?'

'Where's Alex? It's dreadfully important.'

'I haven't seen him for ages, Tina. I thought you were with him?'

'I was, but we lost sight of each other. If you do see him, tell him to come looking for me – and not to do anything stupid!'

She ran off, and then walked over to the boat dock. As she did so, Joss came up from behind and lit the firework that she had held, seemingly forever, in her hand. When Tina turned around, she threw it!

The explosion blew Tina down onto the decking, where she hit her head. She was out cold! Joss received some of the blast as well, and went running off, hugging her breasts. With all the other activity going on, no one noticed... No one except a certain interested party who had been following Tina at a distance.

Roddy Donovan made his way warily over to the dock, and knelt down beside her. She had a cut on her forehead, and singed hair and eyebrows, but other than that she was just groggy. As she began to come around she saw Donovan kneeling over her, and began to scream. Donovan clamped his hand over her mouth, and making sure he wasn't seen, dragged Tina over the side of the deck and into the water.

Struggling was a waste of energy. Donovan was as strong as an ox, and he was an excellent swimmer. Tina felt his arm around her throat as he swam away from the dock. The water was cold, and she began to shiver in the night as they travelled further and further from the beach. Donovan's plan was to swim south for a hundred yards, then head west and fetch up somewhere along the coast, away from Middleton beach. Once he got her ashore he could then argue with her without being interrupted by Prittik or his cronies.

'What do you think you're doing? You'll go to jail for this,' Tina gasped out, as she tried to fight free of his arm. But he was too strong for her.

'I told you I'd get you, you bitch! I'm gonna get that bastard Prittik, too,' he replied, haltingly. It was taking a lot of effort to swim and control Tina at the same time.

'I'll fucking kill you for this, Roddy. Let me go… I've got to see Alex!'

'Oh-you-got-to-see-Alex,' he mimicked, and then he let out a sound like 'whooofff!', as if the air had been suddenly belted out of his chest.

Tina felt his grip go slack, and she floated out from under his arm. Donovan was upright in the water, his eyes staring directly at her as she backed away. He opened his mouth to speak, and a huge gobbet of blood belched out of his mouth, into the water. It was then that she saw the fin.

Her first instinct was to scream. Donovan was pulled savagely under the water, and came up again like a cork, one of his arms missing. Then he flopped onto his back, and Tina could see that there was nothing left below the waist. The fin turned and came back at him again, and Tina turned to swim for her life, certain that her next few moments would be her last.

II

As Joss ran away from the boat dock, she cursed that she hadn't planned that a bit better. It was no joy to be hurt yourself, though Tina had certainly got the worst of it. She wished that she could have hung around, taunted her enemy when she woke up. But she had received a blast in the chest that had really hurt her pride and joy. She was worried that she might have marked her breasts, and was going to go back to the house to check herself out.

As she came into the clearing, she saw Alex, looking much the worse for wear, a new bottle of Jim Beam in his hand. He was staggering, but he was obviously looking for someone, too.

'Joss, for god's sake,' he said, as she approached him. 'Have you seen Tina? I can't find her anywhere.'

'As if I really care,' said Joss, punching at him on the way past. Instead of letting it go, Alex turned and ran after her. He grabbed her by the hair, pulled her back towards him and then spun her around. She looked at him fearfully.

'You're a right bitch, Jocelyn,' he said, and slapped her hard around the face. 'I should have done that the day I found out about you and McRae.'

Joss staggered back in shock... he'd never hit her before.

'You bastard, Alex! Well it serves you right! I'm glad I did it, glad! And he wasn't the only one, Alex. He was just one of ten,' she sneered at him.

Alex drew back his fist and punched her in the side of the head, and she went down like a skittle. He waited for her to get up, but she wouldn't be going anywhere for a while. He went staggering off towards the beach, the front of his shirt now covered in his own blood.

'It's all over now,' he muttered to himself, 'all over!'

The next lot of Catherine wheels were spinning on their posts, and a series of rockets with siren-like squeals were taking off at ten-second intervals. At about two hundred feet they exploded a dense layer of stars over the water.

Alex looked at his watch. It was 2.20am. Another eleven minutes, and he didn't care what happened after that. Hilda, Tina and Jack would share the residue of his estate between them, and St. Paul's would get their lousy organ. Everyone would be happy... except Joss... except McRae and Janelle... except Doctor Proust! Fuck 'em all,' he thought, and began to head for the road.

Jack Delaney suddenly loomed up in front of him, and grabbed his arm.

'You look like shit, mate! Let me help you inside.'

'Not there! Down to the cave, Jack. You promised!'

'But I saw Tina... she was looking all over for you. She said not to do anything stupid!'

'Well, it's too late for that, old mate. Take me down to the cave. Let's get this over and done with. I'm just about done for… put me in the Cathedral, and blow the entrance.'

Jack looked worried.

'I don't know if I can, mate. You're not dead! How can I blow the entrance if you're not dead?'

'Don't pike out on me now, Jack! Take me down to the cave.'

Jack nodded in defeat. Alex put his arm over Jack's shoulder, and the two of them limped off towards the cliff.

In the house, Joss was inspecting her very tender breasts in the mirror. She had only been out for a few minutes, and then had woken up with murder in her soul. She was bruised across the top of each breast, and that, to her, was like a disfigurement. She had a bruise coming up on her temple, where Alex had hit her, and she stood in front of the mirror swearing vengeance. She would get those two, one way or another!

Changing into a less revealing top, she made her way outside and walked over to the boat shed. It was empty now, except for a few canisters of black powder and various bags of chemicals. The three workers were still finishing off the display as far as she knew. It was 2.44am, and it would all be over within the next ten minutes.

Putting the light on, she grabbed one of the spare two-inch casings, and placed it on the bench. There was no powder lying around, so she lifted one of the new canisters up onto the table, and opened the lid with a screwdriver. After watching Colin do this, she thought it would be a breeze. All you had to do was pack it tightly into the tube, seal the end and then fix up the touch-paper.

She'd watched Colin pressing the powder down into the smaller tube, using a rammer and a small ball-peen hammer. She resolved to do the same. Taking a small paper cup, she scooped some black powder out of the top of the canister, and poured it into the casing. Two more scoops and it was full. So far so good! She tried pressing it down with her thumb, and this made a little more space, so she topped it up and then put the rammer in place, over the casing. Carefully tapping the mixture, she gradually compressed it down, and was so involved with the work that she didn't notice the door opening behind her.

McRae and Janelle were looking for somewhere private to conduct a little intimate foray into each other's libido. With so many people around, it was hard to find somewhere that wasn't already occupied. They backed into the shed, thinking that it was bound to be empty, as the workers were out there, setting off fireworks. It was only when the door shut behind them that Joss looked up, and as she did, she jumped! Janelle and McRae jumped as well, and McRae had just enough time to say, 'Oh, shit!'

The hammer came down a little harder than expected, and chipped at the edge of the rammer. One solitary spark flew off the hammerhead, and headed unerringly into the powder spilt on the table.

That's the theory, anyway! No one will ever really know, because those that were there at the time are no longer with us. All anyone knows is that at precisely 2.58am the boatshed on Crab Island went up in an explosion that made the fireworks display look like amateur night. When the smoke cleared, nothing remained of the boatshed, and pieces of bodies were still floating out in the bay ten days later. The police launch was eventually towed over from Port Lincoln, and a gruesome day was spent both in collecting the floating human detritus, and in diving for those pieces now lying on the bottom. But that was later!

Tina had just crawled ashore, and was being helped out of the water by some friendly partygoers when she immediately collapsed in hysterics, and it was some time before those around her could make out the words 'White-Pointer!' as she stared and gestured, horrified, out into the bay.

Then the boatshed went up, and she was left standing there by the rush of people heading for the scene of the carnage. She took off along the beach, pushing her way through the crush, in the opposite direction to the general mass of people. She made it up onto the road and ran past the Bishop, whose internal organs were already suffering the strain of thirteen sausages and four steaks as he headed for the toilet. The explosion had sent his bowel into a quiver, and he was afraid he wouldn't make it if he didn't move now.

On the small lawn at the back of the house, Bagwort stopped to pick up a pair of shattered spectacles that looked surprisingly familiar. They belonged to Doctor Proust, who had been leaning against the wall of the boat shed sipping Brut de Brut, only minutes before. But what made the Bishop gag, and almost bring up every sausage one by one, was the eyeball stuck to the broken lens, and now staring at him, accusingly.

Alex was making his way along the tunnel to the Grotto, while Jack, standing at the entrance, was waiting for him to call out his final instructions. He stood and looked up at the stalactites for the last time, only barely visible at night in the gloom, then he turned on the spot and yelled out to Jack - 'Do it!'

Jack shook his head sadly, checked his watch for accuracy, and then walked along the ledge to where he had placed the plunger. He gave the handle a twist, and was barely aware of the fact that it was Tina, who came stumbling and sliding down the cliff path, as he pushed it home.

'Stop!' she yelled, but her cry was drowned out by several hundredweight of black powder and ten sticks of dynamite, that roared as if in unison, and the sky was filled with flying rocks and debris for a good two minutes after that.

Tina got up and walked around the corner, to find the opening to their favourite cave well and truly sealed. Her legs buckled under her, and she collapsed on the spot. When he finally regained his sense of hearing, all that Jack could hear was the sound of Tina, sobbing bitterly in the night.

Alex had yelled out 'Do it,' and had then taken another swig from the neck of his bottle of Jim Beam. When the explosion came, he wasn't as prepared as he'd thought. The blast raced along the tunnel and hit him full in the face. It lifted him off his feet with the force of a tornado and threw him backwards into the deep pool, where Tina and he had swum naked, once… so long, long ago! He went straight to the bottom, burnt and blackened with black powder, the wind knocked out of his lungs, and in a strange, trancelike state that convinced him that he was already dead. It seemed forever that he lay in that pool, and though he feebly struggled, all he succeeded in doing was entangling himself in weed from the bottom, and as he slowly rose to the surface he looked like a blackened version of Neptune, the sea god.

Up above, in the privacy of the Prittik's toilet, Bishop Bagwort was seated on the podium, trying desperately to expel all that he had previously shovelled in at the other end for the past five hours. There was what appeared to be a grumbling in his bowels that grew louder by the moment, and this grew into a mighty roar before the floor suddenly opened up, and Bishop Bagwort found himself careering downwards, along with the floor and the toilet intact, into some veritable cavern of Hell's nethermost depths.

Alex came up as the Bishop went down, and the sight of this dark nemesis, draped in weeds and blackened with powder, rising up to claim his everlasting soul in some deep grotto of Lucifer's minions, was just too much for the Bishop's faint and guilty heart. He expired before he even toppled off the toilet, and dived neatly down into the depths of the pool, followed closely by a rather long and pointy stalactite.

Alex didn't even look back! He climbed up into what remained of his house, and flung off the hands that were reaching down to lift him free.

'Can't a man even *die* in peace around here?' he bellowed, and then promptly collapsed on the floor of the lounge, which, fortunately, had been built on good, solid ground. When Jacob brought his boat across, Alex Prittik was one of the first to be ferried ashore.

III

Tina sat over by the window, trying to catch a little more light so she could read the paper in comfort. Alex lay in bed, swathed in bandages, the medication for his ulcer standing starkly on the side table.

'We'll try Boston first,' he was saying. 'I believe there are some first class medical research facilities in Boston.'

Tina looked around briefly, smiled once, and then went back to her paper.

'What's up with you? Aren't you talking to me,' he said, aggrieved. 'What? Is it different now... now that you've got to put up with me for the rest of your life?'

Tina looked around again, and sighed.

'Don't you ever shut up, Alex Prittik? What do you want from me - blood?'

Alex looked hurt.

'Now that's not very nice. After all I went through, at least I should be able to expect a bit of conversation!'

'You talk enough for both of us, Alex! I've been sitting in this room for a week, and I'm all talked out.'

'Yes, well... I remember what you said, that day down on the dock. *We can live for every moment we have left...*'

'I remember,' she said, nodding. '*I remember!* And that's exactly what I intend to do, Alex Prittik, because I will love you 'til I die!'

She got up and walked over to the bed, bent over and kissed him gently on the cheek. He reached out, and took her by the hand.

'And if I have any say in it,' he said, squeezing her gently, 'then we're both going to live forever!'

www.ingramcontent.com/pod-product-compliance
Lightning Source LLC
Chambersburg PA
CBHW050657290626
47170CB00015B/1052